"*Alice* takes the darker elements of Lewis Carroll's original, amplifies Tim Burton's cinematic reimagining of the story and adds a layer of grotesquery from [Henry's] own alarmingly fecund imagination to produce a novel that reads like a Jacobean revenge drama crossed with a slasher movie."   —*The Guardian* (UK)

"A psychotic journey through the bowels of magic and madness. I, for one, thoroughly enjoyed the ride."

—Brom, author of *The Child Thief*

"A horrifying fantasy that will have you reexamining your love for this childhood favorite."   —RT Book Reviews (top pick)

Praise for

RED QUEEN

"Henry takes the best elements from Carroll's iconic world and mixes them with dark fantasy elements. . . . [Her] writing is so seamless you won't be able to stop reading."

—Pop Culture Uncovered

"Alice's ongoing struggle is to distinguish reality from illusion, and Henry excels in mingling the two for the reader as well as her characters. The darkness in this book is that of fairy tales, owing more to Grimm's matter-of-fact violence than to the underworld of the first book."   —*Publishers Weekly* (starred review)

LOOKING GLASS

· THE CHRONICLES OF ALICE NOVELLAS ·

Christina Henry

ACE

New York

ACE
Published by Berkley
An imprint of Penguin Random House LLC
penguinrandomhouse.com

Copyright © 2020 by Tina Raffaele

Library of Congress Cataloging-in-Publication Data

Names: Henry, Christina, 1974– author.
Title: Looking glass: the chronicles of Alice novellas / Christina Henry.
Description: First edition. | New York: Ace, 2020.
Identifiers: LCCN 2019040132 (print) | LCCN 2019040133 (ebook) |
ISBN 9781984805638 (paperback) | ISBN 9781984805645 (ebook)
Subjects: LCSH: Alice (Fictitious character from Carroll)—Fiction.
Classification: LCC PS3608.E568 A6 2020 (print) |
LCC PS3608.E568 (ebook) | DDC 813/.6—dc23
LC record available at https://lccn.loc.gov/2019040132
LC ebook record available at https://lccn.loc.gov/2019040133

First Edition: April 2020

Printed in the United States of America
1 3 5 7 9 10 8 6 4 2

Cover art by Pep Montserrat
Cover design by Judith Lagerman

For all the girls who save themselves
And all the girls still learning how

CONTENTS
. . .

Lovely
Creature

Elizabeth Violet Hargreaves trotted down the stairs in her new blue dress, her blond hair neatly done up in curls and ribbons. She couldn't wait to show Mama and Papa how pretty she looked. Elizabeth had spent several moments admiring her appearance from all angles in her looking glass, until her maid Dinah had told her enough was enough and that she should get downstairs else she would miss breakfast.

Elizabeth did not want to miss breakfast. She was a hearty eater, somewhat to her mother's dismay, and breakfast was her favorite meal. There were always pots of jam with breakfast, and a sugar bowl for the tea, and Elizabeth never missed a chance to add an extra dollop of jam to her toast or sneak another lump of sugar.

If her mother caught her she would make that hissing snake noise between her teeth and tell Elizabeth if she kept eating like that she would become rounder than she was already. Elizabeth didn't mind much that she was round. She thought it made her look soft and sweet, and she'd rather be soft and sweet than hard and clipped, like her mother.

Of course, Elizabeth thought Mama was beautiful—or rather, she was beautiful underneath all her planes and angles. She had the same blond hair as Elizabeth, long and thick. When she took it down at night it would fall in rippling waves to her waist. Some of those waves had turned silvery grey, though Elizabeth didn't think Mama was that old, really, and the silver was sort of pretty when it caught the light.

Elizabeth had her mother's eyes, too, clear and blue. But Mama used to laugh more, and her eyes used to crinkle up in the corners when she did. Now there was always a furrow between her brows, and Elizabeth couldn't remember the last time she laughed.

No, that isn't true, she thought to herself. She could remember the last time Mama laughed. It was before That Day.

"That Day" was how Elizabeth always referred to it in her mind, the day that she came downstairs for breakfast to find her father at the table looking like he'd aged twenty years in a minute, his face the color of old ash in the fireplace. In front of him was the morning newspaper, freshly ironed.

"Papa?" she'd asked, but he hadn't heard her.

Elizabeth had crept closer, and seen the paper's headline.

FIRE IN CITY ASYLUM
No Survivors—Tales from Terrified Onlookers

Underneath these interesting bits was a photograph that showed the asylum before and after the fire. Elizabeth stared at the "before" picture. The building seemed like it was staring back at her, like something was rippling under the walls, some-thing that wanted to reach out and grab her and drag her inside.

"Elizabeth," Papa had said, and folded the paper hurriedly, pushing it to one side. "What is it, my darling?"

She indicated the food spread out on the table before him. "It's breakfast. Did Mama eat already?"

"N-no," Papa said. "Mama isn't feeling well. She's still asleep."

That was strange, because Elizabeth was certain she'd heard Mama's voice downstairs earlier. But Papa seemed to have some-thing on his mind at the moment (that was what Mama always said, that Papa had Something on His Mind and Elizabeth Wasn't to Bother Him) so perhaps he'd forgotten that Mama had been here already.

Elizabeth climbed into her seat and laid her napkin on her lap as she was supposed to do and waited for Hobson to serve.

The butler came forward and Elizabeth said, "Eggs and toast, please, Hobson."

He nodded, and lifted the cover off the eggs, and Elizabeth noticed his hand trembled as he scooped the eggs onto her plate with a large silver spoon. He plucked two pieces off the toast rack with tongs and placed them next to the eggs.

"Jam, Miss Alice?" Hobson said, offering Elizabeth the jam pot.

"*Not* Alice," Papa hissed through his teeth, and his voice was so harsh it made Elizabeth jump in her seat. "Elizabeth."

Hobson brought one of his shaking hands to his face, and Elizabeth saw with surprise that he wiped away a tear.

"Hobson, are you all right?" she asked. She liked the old butler quite a bit. He always saved extra sugar lumps for her in a handkerchief and passed them illicitly at dinner.

"Yes, Miss Al—Elizabeth," he said firmly. "I'm quite all right."

He placed the jam pot near Elizabeth's teacup and went to stand against the wall behind Papa. Elizabeth watched him, frowning.

"Papa, who's Alice?" she asked.

"No one," Papa said in his No Arguments voice. "I think Hobson must have been thinking of something else."

Elizabeth ignored the No Arguments warning. "But then why did you get so angry when he said 'Alice'?"

Papa's face looked strange then, a kind of cross between chalky and mottled, and he seemed to be swallowing words trying to escape out of his mouth.

"It's nothing for you to worry about, Elizabeth," Papa said finally. "Enjoy your breakfast. You can have extra jam if you like."

Elizabeth returned her attention to her breakfast plate, pleased to have permission for all the jam she liked but not so silly that she didn't realize Papa was trying to distract her. Still, she supposed she could let herself be distracted for the moment.

And in truth, she *had* nearly forgotten the Incident at Breakfast until later, when she climbed the stairs to get a book and heard Mama making muffled noises in her bedroom. Elizabeth had put her ear close to the keyhole and listened.

"Alice, Alice," Mama said, and it sounded like she was sobbing.

"Alice," Elizabeth said to herself, and tucked the name away. It meant something. No one wanted her to know what it meant, but it certainly meant something.

Elizabeth didn't know why she was now thinking of That Day as she tripped down the stairs in her lovely dress. That Day had been strange and confusing, all the adults in the house speaking in hushed voices.

Her older sister Margaret had even come from across the City in a carriage to confer with their parents in the parlor and Elizabeth had been told in no uncertain terms to go to her room and stay there while this interesting conference occurred.

Margaret was quite a lot older than Elizabeth—twenty years older, in fact, and had two little girls of her own. These girls were ten and nine years old to Elizabeth's nine but had to call her "Aunt Elizabeth" and she did rather enjoy exerting the authority that came with being the aunt. It meant that when she said that they had to play a certain game they had to listen or else she could tell them off without getting in trouble for it.

They would see Margaret and her husband Daniel (who always called her "Sister Elizabeth" and made her laugh by tickling her cheeks with his mustache) and the girls today at Giving Day. All of the families of the City gathered in the Great Square for their children to receive their gifts from the City Fathers.

Elizabeth had noticed last year that some families—her own papa, even—also gave something to the City Fathers in return. She couldn't tell what it was, though, because it was a sealed envelope.

She paused outside the door of the breakfast room, to make certain that Papa and Mama were both in there so she could make her grand entrance and hear both of them ooh and aah at how pretty she looked. The two of them were murmuring quietly to each other as they passed the jam and the butter.

Elizabeth swept into the room and paused just inside the door, holding the hem of her new dress in both hands. Mama hadn't even seen the dress because Dinah had gone with her to the shop to choose it. Elizabeth wanted it to be a surprise for everyone, and of course her hair had never looked quite so nice as it did just then. Dinah had taken extra care on it that morning.

"Ta-da!" Elizabeth said, and waited for the applause.

Instead her mother gasped and said, "Alice!"

Papa's face went from ruddy to white in a moment, and he looked at Mama and said, in a warning voice, "Althea!"

Mama covered her mouth with her hand, and Elizabeth heard little coughing sobs leaking out from behind her fingers.

Alice again, Elizabeth thought. This time she was not curious about the name so much as annoyed. Who was this Alice to steal Elizabeth's thunder? Where were her "oohs" and "aahs"?

"What's the matter, Mama?" Elizabeth asked. "Don't you think I'm pretty in my new dress?"

Papa took a very long draught from his teacup and put the cup back on the saucer with a clatter. Then he held his arms out to Elizabeth, who went to her father and climbed into his lap.

"Of course you look pretty, my sweetheart. I've never seen a creature so lovely as you." He winked at her. "Except your mother, of course. And you are just the image of her."

Elizabeth smiled proudly across the table at Mama, who seemed to be struggling to get herself under control. She stared at Elizabeth as if she were a ghost instead of her own daughter.

"You look very pretty, too, Mama," Elizabeth offered.

Mama did look pretty in her white gown, the same one that she always wore to Giving Day. It was her nicest one and it never was taken out except for this special day once a year. Mama usually wore it with a pink sash around her waist but that sash had been replaced by a blue one that was a little darker than the blue of Elizabeth's dress. Elizabeth wondered what happened to the other sash.

"Elizabeth said you look pretty, Althea," Papa said.

The way he said it was like he was talking to a child that needed to be reminded of her manners. Elizabeth had never heard Papa talk to Mama this way before.

Mama closed her eyes, gave a shuddering breath and then opened them again. When she did the ghost hadn't left her face entirely but she looked more like Mama again.

"Thank you very much, Elizabeth," Mama said. "You look charming in that dress."

If Mama had said this the way that she usually said it Elizabeth would have wriggled with pride but it didn't sound the way Mama usually said it. It was stiff and hard and Mama didn't mean it. Elizabeth could tell.

"Why don't you have some breakfast?" Papa asked, kissing the top of her head. This was the signal for her to hop off his lap and go to her own chair.

She did, though a lot of the joy of the day had been drained out already. Well, perhaps Daniel and Margaret would compliment her dress when they arrived.

Still, Elizabeth thought as she put an extra-generous dollop of marmalade on her toast, *I must discover who this Alice is.*

Elizabeth was tired of Alice spoiling her days.

After breakfast Elizabeth went into the garden to wait for Margaret and Daniel and her nieces to arrive.

"Mind you don't get your dress dirty," Mama said. She sounded almost normal when she said that.

The roses were in the fullest bloom, all of them fat and red and giving off thick perfume that made Elizabeth feel dreamy and drowsy. Mama loved her roses, never let the gardener go near them but insisted on tending them herself.

And of course the roses were the crown jewels of the garden, more luscious than any of the other flowers. The dahlias and tulips always looked like sad little broken soldiers next to Mama's roses.

Elizabeth found her favorite place in the garden, a little nook underneath one of the rosebushes with just enough room for her to sit without anyone spotting her from the house. It was the perfect place because there was space between her hair and the catching thorns of the roses. In fact, she was so well hidden that if you didn't know she was there you would walk right by the rosebush and never see her.

Though if she got any taller she likely wouldn't fit anymore, Elizabeth reflected. She'd grown a little in the last year—not much, but she was hoping to be very tall like Papa. Her mama was slender and delicate and not too tall, but taller than the average neighbor who called for afternoon tea.

Elizabeth wanted long legs and long arms, though she suspected that if she got tall she'd lose some of her roundness.

Well, she thought, *it would be a small price to pay for being tall.* And of course, if she ate enough cake she could make herself as round as she liked again. At least, Mama seemed to think it was Elizabeth's love of cake that made her so. Maybe it wasn't true. Maybe Elizabeth was just naturally that way.

Elizabeth wanted very much to be taller than almost all the boys on the street. She wished to stare down at them imperiously and make them cower. Then maybe they wouldn't say rude things about her face and her soft arms and her round thighs. It didn't bother her to be this way until they said something about it. Though it only bothered her because she felt she ought to be bothered, not because they made her feel bad, really.

Not really.

Besides, it was only poor people in the Old City who should be very thin. Elizabeth had seen some of them pushing up against the bars whenever they drove past the border. They always appeared so pale and spindly and desperate that Elizabeth wanted to stop the coach and hand out all of her pocket money.

She said this to her parents once and her father had scoffed. "Charity is all very well, Elizabeth, but any money you gave those creatures would end up in a bottle. Don't let your sympathy be misplaced."

Elizabeth hadn't understood what Papa meant by "in a bottle" so she'd asked Dinah later and Dinah told her that it was someone who drank a lot of spirits.

"And those Old City folks, they're nothing but shiftless drunkards and murderers, your father is right about that," Dinah had said as she brushed out Elizabeth's hair. "No need to worry yourself about them."

This had seemed very hard-hearted to Elizabeth, but all the adults in her life said it so it must be true.

A little orange butterfly flew into Elizabeth's secret nook and landed on her knee. It flapped its wings at her for a moment, as if giving her a friendly greeting, and then flew away.

A red rose petal floated down from the bush and landed on her knee in the exact place that the butterfly had landed.

I wish that rose was a butterfly, too, a beautiful red butterfly with wings like rubies.

And of course because she wished it, it was so.

The petal seemed to swell, then split, and a moment later there was a lovely butterfly with wings the size of Elizabeth's palm waving its antennae at her.

Elizabeth wasn't surprised by this. Her wishes tended to come true, though she needed to really mean them. If she said idly that she wished for ice cream then ice cream would not appear just because she said it.

Her wishes also came true more often when she dreamed under the roses, though she did not know why this should be. Perhaps because Mama tended them and put her love into them, instead of the gardeners who always seemed to be having their elevenses even when it wasn't the proper time.

She carefully picked up the butterfly from her knee and let it rest on the flat of her hand. It showed no inclination to fly away.

"But butterflies must fly away," Elizabeth said. "They aren't for keeping."

Unless their wings are broken.

She looked all around, startled. That was not her own voice she'd heard. It was someone else's.

Someone terrible, she thought. *Who would break the wings of a butterfly?*

A jealous Caterpillar who can never fly, the voice said.

"Are you the jealous Caterpillar?" Elizabeth asked.

She wasn't certain where the voice was coming from, but it

was definitely not inside her head, as she first thought. That was a comfort, because she was old enough to know that only mad people heard voices that were not their own.

Me? The voice was richly amused by this question. Elizabeth heard the laughter in that single syllable. ***Oh no, not me, never me. I am jealous of nothing and no one for I am the one who keeps all the stories and stories are more valuable than rubies. All the knowledge of the world is in stories.***

"So who is this Caterpillar who breaks butterflies, then?" Elizabeth said.

She thought the voice sounded like a know-all and since Elizabeth had an older sister she didn't need to associate with any more know-alls. Still, if he told her a story it might make the time pass until the carriage came around to take them to the Giving Day ceremonies.

He was very naughty. Very, very naughty indeed, but Alice made him pay for his sins.

"Alice?" Elizabeth asked, her eyes widening and her heart leaping at the sound of the name. "Do you know Alice?"

Perhaps now she could discover the identity of this troublesome Alice, this spectre who left her mother's eyes haunted and her father's face white.

Of course I know Alice. Once she was the Rabbit's Alice. The voice had gone all singsong croony. ***Pretty little Alice with a pretty axe murderer at her side. Pretty Alice who cut the Caterpillar's throat and made it all fall down.***

"But who *is* Alice?" Elizabeth asked impatiently. *And why does no one want me to know?*

Alice swam in a river of tears and waded through streets

that ran with blood and found a cottage covered in roses. Alice walked the forest at night and danced with the goblin and took the queen's crown.

"No, I don't want riddles. If you're not going to tell me properly then I don't want to talk to you at all," Elizabeth said impatiently, and crawled out from under the roses.

The butterfly in her palm flew away and landed on an open flower. Its wings were the same red velvet as the rose, matched so closely that you wouldn't know it was a butterfly at all except for the antennae waving in the breeze.

She dusted the grass and flower petals from her blue dress, feeling that the day was not going at all according to her plan. Everyone was supposed to love her new dress and instead she'd had to drag a compliment from her parents. This annoying voice had come to intrude on her dreaming time under the roses and instead of telling her what she wanted to know it only left more questions in its wake.

And always, always, there was Alice.

"Who is Alice?" she asked, though she didn't expect an answer. She just wanted a chance to show the strange voice that he hadn't distracted her.

Why, Alice is your sister, of course.

Elizabeth was squashed up against the door of the carriage because her nieces Polly and Edith had demanded she ride with them and Margaret and Daniel instead of in her parents' carriage.

Normally she would have been well pleased to play with them instead of straining to listen to her parents' murmured conversation, but she wanted to think quietly about what the voice had told her and it was impossible to think with Polly squealing because Edith kept tickling her.

"Edith, stop that this instant," Margaret said, frowning at her younger daughter.

Edith obligingly folded her hands in her lap, but everyone in the carriage knew that as soon as Margaret's attention turned to something else she would start in on Polly again. Polly was astoundingly ticklish—if you even brushed her cheek with your fingers she would start giggling uncontrollably.

"What's the matter, Elizabeth?" Margaret asked, turning her frown on her sister. "Are you feeling poorly? You're not usually this quiet."

"Yes, I thought some cat had come to steal your tongue away in the night," Daniel said, and winked at her.

Elizabeth dredged up a half smile for him, because she really did like her brother-in-law very much. "I think perhaps I am just a little tired. I didn't sleep very much last night, thinking about today. I was so excited."

Of course this excuse was patently ridiculous. Elizabeth was an exceptionally good sleeper. She could fall asleep in any circumstance, in any position and surrounded by any kind of cacophony. Even if she was overly excited about Giving Day she still would have slept straight through the night and woken up refreshed.

Margaret, however, accepted this reason without considering

it for a moment. Daniel gave Elizabeth a sideways glance that told her he wasn't certain she was telling the truth, but was too polite to say so.

Her sister's carriage joined the line of vehicles inching toward the Great Square. Of course they would have to leave the carriage behind and walk part of the way, though their higher status would allow them to park closer to the ceremonies.

There were soldiers everywhere, strictly enforcing this policy. No amount of wheedling or unsubtle offerings of notes would affect one's placement among the vehicles. Elizabeth had once asked Papa how the soldiers knew where every person belonged.

"It's because of our seal," Papa said. "There is a very tiny mark on the carriage, one that every owner is required to have when they purchase a vehicle of any kind. The soldiers use them to rank each family accordingly."

And the next time Elizabeth was in the stables she'd asked Phelps, the groom, to show her the mark. It was indeed very small, placed in the bottom right corner of the door, and raised like the surface of the seal that Papa used to mark wax on envelopes.

Once their carriage was parked—a few minutes' extra distance farther than Papa's carriage, for although Daniel was connected by marriage to an old family his own family was less prominent than Papa's. His wedding to Margaret had raised his standing, but his own name limited how far he could rise without some significant contribution to the City.

Elizabeth did not believe Daniel ever would rise very much higher. It wasn't that he lacked intelligence—he had plenty of it—but he did seem to lack drive. Elizabeth had often heard Margaret remark that he ought to spend less time laughing and more time working. This reprimand never seemed to affect Daniel, though—he'd only grab Margaret around the waist and spin her until she was flushed and giggling like a girl.

When Elizabeth saw them like that she understood a little better why Daniel had married Margaret in the first place, because her sister often seemed too dour for Daniel's happy nature. Margaret kept her joy tightly wrapped and hidden like a secret present, and only Daniel knew how to find it.

Mama and Papa lingered near their carriage until the rest of the family caught up with them and then they all proceeded together in the direction of the Great Square.

In a proper city the Great Square would have been the geographical center, but the New City wasn't like other cities that Elizabeth had read of in books. The New City had been built when the grandfathers of the City Fathers wished to escape the crime and degeneracy (this was Papa's word; Elizabeth wasn't entirely sure what degeneracy was but Papa's tone indicated that it was a Bad Thing) that was spreading ever outward from the heart of the City. It had been decided that the heart of the City would be walled off and a fresh New City built around it like a ring. Only families of wealth and breeding were permitted to reside in the New City, and all the thieves and murderers were left inside "away from decent folk," as Papa said.

Elizabeth thought that probably there were more than just thieves and murderers left in the Old City, that there were decent folk who just didn't have enough money to make it out. This was a Very Controversial Opinion, for when she expressed it she was immediately shouted down by any grown-ups in the vicinity who assured her that "only filth lives in the Old City."

The ring of the New City accomplished its purpose—the crime-ridden streets no longer spread outward from the center. But dark things grow even in the absence of sunlight, and the denizens of the Old City began stacking floors on top of other floors, and buildings on top of other buildings, until the whole thing looked like a tottering child's toy ready to fall at the touch of a well-placed kick.

The rooftops of the Old City were now higher than the tallest building in the New City—the six-story Home Government building, a gleaming beacon of shining white marble that was meant to be visible from anywhere in the New City. Now, owing to the increased height of the Old City, those residents who lived directly across the ring from the Home Government building could not see the glimmering edifice—only the crooked towers and plumes of dank smoke that emitted from the Old City.

The Home Government building was set at the northern side of the Great Square. The other three sides were residence buildings for the City Fathers, twelve identical three-story brick buildings set four to each side.

The cobblestones that paved the rest of the City were not present in the Great Square. Instead, the ground was composed of large pieces of marble that matched the Home Government building. This marble was cleaned every day, three times a day, by twenty-four servants who scrubbed on their hands and knees at even the most minute scuff in the field of white. There were to be no imperfections in the Great Square.

The twelve City Fathers, descendants of those original forward-thinking men who had stopped the swelling pustule of crime (this was another phrase Elizabeth had overheard, though it wasn't one of Papa's—Papa didn't state things in such a poetic manner), waited on a dais in front of the Home Government building to greet the families of the New City. Beside each Father was a servant holding a bag that contained coins for the children.

Every family lined up according to their housing parish number—there being one Father for each parish. Strictly speaking each Father was a sort of governor for his parish, although as far as Elizabeth could tell all the actual work was done by the Father's representative in the parish.

In Elizabeth's parish that was Beadle Kinley, a horrid old man who smelled of mothballs and always insisted that Elizabeth sit on his lap when he came to visit her papa. She'd tried very hard to avoid this task on his last visit, arguing that she was far too grown-up for lap-sitting. But the Beadle had given Papa a look with his piercing blue eyes, a look that Elizabeth could not read but that her father understood.

He'd swallowed visibly and said, with the tiniest of tremors in his voice, "Go on, Elizabeth. You're not so grown-up yet."

Mama had looked away as the Beadle slid his damp hand down Elizabeth's curls and onto her back. Elizabeth had wanted to wriggle away from his foul touch, but she had learned that he seemed to enjoy this (he always chuckled wheezily in a way that passed for happiness, anyhow) and since she wanted it over with as soon as possible she sat very still and hoped he'd have his fill of her company soon.

Elizabeth shook away the memory of the Beadle as she and her family joined their line. Polly and Edith tried to jostle in front of her in order to receive their coins first, but Margaret reprimanded them sharply and they fell into line behind. Elizabeth was so preoccupied with thoughts of Alice and the mysterious voice (and the creeping memory of the Beadle that seemed to hover like an infected thing in the back of her mind) that she hardly noticed. Of course it was only right that she go first—she was the girls' aunt, after all, and her father was more important than Daniel—but at the moment she couldn't say that she cared.

She only wondered about Alice.

The voice said that Alice was her sister.

Mama and Papa had always said that Elizabeth's only sister was Margaret.

And nobody ever spoke of a person called Alice.

Except on the day that the newspaper brought news of the fire in that hospital.

And today, when Elizabeth came down the stairs in her new blue dress.

Alice must have been my sister once, but she was sent away to that hospital. But if she was sent away, why did no one ever say so? Why did no one ever visit her?

It was very possible the voice was lying to her.

Or, if you are perfectly honest with yourself, Elizabeth Violet Hargreaves, there was no voice at all. Only a phantom you made up to amuse yourself in the garden.

It was certainly possible that the voice was just her own imagination, trying to explain why everyone kept mentioning a person called Alice and then shushing the name away.

Elizabeth moved forward with the line, hearing the *clink-clink-clink* of coins and the numerous happy cries of "Thank you, Father!" echoing all around the Great Square.

The marble tiles made quick walking an impossibility. The material was slippery—not less so for the daily polishing—and it forced everyone who walked upon it to take tiny, mincing steps. There was no striding confidently across the Great Square. That was likely by design, as it was probably best to get one's inferiors in the correct state of mind before they met with one of the Fathers.

Polly and Edith fidgeted behind Elizabeth, tugging on her curls and ribbons to try to make her turn around. But Elizabeth only waved them away with an impatient hand. She didn't have time for her nieces' teasing. There were a lot of things she needed to consider just at the moment. She half wished it wasn't Giving Day at all, for to be surrounded by a jostle of people who expected her to smile and make conversation was very tiresome at present.

After what seemed like a very long while (but was probably not more than a quarter of an hour) Elizabeth and her family reached the front of the line. The City Father for their parish, Mr. Dodgson, smiled down at her as he presented her with a shiny gold coin.

"You are the image of your sister today, Miss Hargreaves," he said.

There was something very odd in the way he said this, a kind of undercurrent that Elizabeth only just sensed. She did feel certain, however, that the sister Mr. Dodgson referred to was not Margaret.

He's talking about Alice. And that's why Mama looked so shocked when I came into the breakfast room this morning—because she looked at me and saw Alice.

So the voice wasn't lying to her. Although that didn't necessarily mean there *was* a voice, after all—it might have been her own cleverness that drew the proper conclusion.

Although I don't know what all the business about the Caterpillar and the throat-cutting was—perhaps a remnant of a nightmare I'd only just remembered.

Mr. Dodgson was gazing at her expectantly and Elizabeth realized she'd been standing there like a goose, holding the coin and staring into nothing.

"Thank you very much, Father," she said, dropping into her prettiest curtsy. She sensed rather than saw her parents' relief.

It was only then, for the first time in her life, that she realized her parents feared the City Fathers. And more than that, too— everyone feared them. The Fathers' censure could destroy a family, drive them from the New City and out in the wild plains or out onto the unforgiving sea—or worse, into the terror and darkness of the Old City.

"Mr. Hargreaves, I'd like a word," Mr. Dodgson said, grasping her father just above the elbow and pulling him back a discreet distance so their conversation could not be overheard.

It was not unusual during Giving Day for this to happen— Mr. Dodgson often used Giving Day as an opportunity to speak with Papa about some issue or other. But Elizabeth felt this time was somehow different. Perhaps it was the tautness of Mr. Dodgson's jaw, or the deep coldness in his eyes. Perhaps it was the way that Papa seemed to flinch away from the words Mr. Dodgson said.

Or perhaps it was that Elizabeth saw, very clearly, Mr. Dodgson's lips form the word "Alice."

Alice, Alice, Elizabeth thought crossly. *Why is Alice haunting me today?*

It was hard not to feel that this Alice, who was possibly (*probably*) her sister, was trying her hardest to spoil the perfect day Elizabeth had envisaged that morning.

Elizabeth felt suddenly that she was thirsty and her shiny patent leather shoes pinched her toes and the ribbons pinned in her hair made her scalp itch. She wanted to go home and have lunch—Margaret and Daniel and Polly and Edith would stay, for Giving Day was a feast day in the New City and after lunch there would be an extra-special pudding and then the family would give gifts to all the servants, and the adults would have presents for the children.

She didn't want to be troubled with worries over a ghost sister and her father's cowering and Mr. Dodgson's cold eyes. She wanted to stuff herself silly on roast duck and potatoes with lots of butter and gravy and then have the largest serving of pudding she was allowed. She wanted to tear open a box from Mama and Papa and find a new doll or a stuffed toy and then spend the rest of the afternoon keeping it out of the hands of her nieces. She wanted to pretend that all the uncomfortable knowledge she'd gained today was just some silly fancy, imagination run wild while she dreamed beneath the roses.

She might even still be there now, under the roses and sound asleep, and soon she would wake up when she heard Mama calling her and saying it was time to go to the square.

Papa and Mr. Dodgson returned then. Mr. Dodgson gave Mama a polite nod and smile and Mama nodded in return. Margaret and Daniel stepped forward with their daughters, and

Elizabeth's group moved off to the edge of the square to wait for them.

Mama and Papa immediately put their heads close together and began speaking through the bottoms of their teeth so that Elizabeth couldn't hear. When Elizabeth turned her face up in curiosity Mama waved her away.

"Go and play while you wait for Polly and Edith," Mama said.

This was Elizabeth's cue to Leave the Adults to Adult Business, and on reflection she decided it wasn't any hardship to do so. She wasn't interested in any more uncomfortable thoughts. She'd had her fill of those today, thank you very much.

She scuffed her shoe soles along the polished marble, wondering if she might leave a mark there that no one would be able to clean.

That would serve Mr. Dodgson right, she thought. *His house is just there, and every day he would have to cross over a black mark as he goes into the Home Government building. And he would know that everything isn't perfect and proper and ordered in his little world, and it would keep him up at night, a tiny thing under his mattress like the princess and her pea.*

Her chest was full of heaving anger all of a sudden, and it was mixed up with shame at seeing her father quail away from the City Father and the helpless frustration of knowing there was nothing that could be done about it.

"Don't go far, Alice," Mama said absently.

Alice again. Always Alice. I'm not Alice. I'm Elizabeth.

She put the toe of her shiny black leather shoe against the perfect white marble and stared at it.

The color from the shoe drained away, starting at the back of her heel, and poured onto the marble walk. In a moment her right shoe was a dull pinkish white and beneath her sole was a giant black stain. It wasn't a puddle, either—it sank into the marble and set there. Elizabeth gave it a fierce grin. No amount of polishing would ever remove that mark, and every year when she came to Giving Day she'd see it there and know that she, Elizabeth Violet Hargreaves (*not Alice*) did that.

Although she did regret the time that the servants would spend trying to fix it. Perhaps if she wished hard enough Mr. Dodgson would scrub at it himself, scandalizing all the servants and the other City Fathers.

She lifted her gaze up to the place where Mr. Dodgson stood. Daniel and Margaret and Edith and Polly were still there, taking an inordinate amount of time for a short Giving Day meeting. Margaret had her hands on Polly's shoulders and Daniel's were on Edith's, as if to keep the girls from shooting off into the plaza now that they had their coins in hand. The adults had their eyes fixed on Mr. Dodgson's face and even from this distance Elizabeth could see the nervous twitch at the corner of Margaret's mouth.

He really is an old monster, Elizabeth thought. *Yes, I think I shall wish that when he sees this stain he will spend all his days and nights attempting to clean it and never succeed.*

Elizabeth had never tried one of her wishes on a person before, but she was certain it would work if she put enough force into the wish. She had so much hate swelling in her at that moment that she thought she could set the dais aflame if she looked at it long enough.

When you walk to your home this evening you'll glance down at the marble when you reach this exact spot. And when you see the stain that has spread all over the marble you'll call the servants and tell them to clean it. And tomorrow morning when they aren't able to clean it you'll fall to your knees and take the rags and polish and say, "I'll do it myself, I'll stay here as long as necessary." And so you will never leave this place—you'll stay right here scrubbing away until you starve and die.

It was a lot of wish to send out, but Elizabeth wanted it to happen exactly as she saw it in her head. She wrapped the wish carefully in her mind, like a brown paper package delivered by the postman, and she pointed it at Mr. Dodgson.

His head jerked back, as if he'd been slapped, and whatever he was saying to Daniel and Margaret seemed to trickle and die on his lips. The blood drained out of Mr. Dodgson's face. Elizabeth saw Daniel reach toward the City Father as if to brace Mr. Dodgson and then pull his hand back as if thinking better of it. Mr. Dodgson would not appreciate such familiarity.

Mr. Dodgson shook his head from side to side, as if trying to dislodge an unpleasant thought.

You'll never dislodge that thought, oh no, that's what you get for terrorizing my papa.

Elizabeth turned her head away so that Mr. Dodgson wouldn't see the triumph on her face. If he suspected her of any kind of wrongdoing he might punish her family, and even though her family was sometimes tiresome and often mysterious she didn't want anything bad to happen to them. They were her family, after all, and she supposed they all loved each other even when they didn't act like it.

Aren't you something, sister of Alice.

There was that voice again, that horrible know-all voice that came uninvited and went away only when it felt like it. She resolved not to talk to it this time.

Not speaking to me, sister of Alice?

I'm not sister of Alice. I'm Elizabeth, she thought angrily, and then chided herself for not keeping her promise to herself.

Very well, Elizabeth, the voice said, and Elizabeth was annoyed because it was clear that the voice was only humoring her. She could hear the laughter underneath.

Just then Elizabeth saw a strange thing, a thing that shouldn't be anywhere but certainly not in the Great Square on Giving Day.

There was a small walkway, almost like a little tunnel, in between each of the City Fathers' homes. These walkways were always there—there was nothing much to remark in that.

What was remarkable was that there was a man standing in one of them, and he wasn't wearing the livery of the City Fathers' servants, and he wasn't dressed in his best suit like all the men in the square. He wore a pair of trousers that might have been some other color once but were certainly grey now, grey because they'd clearly never been washed, and over them he had a ragged blue coat that was too large at the shoulders.

And still this wasn't what had drawn Elizabeth's attention.

The man had his back to her and the rest of the square. And this man had the tail of a bird—a long, white-feathered thing that arced up from under the hem of the coat. Elizabeth was almost certain that the bare ankles visible beneath the trouser cuffs were the same scaly yellow as the chicken feet for sale at the Saturday market.

She took a few steps toward the man-bird, astonished that no one else seemed to notice him. Surely someone that raggedy should have drawn the notice of the guards that patrolled the square. But the only person who appeared to have noted him was Elizabeth.

The man's white tail floated away into the darkness in the back of the walkway. He was leaving, and Elizabeth hadn't gotten a proper look at him at all. She wanted to know if he had the face of a bird, too, or just the feet and tail.

She picked up her pace, but the marble made it impossible to run without falling flat on her face, so she had a kind of awkward hurried shuffle that surely appeared ridiculous to anyone who saw her.

When she reached the edge of the square and the regular cobblestones she paused, squinting into the deep pools of darkness between the buildings. She thought she saw the white tail flash in the shadows, but she wasn't certain. Elizabeth took a few more steps, feeling terribly daring. No one was supposed to approach the City Fathers' homes without express permission.

She glanced back over her shoulder to see if Mama and Papa were watching, because she was sure to be chastised if they were. Margaret and Daniel had joined them now and the four of them were having a Very Serious Conversation—Elizabeth could tell by the way they all stood close together and bent their heads toward one another so no passersby could eavesdrop. Polly and Edith were on their hands and knees trying to spin their new coins on the marble, and Margaret surely hadn't noticed this else she would have told her girls to get up before they dirtied their dresses.

Nobody will notice if I just dart away for a moment.

Elizabeth didn't look around again to see if anyone was watching. She ran into the walkway between the buildings and then paused, waiting for the alarm to be raised.

No one appeared to have noticed her exit from the square.

No one, that is, except for the Voice.

What are you doing, sister of Alice?

I told you I'm Elizabeth, not sister of Alice.

Elizabeth felt pleased that the Voice sounded alarmed. She took a few more steps, waiting for her eyes to grow accustomed to the shadow. She couldn't see the white-tailed man any longer, and there was a little rush of disappointment. Perhaps she wouldn't find out if he had the face of a bird, after all, and she would have to go back and spin coins with Polly and Edith until Mama and Papa decided it was time to return for the feast.

There was a scratching of footsteps in the dirt, and the gleam of eyes near the very end of the walkway. Then Elizabeth saw the white-feathered tail disappear around the corner behind the left-hand house.

If I only hurry, I can catch him and see, she thought, breaking into a run.

No, don't, sister of Alice! Don't follow the white tail.

"Why ever not?" Elizabeth said, huffing as she ran. She wasn't an active-running-about sort of child and she was already hot and out of breath.

I am the keeper of the stories and I've heard this story before.

"My story isn't the same as anyone's," Elizabeth said.

Stories are retold more often than people think, because they don't listen to stories and learn properly.

Elizabeth reached the end of the walkway, which was much longer than she'd expected. She thought she would find herself between two back gardens (she'd expected the City Fathers to have the largest, most elaborate gardens imaginable), but instead she had arrived at a T-junction with another walkway.

She glanced to the left and saw the white tail bobbing away behind the buildings.

Elizabeth ran again, certain that she would catch up to the bird-man in a moment. He was only walking and she was running. The moment she caught him she'd tap his shoulder and he would look directly at her and then she would know for sure whether he was a bird or a man. And once she did she would run right back to Mama and Papa and no one would ever know where she'd gone or what she'd done.

That's what Alice said, too, the Voice said.

"Oh, do go away," Elizabeth told the Voice. "It's not polite to eavesdrop on someone's thoughts."

I only meant to say that Alice followed someone she oughtn't have and she wasn't the happier for it. You may not be either.

"I told you, go away," Elizabeth said.

The Voice was distracting her when she needed to pay attention. It seemed that no matter how fast she ran the bobbing white tail never got any closer, though she watched carefully and the bird-man didn't seem to be running.

Elizabeth was only half aware of what was around her. The bird-man turned another sharp corner and Elizabeth huffed out an irritated breath.

At this rate I'll never catch up with him. Perhaps I should just turn back now.

(But then you'll never know for certain if he really is a bird-man, or just a man with a feathered tail stuck under his jacket, and if he is just an ordinary sort of man don't you want to know why he's done such a silly thing?)

A stitch had formed under her right ribs, and it made little shooting pains with every step she took. She was starting to get hungry and cross, too, and felt that she'd been gone long enough that when she went back all the grown-ups would shout at her for sneaking off.

Yes, I should just go back, Elizabeth thought, but as she thought it she reached the turning where the bird-man had disappeared.

Just as she arrived she saw a flash of orange and one bright black eye flash around the next corner, which was about ten steps from where she stood.

"Wait!" Elizabeth called. "Oh, wait, please. I won't hurt you! I only want to talk to you for a moment."

Elizabeth sprinted to the corner. Her dress was sticking to her back and she tugged at it as she ran. She was certain her beautiful curls and ribbons were all bedraggled, too. But the bird-man was so close. She'd only just seen him. He couldn't be more than a few steps away now.

Elizabeth rounded the corner and stopped.

She'd reached an odd sort of intersection. She stood in a circle with many alleys shooting off it in all directions, like she was in the center of the sun and its rays.

Elizabeth peered down one of the alleys. There was nothing much to see there—the light petered out a few steps beyond where she stood and the rest of the alley was hidden in shadow.

Just like the walkway where I first saw the bird-man.

She peeked into another alley, and saw the same thing. She went all around the circle only to discover that every path looked exactly the same. It was only then that she finally noticed she couldn't see any buildings around her, or hear the noise of people, or smell the Giving Day feasts that were surely being cooked in every home.

All around her were high faceless brick walls, and above her was an identical brick ceiling.

She wasn't in an alley, running behind buildings in the New City. She was in a tunnel. And all the exits from the circle where she stood were identical.

Including the one that would lead her home.

Elizabeth felt the first stirrings of fear. Where in the City was she? She'd never heard of a brick tunnel anywhere—if she had, she might be able to determine just how far she'd gotten from the Great Square.

Mama and Papa and Margaret and even Daniel, who never ever yells, are going to be very put out with me when I get back.

She didn't doubt at all that she *would* find her way back. The path wasn't obvious at the moment but soon she would remember which direction she'd come from and then simply retrace her steps.

And even if I choose the wrong path, I'm sure to come out on a street. And streets have cabs. I shall simply order the driver to return me home and then Hobson will use some spare change to pay for the cab. I might get a scolding, but I shall also have a wonderful story to tell Polly and Edith. They shall be ever so jealous to see me riding up all by myself in a cab like a queen.

"Yes, that's just what I shall do," Elizabeth said.

She took a few steps into one of the paths, cocking her head to one side to listen. It was certainly very strange, the way she couldn't hear anything from the other end of any of the tunnels. It would be easier to make a choice if all the choices weren't precisely the same.

But they aren't all the same, Elizabeth thought. *Each tunnel leads to a different place. I just don't know what that place is yet.*

Elizabeth realized that if she considered it properly this was all just an adventure, and there was really no need to be frightened at all. When she got through the tunnel—whichever tunnel she chose—she would find someone who would help her find her way home.

That's how things worked in the New City, after all. Everyone was part of the same community, even if you'd never met them before. And she knew for certain that if she mentioned Papa's name people would hasten to assist her. It always happened whenever they went out shopping or to a restaurant or some such thing. There would always be a bowing or curtsying worker eagerly saying, "Yes, Mr. Hargreaves. Whatever you would like, Mr. Hargreaves."

Elizabeth could just imagine someone holding the door of a cab open for her, saying, "Please take care, Miss Hargreaves." The driver would gently settle a rug over her knees and just as he climbed up onto his seat someone would run up and hand her a cake from a tea shop and say, "I would be ever so grateful if you would take this, Miss Hargreaves," and Elizabeth would nod and ask what shop it was from so that her family could return and patronize it at a later time.

The thought of the tea cake made Elizabeth's stomach rumble. She really ought to be in her own carriage right now, nearly home and ready for the feast.

"Well, Elizabeth Violet Hargreaves, the sooner you choose the sooner you'll be home."

She stood in the center of the circle, closed her eyes and pointed her arm straight out like the hand of a clock. Then she spun in a slow circle for a few moments before coming to a stop. Elizabeth opened her eyes.

The tunnel she pointed at looked the same as the others. Elizabeth shrugged and went inside.

Be careful now, sister of Alice! Be so, so careful!

Elizabeth wasn't certain if she actually was hearing the Voice now. It would sound tinny and far away and then somehow close and clear.

Besides, she didn't need the advice of a mysterious Voice to know that she ought to be careful. She was going into a dark tunnel and the possibility of falling and hurting herself in the darkness was very great.

She strode forward confidently, certain that she would see light at the other end of the tunnel any moment.

Elizabeth was already looking forward to sitting in a cab. Her patent leather shoes, which had looked so smart that morning, pinched her feet. They weren't meant for running. They were only meant for sitting at tea and standing in line to meet the City Fathers. If she looked down she could see the shoe that lost its color faintly glowing in the light from the entrance.

I wonder how I will explain to Mama what happened to it, she thought. Elizabeth knew she could never tell her mother the truth. Mama would never believe—not even if Elizabeth demonstrated with the other shoe right in front of Mama's eyes.

Mama only saw what she wanted to see, and everything else resulted in "Run along, Elizabeth."

It didn't matter, really, if Mama was upset about the shoe. What mattered was Elizabeth's wish. When she thought of Mr. Dodgson and that terrible fear on Papa's face she felt a fierce delight that Dodgson would spend the remainder of his days on his knees, scrubbing at a stain that could never be cleaned. That would be worth any scolding she got from Mama about her shoe.

Elizabeth was so caught up in thinking of Mama and Mr. Dodgson and her shoe and the anticipated relief of a cab and a cake that at first she didn't notice just how dark it was inside the tunnel. And it was very dark, much darker than she'd expected. There was no light in the direction she was heading, and when she looked behind, the entrance of the tunnel seemed to have shrunk to just a pinprick.

"But that can't be," Elizabeth said, frowning. "I haven't come so far."

She started back toward the entrance, determined to prove the truth of this statement, but the pinprick shrank even more as she looked at it.

And then it disappeared entirely.

There was no exit that way.

Cold fear washed through her.

Just what sort of mess have you gotten yourself into, Elizabeth Violet Hargreaves?

How very foolish she'd been, chasing after some strange man because she wanted to see his face. At the time it had seemed like a harmless lark, a moment's diversion.

Now she was trapped in a tunnel far from home and the way back was closed.

The only possible direction she could go was forward.

But what if she reached the other side and found that it was closed, too? Would she die in this place, a brick mausoleum, withering without light and air?

Elizabeth clenched her fists. "No, I will not."

She marched forward, her heels ringing on the pavement. She was going home to Mama and Papa and when she got there she vowed she would be very sensible from now on.

"I shall be so sensible I might even be called boring," she said.

Her voice echoed off the walls and returned to her, seemed to press up against her ears and make her shiver.

Sensible, sensible, sensible, boring, boring, boring

"That's right. I shall be eminently sensible. I shall always do what I am told and I won't take any extra marmalade at breakfast. I'll discreetly refuse sugar cubes when Hobson tries to hand them to me. I'll never make a fuss about anything again." She paused, thinking hard. "Well, perhaps about sitting in the Beadle's lap. I don't think that's something I should have to do."

A voice said out of the darkness, a voice that scraped like grain in a grindstone, "He only wants you to do that because he's a dirty old man. When you sit there and wriggle, his dead staff comes to life again."

Elizabeth screamed. She couldn't help it. She'd had no notion that she wasn't alone in the tunnel. Then she was angry because she'd screamed—angry at herself and more angry at the person who startled her.

"Who's there?" she demanded, using her best Hargreaves voice. People generally obeyed the Hargreaves voice.

"Yes, he likes it when you wriggle this way and that, and he can smell the sweetness of your hair and think about what he would do if only your parents would leave the room," the voice said again. "He would like that very much, although I expect you wouldn't. Most girls don't, you know."

The voice sounded closer this time, though Elizabeth hadn't heard any movement in the darkness.

"Who are you?" she repeated. "If you're not going to introduce yourself properly I don't want to speak to you. I don't need to stay here and listen to you speaking about filthy things."

The things the voice said made her skin crawl, made her feel like hideous bugs marched inside her ears with the words.

Of course she'd known, deep down, that what the Beadle did was wrong. She didn't completely understand what was wrong about it but she knew that it made her feel ill and that was enough.

The voice cackled, and Elizabeth started away, for it had been just at her right shoulder—close enough for her to feel its breath. This wasn't like the other Voice, the mischievous one in her head. This voice was a cruel and malignant thing, harsh and grating. This voice had never seen sunshine.

"But filthy things do happen here, Miss Hargreaves. Filthy things done by filthy people."

Elizabeth didn't turn around, though the owner of the voice stayed very close to her. She wasn't going to give him the satisfaction of her attention. Whoever it was obviously wanted to terrorize her and she was not going to be terrorized and that was that.

"I'm not interested in filthy things. Filthy things only happen in the Old City," Elizabeth said primly, marching forward.

"And just where do you think you are then, little Alice?"

She couldn't see him because the dark was an absolute thing, a cloak over her eyes but she could feel him, so very close, close enough for his long fingers to scrape over her upper arms.

The terror erupted then, made her heart pound and her hands shake, made her want to run and scream and cry and call for her papa to save her, but she kept her voice as clear and even as she could make it.

"I'm afraid you are mistaken," she said. "My name is not Alice."

"Oh, you're an Alice, all right. Too curious by half, and foolish with it. So full of magic that you practically glow in the dark, so full of it that you're calling all the hunters to you without even knowing it, little rabbit. And rabbits who wander from their warren get caught by foxes."

He did grab her then, closed his fingers around her arms and squeezed hard enough to bruise. He had long, long fingernails that tore the sleeves of her dress and cut into her skin. She felt like he'd branded her there, marked her as his own.

Elizabeth was scared, she was more scared than she'd ever been in her life, but she was angry again, too. Angry because there was that *name* again and somebody insisting that she was someone she was not.

"I. Am. Not. ALICE."

The last word was not a scream but a yell, a primal thing that came from her heart instead of her throat. The man holding her jerked away, releasing her. There was an awful smell of burning flesh, sour and smoky.

"My hands!" he screamed. "What have you done to my hands?"

Elizabeth didn't know what she'd done, but since she couldn't say she was sorry it happened, she didn't stop to investigate. She ran, harder and faster than she'd ever run before, ran until the howls of pain and rage faded away into the shadows of the tunnel behind her.

"How *long* is this horrible place?" she said, stopping to try to catch her breath when she thought she was far enough away from the man with the long nails and the grating voice.

For all she knew the tunnel might not be a tunnel at all but a labyrinth, or a circle. She might run forward only to crash right into that man again from the other side.

Think, Elizabeth. Think, think.

"There has to be a way in and out. Otherwise that man would never have gotten in here in the first place. So there are exits, but they must not be very obvious ones."

She hesitantly reached out to her left, waving her hands in the blackness until she felt the rough scrape of brick under her fingers. She had an idea that there were openings in the wall, if only she could find them.

But what if I'm walking along here, searching for a door, and it happens that the door is on the opposite side and I never notice it?

Elizabeth shook her head. If she worried about all the possibilities, then she would never get anywhere—she'd just stand there like a frightened goose until that man caught up with her again. She rather thought he would be more determined to catch her the second time, too, and she wasn't certain she could duplicate whatever it was that hurt him the first time.

Elizabeth crept along, sweeping her arms up the wall as far as she could reach and then down again in big half circles. Every few moments she would stop and listen for the sound of someone creeping up behind her. She wasn't going to be taken by surprise again.

After several moments (in which her stomach began making extremely noisy groans that were loud enough to drown out the possible presence of another person) she halted in frustration. There wasn't any door in the wall. At this rate she'd just go on creeping forever and the only thing she would detect would be plain brick wall.

She put her back to the wall and lowered herself until she was sitting. Her feet hurt so badly that she wanted to take off her shoes, but she knew that wouldn't be a wise thing to do. She might step on a nail or a piece of broken glass, and if her foot were hurt or bleeding she wouldn't be able to run if she needed to run. And she might need to run, though she hadn't the faintest notion where she might run to. There wasn't anything here except shadows and brick that went on and on and on.

But how did that man get in here? The exit behind me is closed, and the way ahead is dark.

A tear slid out of her right eye, and she knuckled it away impatiently. Crying wasn't going to solve anything. And no one was going to come and save her, because no one had any notion where she'd gone.

Except the Voice. That Voice knew where I was going, somehow.

It felt very lonely there with the dark pressing all around her and her feet hurting and her stomach growling. She would have welcomed the presence of a bossy Voice just at the moment. At least she would have felt less like she'd fallen into a hole with no bottom.

You have to stand up again, Elizabeth. You have to keep going.

But it was very difficult to feel that going forward mattered at all. Why tire herself out if there was nowhere to go?

Just then she felt something furry nosing around the fingers of her left hand. It was only a tiny thing, making equally tiny squeaking noises.

She lay the palm of her hand flat and felt its paws as it climbed on, and then when it scurried off again quickly. A mouse.

"Hello there, Mr. Mouse," she said. "Don't run away. I won't hurt you."

She heard the mouse hurrying back. Its forepaws climbed onto her palm again. Elizabeth couldn't see the mouse, but she imagined it perching there, half on and half off, staring up at her with bright little button eyes.

"That's what Big People always say, that they won't hurt us, but then they set out traps that catch or hit us with great brooms or put the cat on us," the mouse said, in a rather squeaky little voice.

"Well, I haven't got any traps or brooms or cats in my pocket," Elizabeth replied, and then a moment later she realized she was talking to a mouse. She was *talking* to a *mouse*, and the mouse understood her and she understood the mouse.

She'd thought the day couldn't be any stranger, but she supposed one must be prepared for strange things to happen on a day when one chased a bird-man into an endless tunnel.

"You could still stomp on me with your feet," the mouse said.

"I would never do such a thing!" Elizabeth cried, insulted at the very thought. Then she amended, "Leastways, not on purpose. I might accidentally tread on your tail in the dark, but I wouldn't mean it. It's very dark in here, you know."

"Not for me," the mouse said, and Elizabeth noted the pride in his voice. "I can see everything just as clear as sunshine."

"Might you help me, then, little mouse? I want to get out of this place more than anything. Have you seen an exit large enough for a person to pass through?"

The mouse made a series of little squeaks that trilled up and down, and Elizabeth realized he was laughing.

"Silly little girl," the mouse crowed.

"I'm not a silly little girl," Elizabeth said, stung. "And that's certainly not a polite thing to say to someone you've only just met."

The mouse sobered immediately. "No, you're right, of course. I'm terribly sorry for laughing. It's only just that you don't have to stay in here if you don't want to."

"What do you mean?" Elizabeth asked.

"Well, you're a Magician, aren't you?"

"Am I?"

What on earth is a Magician? Elizabeth thought. She didn't like to ask, though, for she felt the mouse might laugh at her again and she wasn't in the mood for feeling a fool.

"I can smell the magic on you," the mouse said. "Don't you know that you have it?"

"Well," Elizabeth said slowly. "I know that I can do certain things, things that other people don't seem to be able to do. Like change a rose into a butterfly."

"Then surely," the mouse said, with infinite patience in his voice. "You can change a wall of brick into a door."

When he said it like that she felt very silly for not thinking of such a thing in the first place. Her only excuse was that she was tired and hungry and confused and she'd had a rather bad fright, which might make anyone silly.

"Thank you, Mr. Mouse," Elizabeth said. "I'm going to do just as you suggest."

"I don't suppose," the mouse said with a touch of wistfulness, "that you have a crumb or two in your pocket?"

"I'm terribly sorry," Elizabeth said. "I haven't got anything today. Mama said I wasn't to put toast in my pockets as I usually do, else I would ruin my splendid dress."

"Ah, well. No matter. I can find a crumb here and there," the mouse said.

"Do move away now, so I don't accidently step on you. That would be a poor repayment," Elizabeth said. "Unless you'd like to come out of the tunnel with me? If you do, you could go in one of my pockets."

"I suppose I'd better," the mouse said. "You seem like the sort who might need advice again, and I'm just the mouse to give it."

"Very well," Elizabeth said, though she didn't think she'd need the advice of a mouse again. Still, once she left the tunnel she might be able to find some food to share. It would be a nice thing, since the mouse had been so helpful.

She gathered the mouse up and carefully slid it into the large pocket on the front of her dress. The mouse wriggled around a bit and then seemed to settle down at the bottom of the pocket.

Elizabeth stood and faced the brick wall again. She put both hands on the wall and thought, *I wish there was a door, just here.*

Nothing happened.

"You'll need to try a little harder than that," the mouse said, its voice muffled by the cloth of her dress.

Oh, do be quiet, Elizabeth thought. All of this was hard enough without the mouse commenting on every little thing she did or didn't do, but she held her tongue. It wouldn't be in the least helpful to start an argument when she was trying to solve this problem of the wall.

The thing of it was that she'd never really thought of what she did as *magic*. It was only wishes, gentle thoughts that sort of drifted out of her and made things happen.

(Although that thought about Mr. Dodgson wasn't gentle, no it was not at all.)

Now it was like her wishes were in a bottle and the mouse had put a stopper on it by calling her a Magician. Magic wasn't real; it was a faraway thing done by fairy godmothers with pumpkins or snow queens with mirrors on high mountains. Magic wasn't something that Elizabeth had at her fingertips.

She thought about asking the mouse his opinion on what to do next, but a small, delicate rumble shook Elizabeth's pocket. The mouse had fallen asleep, and she rather thought it was snoring.

Do mice snore? It was no stranger, she supposed, than a mouse sitting up on its hind legs and talking.

She shook her head. If she didn't stay focused on the task at hand she'd be stuck inside this tunnel forever, and the mouse would laugh and laugh at her ineptitude.

No mouse will laugh at me again, she vowed, and placed her hands flat against the brick.

I wish there was a door here, she thought, but this time she pictured the door in her mind. It was just a little taller and wider than she was herself, and it was made of wood that had been painted white. The frame all around was as blue as her dress, and the doorknob was a pretty silver color. It would open on noiseless hinges and—best of all, in Elizabeth's opinion—no one bad would be able to see that it was there.

That man who grabbed her, or anyone else like him, would never notice the door, even if they touched it. To them it would just be another section of the brick wall.

Elizabeth felt the rough brick shift under her fingers as it transformed into the smooth painted surface of her door. And just in time too, for there was suddenly a noise coming from farther down the tunnel—from the place where the man had been.

"I'm going to get you, you little witch, and when I do you're going to wish you'd never been born!"

Elizabeth grasped the knob of the door, which was just where she'd thought it would be, and opened it, stepping quickly out of the tunnel and slamming the door behind her.

But not before she heard the last thing the man was shouting.

"You'll wish you'd never been born! *Just like ALICE!*"

Elizabeth patted the door behind her, confident that it was shut tight. If her wish was true then the man wouldn't find the door, and even if he did, she had more opportunities to escape him out in the open. Surely someone would help her if a man ran at her and tried to take her away.

She felt unaccountably shaken by his last words. She didn't like to think of Alice wishing she'd never been born. The Voice had made it sound like Alice was someone strong and powerful, someone whom Elizabeth should aspire to be.

Though he also said that Alice had regretted her curiosity.

Elizabeth was regretting her own curiosity very much, but now that she was out in the world again she was certain that everything would be put right.

She rubbed at her eyes, blinking. It wasn't so terribly bright out—it seemed like there was a haze hanging over everything—but she felt like a mole that had just emerged from the ground.

Slowly her surroundings came into focus, and when they did she half wondered if she hadn't been better off in that tunnel after all. Perhaps she should have just gone back the way she came, and never mind the man with the long fingernails who tried to grab her.

The door had opened onto a square, but it was a square like Elizabeth had never seen before. This was no Great Square, or even one of the smaller squares scattered around the New City. Those smaller squares always had parks or zoos or pleasant little fruit markets.

There was nothing pleasant about this square, and Elizabeth felt herself shrinking back against the door she'd just come through, hoping to turn herself invisible.

There were several run-down buildings that faced on the square, all of them wooden, and all of the wood was grey. The bottom floors were certainly businesses—the sharp scent of spirits wafted in the air, mixed with meat pies and something else—something that smelled like desperation.

The upper floors of every structure seemed to be apartments or bedrooms, and some of the buildings had three or four or five floors above the initial one. Elizabeth had never seen buildings so high

(except from far away, in the Old City)

(and that man said to me, "Just where do you think you are?" and I should have known when he said that, I should have known that I've wandered too far from home)

Some of these buildings had porches where sharp-eyed men stood in clumps, smoking cigarettes or holding small bottles or both. All of them wore the rough homespun wool and leather boots that she associated with laborers or sailors, and none of them looked as though they'd bathed in several weeks. Their laughter was a harsh and raucous thing. They seemed to do a lot of it, though Elizabeth heard no joy.

The women were something else, again. All of the ones Elizabeth could see wore bright colors—satins in jewels and stripes, feathers in their hair, petticoats and stockings exposed for all to see. Their lips were too red and their eyelashes were too black and they laughed shrill and long and loud. There was no joy in their laughs either, if you listened properly, though the men all around them appeared to be fooled.

These, Elizabeth knew, were Fallen Women. She'd never seen them before, only heard of them spoken in hushed undertones by the ladies who came to lunch with Mama. They always discussed Fallen Women and Their Offspring, and how they might perform some small act of charity to assist these women and children—though this act of charity would never extend as far as actually going into the Old City to hand out food and clothing personally. No, that was something for the servants to do.

The Fallen Women seemed to be trying to lure the men away from the pubs, and Elizabeth watched, fascinated, as they raised their skirts and flicked open the buttons of their blouses. Some of the men ignored the women, but others got a look in their eyes that made Elizabeth shrink even more, for it was a hard and predatory look. She wanted to shout at the women, "No, run away! They're only going to hurt you!" but then she had a funny feeling that the women knew that, and were resigned to their fate.

I must get away from here before somebody sees me, though she had no notion of how she would do such a thing. She self-consciously smoothed her hair, which was so golden and bright it would attract immediate attention if she tried to move through the square. The thought of one of those hard-eyed predators catching sight of her made Elizabeth shiver.

There was an abandoned cart a short distance away—it looked like it might have once been a place where fruit was sold but now it was just a half-rotting obstacle on the sidewalk. Elizabeth darted toward it and hunched behind, keeping a sharp eye on the crowds of men all around the square. The danger, she felt, would come from there.

Not that there weren't cruel women in the world—Elizabeth wasn't so foolish as to think that. But the women here in the square seemed mostly the sort concerned with their own survival. They wouldn't have the time or the inclination to chase after little girls.

"What I need," Elizabeth muttered, "is a cloak of some sort. Then I can slide around the edge of the square and try to find a cab."

Her eyes darted everywhere, looking for a shop, a line of laundry, anything. Not that she would *steal*, of course. She would leave some money—though the only money she had in her pocket was her Giving Day coin, and she had a notion that she would need that for transportation.

She could leave a note with a promise of payment later—always assuming she could find a sheet of paper and a fountain pen to write with. Elizabeth could make her letters very nicely, and even sign her whole name with a lovely little flourish.

"Just try to find a cab in here that will take you back to the New City," the mouse said, breaking into her thoughts.

She glanced down at her pocket. The mouse had perched its forepaws on the edge of her pocket, and stared up at her. It looked almost exactly as she'd imagined it in the tunnel—small and grey and soft looking, with pink-shell ears that turned in her direction. The only difference was the eyes. The mouse had bright green eyes, like little jewels in its face. She'd never seen a mouse with colored eyes before.

"If I managed to get into this place from the New City then I surely will be able to return there," Elizabeth said with a conviction she didn't entirely feel.

"That's precisely what Alice said, but it didn't quite work out the way she planned," the mouse said.

"Oh, Alice, Alice!" Elizabeth snapped. "All I ever hear about is Alice. How many times must I tell you that I am not Alice?"

The mouse looked up at her, and if a mouse could look crafty then this one certainly did. "Aren't you? Your parents only had you to replace her. Their little Alice had grown up and gone mad and they had to put her in a box so nobody could see her madness and her pain, she had so much pain but they didn't want to know it, but they still wanted a little pet to love so they had you and pretended that Alice never was."

Elizabeth sucked in a breath between her teeth. "That's an awful thing to say. An awful, terrible thing to say. I thought you were a nice mouse, that you were here to help me."

The mouse made a little movement that could have been a shrug. "Sometimes awful, terrible things are true. I always tell the truth, even if it means know-all little girls don't think I'm very nice. I'd rather be true than nice."

"I don't believe it's true at all," she said. "I think you're horrid."

"Whatever you like," the mouse said, unconcerned.

It couldn't be true, what the mouse said. Her parents would never put any child of theirs away when that child was hurting. And they certainly hadn't had her to *replace* Alice. That would be awful in more ways than one.

It would mean that she was nothing to them as Elizabeth, only a swap for another girl who'd become somehow unacceptable. Alice meant so little to them that anyone would do in exchange.

No, I won't believe it, Elizabeth thought fiercely. *I won't.*

But then why did no one ever mention Alice except by mistake?

She wouldn't worry about it just now. She had to get out of this terrible place and back home again. Once she was safely in her room and her belly was full and her hair was clean and washed she would think about all of these uncomfortable ideas.

"Too bad I can't turn into a mouse and dart through the square," Elizabeth said.

"Who says you can't, but then where would I be?" the mouse said.

"You could run along beside me," Elizabeth said. "And guide me, of course."

"Of course," the mouse said.

Elizabeth thought she detected a little bite in the mouse's tone, and she was about to speak sharply back at it—it was riding along in *her* pocket, after all—when it spoke again.

"But it's terribly difficult to transform, and if you don't know what you're doing then I don't think you should try," he said. "Unless you want to have whiskers and a tail for the remainder of your life."

"I'd rather not."

"Well, then, you ought to think about cloaking yourself."

"That's what I already said," Elizabeth said. "But there's no cloak to be had."

"No, no, not that sort of cloak," the mouse said. "Didn't I already say you were a Magician? You could cloak yourself with magic and no one could see you."

Elizabeth frowned. Making a door in the wall had been hard enough. How was she to use her magic to keep all the people— and there were so many people—from seeing her?

"How am I to do that?" she asked.

Again, the mouse made a little movement that was like a human shrug, even though it didn't really have shoulders.

"How am I to know? I'm just a mouse."

Elizabeth muttered a word under her breath that she'd heard Papa say only when he was especially angry. The mouse chuckled softly.

Well, she didn't need some silly mouse to help her. She could solve her problems all on her own, and she was not going to ask again and make herself sound foolish.

Everything she'd done so far was as simple as a wish, but it was harder to wish for something when you were cold and hungry and terrified of being caught. She wanted very much to rely on someone else (though she would never, ever admit such a thing out loud), for when you are a child that's what you are supposed to do—let adults decide the best thing to do. But the only adults around weren't the sort she could trust to make the best decisions for her, and so she'd gone back around to where she started. She was going to have to puzzle this one out on her own.

I wish, she thought, and then realized this thought was a very tentative thing, and that she'd have to put a bit more *oomph* into it if she wanted this wish to go anywhere.

I wish, she thought again, and just at that moment it seemed that one of the men across the square caught sight of her. Perhaps it was just a glimpse of her blond hair or the trailing end of her blue dress but there were definitely eyes upon her now, or at least upon the fruit cart.

Her insides seemed to squeeze together, and she hunched

over in terror, whispering, "You don't see me, you don't see me, you don't see me."

She listened hard for the sound of rushing footsteps, or for the approach of laughter, or the sound of someone calling, "Hey, where are you going?"

If someone comes over here I'm just going to run, run, run and perhaps they'll be so startled that they won't see me.

But that someone might come with friends, friends that would surround her and snatch her up and carry her away screaming and there would be nothing she could do about it then, for she was a small and soft and frightened thing.

"So they mustn't see me in the first place, and they don't see me, don't see me, don't see me, I'm blending in with the wall and the cart and the ground and the sky, whatever they look at it will be like I'm water that you can see through and I won't even seem like a ripple to them, no cruel eyes can see me nor cruel hands touch me, they don't see me, they don't see me, they don't see me."

And then the man was there, and she'd been concentrating so hard on her spell that she hadn't even heard his approach. She saw his boots first, cracked brown leather with protruding nails that clicked on the cobblestones (*I ought to have heard those, I really ought*), and over the tops of the boots was a pair of wool trousers that had seen better days (and could really do with a wash, too, for the smell was something terrible that made Elizabeth want to gag).

Her eyes rose higher, past the brown leather belt with the silver-handled knife hanging off it in a matching brown leather sheath, and then a brown waistcoat over a blue shirt buttoned only partway. He had a long thick scar that went across his chest, and the rest of him appeared no better washed than the trousers. She was afraid to look at his face, to see his greedy eyes, but then she told herself that she wasn't a scared little mouse—even if she felt that way—and went the rest of the way.

His face wasn't shaved, and his eyes were a very hard blue, but they were full of puzzlement now. He stared into the place where Elizabeth huddled and his face was contorted in confusion.

He can't see me, she thought, and it was a wonderful thought that filled her with glee. She could see everything about him, down to the lines around his eyes, but he was looking right at her and he *couldn't see her*.

The man scratched his head with a filthy hand and circled all around the cart.

"All right there, Abe?" one of the other men from across the street called.

"Thought I saw something," Abe replied, but though his boots passed within a whisker's length of Elizabeth he did not realize she was there.

It worked! I did it!

"Told you that you were a Magician," the mouse said, and he sounded terribly smug.

"But you didn't tell me how to do the spell, so don't think you can take credit for this," Elizabeth said tartly. "That was all my doing."

"If you know so much about doing something then you ought to get yourself out of this square before the spell wears off," the mouse said.

Elizabeth would have liked to make a smart reply back, but

she recognized the wisdom of this statement. She'd managed to hide herself from one man's eyes, but it didn't necessarily mean she could hide from them all.

I'll have to, she thought, *else I'm never going to get home again.*

She felt very exhausted then, worn thin in a way that she'd never been. Home wasn't so far away, geographically speaking, but there were so many tasks for her to accomplish in order to get there. And while she was a very clever nine-year-old, she was, in fact, only nine, and not accustomed to fending for herself in this way.

Moaning about it won't fix anything, Elizabeth Violet Hargreaves. Get yourself up and save your own self, because no one is going to do it for you.

That thought sounded like her, but a more grown-up version of her. It was as if her future self was chiding her.

(Or maybe it was Alice maybe Alice is helping me.)

No, she wasn't going after Alice again, even in her thoughts. She had quite enough Voices in her head already.

Elizabeth took a deep breath and stood up. She tried very hard not to think of the brightness of her blue dress or the very golden strands of her hair, because if she did she might suddenly become more conspicuous.

Ah! That's it!

She didn't need to make herself *invisible*. She only needed to make sure no one noticed her, and that wasn't the same thing at all.

Most of the activity in the square was on the opposite side from the fruit cart. There were two possible exits—a cobblestoned road that led away to Elizabeth's left, and a narrow alley opening almost exactly across from her. The alley was set diagonally from where she stood, so she couldn't see into it or see how long it was.

The road would leave her dangerously exposed if the spell wore off. The route to the alley would put her directly in the thick of the crowds, and Elizabeth did not fancy getting trapped in another tunnel. What if there was no exit at the other side?

No, she would have to risk the road. At least she knew there would be somewhere to run—if running became necessary, which she sincerely hoped it would not, for Elizabeth felt she'd had her fill of running for one lifetime. She was not, she decided, a running sort of person. She was a sit-quietly-with-tea-and-cakes sort of person.

It was good to know what sort of person you were, she reflected as she eased around the fruit cart and stepped out onto the road. It helped you save a lot of fuss and bother trying things that you wouldn't like in the first place.

As she walked Elizabeth thought, *You can't see me, you don't notice me, there's nothing here but a bit of air.*

And it did seem that it was working. Not one of the many people gathered in the square appeared to see her at all.

"Be careful," the mouse whispered. "Be so very careful."

She didn't respond because she thought it might draw attention to her, and if someone noticed her voice they might notice her self. It was quite irritating, the way the mouse kept presuming to instruct her on things she already knew. And she half suspected that it had spoken only because it knew she wouldn't speak back just then.

Two men suddenly broke away from the pack, shouting and

laughing. Elizabeth saw them out of the corner of her eye, reeling along and leaning on each other.

Clearly they've overimbibed spirits, she thought disdainfully. She wasn't entirely certain what spirits were, but she knew that they made people smell terrible and do uncharacteristic things.

She'd overheard one of the kitchen maids, Fiona, talking about "my Bert" and the things he did when he had too many glasses of spirits. Bert was one of the stable boys—well, stable men, if Elizabeth was truthful, though they were always referred to as "boys." Elizabeth had snuck into the kitchen to see if she could wheedle an extra cream puff from the cook.

She'd come upon Fiona and Cook sitting at the large table where Cook made pies and cakes. Fiona was crying and she had a black bruise around her eye and Cook was holding her hand and saying soothing things. Elizabeth had decided that was not the correct time to ask for an illicit snack and quietly retreated before either of them noticed her.

The two drunken men staggered about in a crooked line, and Elizabeth had a job avoiding them. Every time she thought she'd gone past them they seemed to reappear beside her, leaning this way and that. She didn't want to run—for she was not a runner, as she had decided, and also because the heels of her shoes would make quite a lot of noise—and she was trying to balance brisk walking with silence.

One of the men reached out, gesturing wildly, and his fingertips brushed against the ribbons tied in her hair.

Elizabeth gasped—she couldn't help it—and then thought quickly, *You don't see me, you can't see me, there was nothing there, only your imagination.*

The man staggered to a halt, so Elizabeth hurried on ahead of him. She heard him say to his friend, "Thought I touched something just now. Like a girl's hair," and his friend responded, "That's wishful thinking, Ed."

"But I heard her," Ed protested. "She made a little noise, like."

Elizabeth didn't stay to hear the remainder of the conversation. The important thing was to get away.

The street that Elizabeth followed didn't seem to be that much better than the square she'd just left. There were a few more-respectable businesses—pubs and bookshops and tailors and things—but just as many of those were houses where women lurked in their smallclothes and gazed at everyone passing with eyes that lured.

There was another odd thing, too—the street seemed to be stained red, especially along the curbs.

Almost as if a river of red had run along there, and left evidence of itself behind.

This thought was followed immediately by *I must get home, where the only red things are my mother's roses or the red ribbons for my hair.*

She walked along, growing increasingly desperate. She didn't think she'd gotten that far away from the New City but the towering structures of this place made it impossible to see what direction she ought to go in. It seemed far too risky to ask someone for help, and she hadn't seen anything resembling a cab.

If she didn't find her way out of here soon then she would still be in the Old City when night fell, and Elizabeth knew enough to know that would Not Be a Good Thing.

Just then something snagged her attention, made her stop in the middle of the street and turn her head.

"What is it?" the mouse whispered. He had been silent for some time.

She didn't answer. She was trying to see if she'd only imagined the thing she thought she saw.

It was purple, whatever it was, and it was at the end of a little alley that she could see into from where she stood. The object seemed to sparkle, to wink, to wave at Elizabeth, but she couldn't quite bring it into focus. The alley was shadowed, though not as dark as the tunnel that had trapped her. Elizabeth could clearly see the T-junction at the end of it, so even if she went into the alley there would be a way out.

And she did want to go in the alley, despite her previous conviction that it would not be a good idea to find herself trapped again (once was really enough for one day). The purple sparkling thing seemed to call her. It tugged under her ribs, made her move toward it without any sense of why she would do such a thing.

"Elizabeth!" the mouse said.

She didn't pay the mouse any mind, because she thought the creature was chiding her for heading off course.

Then the man's arms closed around her, vines that twined and pulled tight and his breath was hot and crooning in her ear.

"Look at this prize I've found just for me. Look at this lovely creature so sweet, so sweet, just waiting to be soured."

He picked her right up off the street like she was nothing but a bit of flour-sacking and he squeezed her so hard that the scream in her lungs was choked away.

What happened what happened how did he see me how did he know oh I know I think that my magic wore off because I was distracted just like a silly magpie by shiny things

(*Panic won't help you, Elizabeth.*)

There it was again, that big-sister voice. And it was so firm and clear that Elizabeth calmed immediately. Once she was calm it was easier to think how to escape.

First she needed to get out of the man's grip. Then she had to run away fast enough that he couldn't catch her again.

Oh, running, I'd rather not run again, all I've done since I left the Great Square is run.

The man paused, shifting her in his grip. Elizabeth kicked back and the hard soles of her shoes connected to his soft flesh. He cried out in anger, but he didn't drop her, as she'd hoped. Instead his arms seemed to pull tighter, like a noose closing around her.

"Try that again and you won't like what I do, my lovely creature."

Elizabeth would not like anything he did—she was very certain of that. And she had a feeling that once she was inside his hidey-hole that she would be gone forever, just a foolish little girl who went following her curiosity and came to a bad end.

She had to force him to release her. She'd done it before, when she was in the tunnel. The man who'd grabbed her then had screamed that she'd done something to his hands. The only trouble was that she didn't know what she'd done and it was hard to think while this other man held her so tight and her head was bouncing all around.

Hurt him.

This wasn't the big-sister voice, or the other Voice, or even a whisper from the mouse in her pocket (who seemed to have gone quiet now that she was in actual peril, or perhaps he'd just fallen out and been crushed by someone's boot). This was Elizabeth's own thought, and as soon as it occurred to her that thought scorched through her like a flame.

A flame, yes, I'm a burning flame and the fire doesn't hurt me but it hurts him, it's making him smoke and burn.

And then she could smell it, the horrible stench of cooking flesh, and the man screamed and dropped her to the ground. She fell heavily and rolled to her side, hurting all over and trying to catch the breath he'd just about squashed out of her.

The man danced in place, flames rising from his arms where they had held her tight and licking over his torso where he'd pressed her against his chest. A crowd had gathered, people pouring out of the buildings nearby or clustering around him from the street. None of them seemed to notice her lying on the ground and she rolled away to avoid their feet.

Elizabeth scrambled up, trying to get her bearings. She didn't think the man had brought her very far but it was vital that she not simply dart off in any direction. If she did that she might end up back in that horrible square and she didn't think she had it in her to make the invisibility spell again.

The smell of the man burning alive made her feel sick and confused. Elizabeth knew he meant to hurt her, that if she hadn't stopped him he would have done something terrible to her and she had every right to stop him from doing that.

But he was dying now, dying because of her, and that wasn't a very comfortable feeling for a small girl to have.

She couldn't see him through the tangled mass of people but she could hear him and suddenly his screams were no longer simply shrieks of pain but words.

"You're not a lovely creature at all! Not at all! And no prize but a punishment! You're a very naughty, naughty little girl!"

Strangely, his words made her feel better. *No prize but a punishment.* Yes, Elizabeth found she rather liked the idea of being a punishment to any man who dared treat her like a doll to be collected.

I'll remember that, she thought fiercely. *I'm nobody's prize, and I never will be.*

And then she heard the calling of the sparkling thing again. For a moment she hesitated, resisting. What good would it do to find out what the thing was? How could it help her get home again?

It might, though. You might walk toward it and discover that the path back to the New City is just around the bend of that alley, and the sparkling thing your guide, like the North Star.

If Elizabeth were truly honest with herself she'd admit that she just wanted to know what it was, just like she'd wanted to know what the bird-man looked like. She couldn't help it. If she turned away from the call of the winking purple object at the end of that alley it would only haunt her endlessly, become a scabbed-over wound that she'd worry and pick at in her mind.

This was her weakness. She needed to know. She could never be content with not knowing.

But it felt different now, less like the call was luring her into a trance, as it had before. Elizabeth was very confident that this was her choice.

She felt more confident altogether. She didn't fear the gaze of the adults that brushed past her, because if one of them touched her she would set them on fire like she had the man who'd tried to kidnap her. Yes, she would do that. She wasn't afraid.

I am *a lovely creature*, she thought. *A creature made of bone and gold and flame, and no one can harm me.*

I'm not like that man in the tunnel said. I'm not an Alice at all.

"Where are you going?"

The question startled her, for at first she thought it came from one of the many people passing her, but then she remembered the mouse. Elizabeth glanced down at her pocket and saw the mouse glaring up at her with those disconcerting colored eyes. Mice shouldn't have eyes like that. Mice probably shouldn't talk, either.

"I thought you wanted to get out of the Old City," the mouse said.

"I do."

"Then you are certainly going the wrong way," the mouse said. "That way is back to the square you just came from."

"I know."

"Where are you off to then, little Alice?"

"I'm not Alice," Elizabeth said, but absently. She was listening for the singing call of the sparkling purple thing. She thought it might be a jewel. Only jewels glittered like that.

Then the alley was there before her—an innocuous-looking path between two buildings.

Just like the one in the New City, where you saw the man with the bird-tail.

The man with the bird-tail seemed so far away now, a thing that had happened long ago to another girl called Elizabeth.

She was vaguely aware that she was drawing attention now. There were eyes on her, eyes that contemplated and coveted.

Those eyes did not concern her. Elizabeth wasn't going to be captured again. The only concern of her heart and mind was finding that sparkling purple jewel. And unlike the man with the bird-tail it couldn't run away from her.

Elizabeth stepped into the alley.

"No, I don't think you ought to do that," the mouse said, and there was a definite note of alarm in his voice. "That is nothing a little girl should want to meddle with."

She heard the mouse's words, but the sense of them rolled off her and fell to the ground. The alley was cool and shadowed but not as deeply dark as the tunnel. Elizabeth could see the shapes of the bricks in the walls, the faint grey-white mortar that held them together. There was no one in the alley except her.

The jewel would belong to Elizabeth alone.

The noise of the street faded away almost instantly as she walked toward the purple object. It wasn't just singing to her now—it was waving, almost frantically. It was sending a signal that only she could decipher.

No one can hear it but me. Nobody knows about it except me.

But that assertion was disproved immediately, because the mouse said, "You stay away from that thing, Elizabeth Violet Hargreaves."

Names have power, especially when you're only nine years

old. Whenever Elizabeth heard someone say her whole name with that kind of authority something inside her would quail, because it usually meant she'd done something wrong and a grown-up had discovered her perfidy.

When the mouse said all of her names it made her halt in the way nothing else could have done. It broke the spell of the song.

She was very angry then, and when she spoke to the mouse she couldn't hide her temper.

"And what do you know of it, little mouse?"

"I know more than you think, little girl," he said, and he didn't sound very mouse-like at all, just then. "I know that Alice defeated it, and she hid it away in a jar, and she took it out of the City altogether. So it shouldn't be here at all now, calling to you."

"Alice *again*!" Elizabeth shouted. "I've had enough of Alice and I've had enough of you. If I want to see what that jewel is then you can't stop me. You're only a little mouse."

Elizabeth scooped the mouse out of her pocket then and placed it on the ground—though not roughly, she didn't want to hurt it, only to make it stop annoying her. "Run away now, mouse. I'm sure someone has left some crumbs out for you to eat."

She spun away from it, ignoring the indignant squeaks coming from the vicinity of her shoe-buckle. Elizabeth felt a tiny prick of regret—the mouse had tried to help her, after all—but then decided she wasn't going back for the creature. She was so very *tired* of all this Alice business.

(and the mouse wasn't even nice all the time, he said that Mama and Papa only had you to replace Alice and he made it sound like they threw Alice away with the litter in the first place and of course that was all a lie)

The sparkling thing was getting closer and closer. It wasn't at all like the white-tailed bird-man, who seemed to disappear into the distance no matter how she tried to catch up to him.

Elizabeth felt a little shiver of anticipation. Even though she'd only discovered the existence of this purple jewel less than an hour before, she felt that her mind had been preoccupied with it for even longer. It was like the knowledge of it had always been in her mind, lurking somewhere behind the best places to hide a sweet bun in her bedroom so Mama wouldn't find it and how to get revenge on Polly for telling Mama about the last hiding place.

As she approached it more details came into focus, like Elizabeth was peering through a spyglass. The sparkling thing was in what appeared to be a glass jar, a very small one with a sealed top. The jar was directly in the center of a little wooden table. But she still couldn't quite make out what was underneath the glass.

A thrill of excitement filled her. Soon she would see what had been calling her, what glittered and winked and waved at her. And she would put it in her pocket and take it home, and it would belong to her forever.

Something made her stop then. Something that wasn't quite right, a little nagging something in her mind like the princess's pea under all the mattresses.

This isn't right, not at all. Why is there a table and a jar right out here in the open where anyone can see it? Is it a trap?

Her footsteps slowed.

What if the bobbies are trying to capture thieves by luring them with this object? And as soon as I pick it up they'll throw a net over me and put me in jail.

Elizabeth considered this. If it was that sort of trap then it could benefit her. A policeman would clearly be able to see that she was a daughter of the New City and didn't belong here. He might even help her get home safely.

But it could be another kind of lure, and there might be a different kind of person waiting with a net.

"Well, no one is going to capture *me*, even if so," Elizabeth said. "I won't let them."

Still she hesitated. Her heels dragged across the ground like the cobblestones were made of molasses.

I thought you wanted it, Elizabeth. I thought you were going to open the jar and put it in your pocket and make it your own.

The idea didn't seem so wonderful, all of a sudden. Maybe it was because she'd left the mouse behind in a huff, and now she regretted it. Maybe it was because something about the way the purple thing waved and winked made her feel ill. The calling song had turned sour and she wished she could stop up her ears so she couldn't hear it.

Now she was right up to the table, and all she had to do was reach out and pick up the jar. Her hand didn't seem to want to move, however, and she wasn't inclined to force it. Elizabeth crouched down so she was eye level with the jar.

"It's not a jewel at all," she said.

It was a butterfly, a little purple butterfly fluttering around in desperation inside the jar. It beat its wings against the glass, darting up and down in the limited space available.

Elizabeth knew she should have felt some sympathy for the insect. She was fond of butterflies, and the sight of one so clearly longing for freedom should have had her opening the jar without a second thought.

But now that she'd seen it the butterfly repulsed her. She had nothing in her stomach but still she felt her gorge rise. All she wished for now was to be away from the horrid little thing. It had tempted her, distracted her from her purpose. Elizabeth glanced up at the sky and thought it might be darkening. She needed to be back home in the New City before night fell.

Elizabeth spun away from the table, determined not to be led astray by such nonsense again.

"Where do you think you're off to?" a voice said. It was a lazy, drawling voice, the kind of voice that you might say was too slow to mean harm. If you said that you'd be wrong, because there was a ripple of menace under those seven words, a dangerous compulsion that made Elizabeth turn back.

"You!" she said, for there stood the bird-man who'd so fascinated her that she'd followed him from her safe place to this dangerous one, all for the promise of seeing what he looked like.

She oughtn't have done it, she realized that now. It wasn't simply that she'd been lured to the Old City. It was also because this was no amusing chimera, no child's playmate who would chirp at her and make her laugh. That, of course, was what she'd been thinking would happen. Elizabeth had imagined a kind of chicken's face crossed with a man's, with a silly little orange beak and orange eyes and a bright red crest that would flop around when he talked to her.

The reality was not connected to this silly fantasy in the least.

First, the voice didn't go with the face at all. It was certainly a bird's face and not a man's, for all that the voice couldn't be anything but a man's. The head was sort of oval-shaped with a high crown and it was all covered in white and grey feathers. In place of a nose there was a medium-sized yellow beak with curved tips that met one another at the end. Those tips were sharp and cruel, made for grabbing and rending.

His eyes were bright and cold and blue with black pupils—a person's eyes, eyes that weighted and assessed. Elizabeth's gaze slid over the man's clothes. His arms looked like a man's arms, not wings, though little bits of feather stuck through the jacket sleeves like the down in her quilt at home.

At the end of his sleeves Elizabeth saw that one hand was a regular human hand—a hand that appeared just as strong and cruel as his beak—and the other hand was a bird's grasping claw.

"You're not going to run off now, are you?" he said, and the long lazy stretch of his syllables made Elizabeth shrink away. "After all the trouble I've had to bring you here in the first place."

Elizabeth knew she shouldn't talk to him, shouldn't stand there frozen like a silly rabbit who'd seen a fox, but that troublesome streak of curiosity made her say, "Why? Why me?"

Underneath the "why me?" was something else, something that seemed like, *Why me and not some other girl, couldn't you have taken some other girl?* And Elizabeth felt her cheeks burn in shame for she should never, ever wish her own misfortune on someone else, not even for a moment.

The bird-man didn't seem to notice this, for he clicked his beak and made a rough noise that could have passed for laughter in another place.

"Why you? Why do you think?"

Elizabeth shook her head. She didn't seem capable of any other movement. She certainly didn't feel like a lovely creature now, a creature of bone and gold and flame. She felt like a soft little girl caught in a hunter's net.

"What do you think is in that jar?" the bird-man asked.

"A . . . a butterfly," Elizabeth said, stumbling over her words.

"No, you don't."

"No I don't what?"

"Don't think it's a butterfly. You *know* it isn't a butterfly. You can feel that it isn't, can't you?" The bird-man glared at her with such furious expectation that she could only nod.

"I want that jar open. And you're the girl to open it for me."

He was coming closer now, looming over her, reaching out with that clawed bird-hand and she felt more helpless than she'd felt all day, unable to run or scream or even set him on fire. The claw closed around her wrist—cold and scaly and tight like a wire.

It was so alien that she didn't even try to pull away. A deep shock radiated from his touch, a shock that froze her muscles, even seemed to stop her blood flowing.

Think, Elizabeth, think. You don't know what's in that jar but you don't want it open so you have to get away.

"Wh-why can't you open it yourself?" Her teeth were chattering and her voice was a tiny thing, a mouse squeak in the dark.

"You think that's just a regular sort of seal on that jar? That jar was closed by a Magician, and only a Magician can open it," the bird-man said. His beak clicked between each word, a sound that was uncomfortably like the ticking of a clock.

Tick-tock goes the clock and so flies the time. You have to get away before he makes you do something you don't want to do because when that butterfly comes out it won't be a butterfly anymore.

"So get some o-other M-Magician," Elizabeth said through her chattering teeth. "Wh-why should I b-be the one?"

"You're a very stupid little girl, aren't you? Why would anyone be interested in you except for one reason? You are the very image of her, after all."

He seemed to smile then, though Elizabeth didn't see how with that beak, but he made a kind of sly smirk that caused Elizabeth's back teeth to grind. She hated the sort of grown-up who acted like they knew everything and that she was a fool simply because she was young.

How could she help being young, after all? She was certain that when she got older she would know more things—perhaps all of the things there were to know—but she hadn't had the time to do so yet.

Getting angry about the bird-man's smirking face seemed to calm her. His cruel grip on her wrist hadn't lessened, and she still couldn't see how she was to escape, but she felt better able to think it all through. She only needed to think faster.

"What, didn't your parents tell you about Alice? How you are just a tiny version of the girl they lost to a Rabbit?"

Elizabeth remembered tripping down the stairs in her new dress that morning—was it really that morning? It seemed like it was one hundred years ago—and her mother's face was so white as she whispered, "Alice."

"Alice, who wandered too far and got lost, just like you. I wonder what they'll do when you don't come home. You were supposed to fill in her space. Perhaps they'll have another golden-haired Alice to fill in your space."

No, I'm not just a placeholder for Alice. I'm not. I'm not.

"But Alice was a little too clever for that Rabbit. He marked her but she escaped, and then she and her hatchet man made him fall down like a domino. Him and the Caterpillar and the Jabberwock. They all fell down, one by one."

Elizabeth's attention snagged on one word, that very funny word. "The Jabberwock?"

"Beware the Jabberwock, that's what they used to say. And he made the streets run with blood. Until little lost Alice decided she didn't want to be lost anymore and put him in that jar."

Little lost Alice decided she didn't want to be lost anymore. Somehow Elizabeth had gotten the impression that Alice was a broken thing, not someone to be admired. But then she remembered the Voice telling her that Alice "made it all fall down."

I don't want to be lost anymore, either. And I don't want to let the rivers run red with blood. What should I do? What should I do?

Alice!

The cry came from her heart and her mind, somewhere in a secret place that wanted an older sister to help her, to look out for her. Margaret was the type who tutted, never saved.

Elizabeth didn't know if Alice could hear her, or if she would even want to hear the little girl who slept in her bed and wore her clothes and took the love that should have been Alice's.

Alice! Alice, help me!

"Since Alice is not here—and it's a good thing for her she is not here, for there are many who'd be happy to punish her for what she's done—I need someone of her blood to open this little jar here, you see? And that means you."

His grip on her wrist tightened and Elizabeth cried out. He leaned down so his beak was just a click away from nipping off her nose.

"If you're a good girl and you do what I ask I'll show you the way to get home again."

No you won't, Elizabeth thought. *Your eyes are lying to me as much as your tongue. I can see the lie.*

"But if you're not a good girl, if you don't help me open this jar, then I might have to put you in a sack and take you down to the wharf. There's lots of men there that would pay good money for a pretty little doll like you."

(Pretty little Alice)

(That's what he said to me. He grabbed my hair and held it tight and called me pretty little Alice.)

That wasn't Elizabeth's voice, or Elizabeth's thought, or even the Voice that came and went so mysteriously.

She saw a flash of images, like a cinema reel turning very quickly. A man with long white ears, like a rabbit but still a man— not unlike Elizabeth's own bird-man. He was snarling and his face was close to someone—*close to Alice*—and then one of his eyes was gone, there was a dagger in its place and a hand with broken fingernails pulling the knife away heedless of the blood.

The last thing was a man, a painfully ordinary-looking man, a man with a black suit and a black cape and very shiny black shoes. He would have looked like he was off to the opera, except that his eyes were pools of night sparking with malice.

And behind him Elizabeth thought she could see great wings that covered the sky, just a hint of them, a shadow playing tricks.

Is that the Jabberwock? He didn't look so very scary, not like the rabbit-eared man, but Elizabeth already knew that cruelty hid behind a kind face. The City Fathers were proof of that.

(Don't believe anything he says. He's going to hurt you no matter what you do.)

I know, I won't. Elizabeth didn't know whether she was hearing the real Alice or only an idea of her, a hope, a wish borne on the fetid breeze.

(You need to make a wish.)

I know how to wish, Elizabeth thought. *I do it all the time.*

(And your wishes come true, don't they?)

The Alice-voice was very faint. Elizabeth was concentrating so hard on hearing it that she half forgot the bird-man holding her wrist. That is, until he shook her hard and made her cry out.

"Are you listening, my little dove? You do what I want and you'll get what you want."

His beak went *click, click, click* as he spoke. It was very difficult not to think of his beak going *click, click, click* and rending all of her soft bits, picking out her eyes, tearing off her nose.

(I made a wish, too, and you can't undo it.)

Then Elizabeth saw one last flash, a memory that wasn't hers at all. It was the man in the cape, and it was like he melted out of the air, and suddenly there was just a little glass jar with a purple butterfly.

(I thought he was gone forever, that he fell into a hole with the goblin and disappeared. You can't let him get out again.)

Elizabeth didn't understand this bit about the goblin, but she did understand that she couldn't let the butterfly turn back into the man.

"All right," Elizabeth said. "I'll do what you want."

She hated the way she sounded, her voice a shrinking cringing squeak. The claw gripping her wrist relaxed just a fraction but Elizabeth still felt the promise of violence.

"No tricks now," the bird-man warned. "I can rip your throat out before you even think about a scream."

He released Elizabeth's wrist and she exhaled a breath she hadn't realized she was holding. It was such a relief not to feel his scales on her skin. Then his bird-hands dug into her shoulders, the claws piercing the sleeves of her pretty blue dress—*it's not so pretty anymore*—and cutting into her skin.

The bird-man turned her toward the table, and it seemed that all she could see was that fluttering purple butterfly beating its frantic wings inside the jar.

He's going to make me open the jar and if I don't do it he'll eat me up oh what am I to do Alice what am I to do?

The voice fluttered into Elizabeth's ear, as delicate as a baby moth.

(Make a wish.)

There were two problems, to Elizabeth's way of thinking. One problem was the Jabberwock, which was an altogether bigger problem than the bird-man even if it didn't seem like an immediate threat. And the second problem was the bird-man, who might kill her out of spite if she didn't do what he wanted.

(Even when it's hard you have to be brave.)

I don't want to be brave, not really. I want to go home.

(Girls like us, we have to save ourselves. Nobody else will get you home.)

I don't want to save myself.

(I believe in you. Make a wish.)

The bird-man jerked Elizabeth's shoulders. "Pick up the jar and open it."

(I believe in you. Make a wish.)

Elizabeth didn't want to touch the jar. She thought she saw the shadow-wings rising up behind it, stretching toward the sky. If she put her hands on the glass the wings would close around her and pull her into the darkness and she'd never go home again.

That's enough now, Elizabeth. If you want to go home you have to save yourself.

This wasn't Alice, or the Voice, or even her own little-girl self. It was some brisk, sensible version of herself, one who knew that the only way to tackle an unpleasant task was to get on with it.

Yes, get on with it, she thought, and closed her hand around the jar. *Make a wish.*

I know what to do. It came to her with no warning, a plan fully formed and delivered. She just needed to make certain he didn't notice the first part.

"All you have to do is ease open that little cork and your job will be done," he said, digging his claws in deeper. His voice was filled with obscene anticipation, his breath puffing out in little pants against Elizabeth's hair.

"Why can't you open it?" Elizabeth asked. She didn't really care about the answer. She only wanted to distract him for a moment, so she could do the thing that was going to make him so angry.

The bird-man shook her again, making her teeth clatter against each other. "I told you, only Alice or one of her blood can open it. And you have to be a Magician on top of it. Do I look like any of those things to you?"

"But why do you want it open in the first place?" Elizabeth asked. Her hand tightened on the jar, her fingers covering the interior. She thought she could feel the desperate beat of the butterfly's wings against the glass.

I wish you to stop fluttering and sink to the bottom of the glass. I wish you to die and never be reborn.

"Why wouldn't I want to let the Jabberwock out?" the bird-man said. "The last time he caused such wonderful chaos, such delightful death. A smart fellow could take advantage of a situation like that. A smart fellow might even get some territory of his own."

So this is all for some venal purpose, Elizabeth thought with contempt. *He wants to be a gangster and he's using me to do it.*

The jar in Elizabeth's hand felt different than it had before, no longer pulsing with magic, or filled with that rapid fluttering.

"Open it!" the bird-man said.

"Very well," Elizabeth said, and opened the jar.

The bird-man released her shoulders and snatched the jar from her hand. She ran a few steps away, but not too far. She still needed him.

The man clearly expected something exciting to occur, some form to rise from the opening like the genie from the lamp. After a moment he lifted the jar to his face to peer inside.

At the bottom of the jar was a purple butterfly, unmoving, its wings curled at the edges and blackened as though they'd been singed.

"What have you done?" the bird-man screamed, turning toward Elizabeth.

For a brief moment she saw her death in his eyes, saw the sharp beak coming for her.

Then she said, "I wish you were a tiny little moth, barely bigger than my thumbprint. You will live in that little jar and talk to me if I want you to and no one will ever be able to open it but me."

It happened so quickly. One moment he was there, reaching for her, beak snapping. The next moment he was gone and there was only the jar lying on its side on the ground, the cork pushed into the top, a tiny white moth fluttering inside.

Elizabeth picked up the jar and brought it close to her face. The purple butterfly was almost gone now, slowly turning to ash. The white moth threw itself against the side in fury.

"There's nothing you can do about it, so you shouldn't bother wearing yourself out trying to escape," Elizabeth said.

The moth unleashed a stream of curses that made Elizabeth tut at him.

"You shouldn't use language like that around a child, you know," Elizabeth chided. "Besides, if you're nice to me, I might let you out one day. But if you aren't then I can always leave you in there."

The moth subsided, though it seemed his fluttering was rather sulky.

"You are quite an Alice, Elizabeth Violet Hargreaves," a voice said.

It wasn't just a voice, though, it was the Voice in her head, the Voice that had been plaguing her for most of the day. But it wasn't in her head any longer. It came from only a few feet away.

There was a man there, small and neat and not much taller than Elizabeth herself. He wore a velvet suit of rose red and his hair was golden brown and curly. But it was his eyes that struck her—bright green eyes, emerald eyes, sparkling curious eyes that looked terribly familiar to Elizabeth.

"You!" Elizabeth said. "If you could turn yourself into a mouse and back again then you could have helped me, you know."

The man shook his head. "No, I could not do any more than I did. You had to discover what you were worth yourself."

That seemed like a very poor excuse to Elizabeth, who didn't think letting a child come to harm was a good way to build character.

"Was this all a plan of yours, then?"

The man looked offended. "No, never. I would never have lured you into the Old City at so young an age. If you recall, I tried to warn you off and you didn't listen."

Elizabeth chose to ignore this, because she wanted to feel annoyed at somebody over her predicament and this person was conveniently at hand.

"Who are you, anyway?" Elizabeth asked.

The man bowed low and then presented her a rose—a very red rose, a rose that could never have come from nature. Elizabeth took it, turning it over in her hand, and as she did she saw a flash of something—a little cottage in the middle of this ugly City, all covered in the same sort of beautiful roses.

"Come and see me one day, Elizabeth Violet Hargreaves. When you're older and wiser."

He winked at her, and then he faded away, until all that was left was the sense that those green eyes were floating in the air, and then those too were gone.

"Well, that was less helpful than it should have been," Elizabeth said, huffing out a breath.

She tucked the curious rose into one of her pockets. Her stomach rumbled as she peered up at the sky. Night was falling. Mama and Papa were sure to be in quite a state by now, a thing that Elizabeth was sorry for, though a small part of her felt angry and resentful that they had never told her about Alice.

She wondered how much of her story she should tell them, and what they would believe.

Elizabeth had a feeling that Alice had told too much of her story, and so they'd sent her away.

Elizabeth wasn't going to let them send her away—not simply because she didn't want to be, but because she didn't think they deserved to always be safe and comfortable, to ignore what the world outside was really like.

She already felt older and wiser than she had been this morning, though not quite older and wiser enough to go and see the man who lived in the rose-covered cottage.

"But I will, one day," she said.

I'll be waiting for you, he said.

"Now," Elizabeth said, lifting the glass jar up to her eye level. The moth landed on the side of the jar, waving its antennae at her. "You are going to tell me the safest way home. And if you're very good, and don't lead me astray, I might let you out when we get there."

The moth said, "And if I don't?"

"Well. You know what happened to your friend the Jabber-wock, don't you?"

Yes, you are quite an Alice, Elizabeth Violet Hargreaves, the strange little man said.

"I'm not an Alice. I'm myself," she said, with a little tartness in her tone.

The man laughed, soft and knowing.

But I'd like to meet you one day, Alice, Elizabeth thought. *One day we two girls will have tea and cakes, the loveliest tea party you can imagine.*

(I'll be waiting for you), Alice said, or maybe it was only something Elizabeth hoped she heard.

But she had a kind of vision then, of a cottage by a lake at the edge of a field of wildflowers, and Alice waving to her from the doorway.

I'll come and meet you, Alice. When I'm older and wiser.

Girl in
Amber

Alice woke from something that felt not quite like a dream but not quite a memory, either. She thought she'd been speaking to a little girl, a girl who looked almost exactly like she did when she was young, and that girl was in terrible danger and Alice had helped her somehow.

The dream-memory was already disappearing, like broken cobwebs drifting to the ground in the weak sunlight filtering through the trees. Hatcher was gone, though the blankets were still warm in the place where he'd slept. His rising might have even been the thing that woke her, though he surely had done it without making a sound. Even in sleep she could tell whether he was near or far.

Alice wished he were near, because she wanted to tell him about the little girl who looked so like herself. Not that he would necessarily have advice or wisdom to share on the subject. Hatcher wasn't talkative at the best of times. But it was still a comfort to see his grave face across the fire, with that intensity in his eyes that told her he was really listening and not just waiting for his chance to talk.

That was how most conversations went, in Alice's experience—people didn't listen but only waited for their turn to speak. Not that she had so much experience, really, having spent the better part of her adulthood in a hospital with a wall between her and her only companion. But she'd spent a lot of time watching other people since she and Hatcher left the Old City, watching how the people in all the doll-sized villages behaved with one another, and she'd collected some interesting impressions.

The morning was cold, cold enough that her face felt a little raw. There had been a winter festival at the last village Alice and Hatcher passed through, and Alice had purchased a heavy knitted cap in grey wool and a thick sweater to match. Hatcher had consented to a sweater but wouldn't have the hat—he said it would cover his ears and he needed them.

The woman selling the knitted goods had looked at him askance and Alice had paid for their items and hurried Hatcher along before he started talking about turning into a wolf. Not that he would wear a knitted hat when he was a wolf, but his hearing was a great deal more acute than it used to be and he didn't like anything to impede it.

That he *did* turn into a wolf wasn't a subject Alice liked to bring up with regular folk. It tended to make them nervous, because they thought Hatcher was mad (he was, but that wasn't a thing Alice liked to talk about over dinner, either) or they believed in wolf-men and that belief frightened them.

If it was the latter, then the rifles and cold eyes would come out and they'd be chased from the place and of course Alice didn't want that. It was a lot of trouble to escape (it had only happened the one time, but the rumours had dogged them for three villages after that and they'd had some trouble restocking their supplies as a result) and it was never easy to keep Hatcher from killing anyone who threatened her.

Really, it was better if Hatcher did as little talking as possible in mixed company. He just wasn't capable of dissembling, even for his own good.

Their path was leading them ever northward, and the farther north they went the colder it got. Add the regular progression of the seasons, and Alice felt a constant nagging worry about the weather, like a pea under her mattress. She wanted to find a good place to settle for a few months, so they wouldn't have to constantly hunt about for food and warmth and shelter.

Hatcher never seemed to mind sleeping outdoors or spending their days on the move, but Alice was beginning to find it wearisome. She was not as wild as he was, a force of nature barely civilized. Alice preferred a soft bed over a tree root and she liked her food served on plates.

Someday I'll get to my cottage by the lake (the one I've always dreamed of, the one I'm still searching for) and my mattress will be the softest thing imaginable, so squashy that I will lie down upon it and sink into it so far that no one will be able to see me. And then I will cover myself up with the thickest, warmest blankets and sleep and sleep and sleep as much as I want, and never worry about a stranger coming upon me in the night.

Alice lay there for a few moments, imagining the wonderful

sense of security that came with being surrounded by four walls. It was a thing she'd taken for granted for a long time.

Though I don't want anyone but me to lock the door that leads outside, thank you very much. She'd had quite enough of that in the hospital. If there was any locking to be done it would be by her, from the inside.

She was getting colder every moment now, aware of the chill creeping up from the ground and the lack of heat now that Hatcher was gone.

"I'll be warmer if I move," she muttered, and so she forced herself to get up and put on her boots and stamp around until her blood was flowing and everything felt less stiff.

Then she collected some wood for a fire, started it, and set water to boil for tea. They had only tin mugs and no proper teapot, but Alice wasn't moving an inch without a cup of tea. She would have liked a little honeycomb or a lump of sugar to drop into it but it wasn't easy to carry such things about and anyway, the price of sugar was very dear this far from the City.

Elizabeth likes sugar in her tea, too, Alice thought as she toasted a piece of bread over the fire. And then she tilted her head to one side, because she wasn't entirely sure who Elizabeth was but felt that she knew her.

Perhaps I knew her as a child and have forgotten. Alice had a lot of memories like this, half-fragmented things that swirled around, jigsaw puzzles that didn't fit into the larger picture. It usually didn't trouble her, because there were too many to bother about, but this one did. There was a little pain in her heart, like she shouldn't have forgotten this girl.

Hatcher returned while Alice was eating her second piece of

toast and sipping at the too-hot and very bitter black tea. His hair was wet and his face was shiny.

"Did you go swimming?" Alice asked.

He nodded, holding his hands to the fire. "I wanted a wash."

This was code for *I killed something large and bloody and didn't want to come back with the proof on my face.*

Alice confirmed this by asking, "Toast?" and got a head shake in reply. He might have eaten a whole deer, for all she knew. Sometimes he brought back animal bits for her to roast over the fire, but there was nothing today.

"I've been thinking," she said.

He looked up at her and waited.

"I'd like to find a house where we—or at least I—can stay for the next few months."

He nodded. "I've been thinking on that, too. The winter's going to be too hard for you if we sleep rough."

"But if we stay in a village it won't be too good for you, unless you can . . ." She trailed off, for she thought it might be indelicate to say "control yourself."

He grinned. "Avoid eating the villagers?"

"You don't eat villagers," Alice said. "Although you might take an arm off if they offend you."

"Only if they offend *you*," he said. "I can take any insult to myself, but never to you."

"Well," Alice said briskly, trying not to feel pleased about it. She shouldn't encourage the violence that was always just under the surface of his skin. "Do you think you *could* avoid eating villagers for a few months? Or intimidating them with your axe?"

Hatcher rubbed his face, clearly considering. For a while he'd kept his cheeks clean-shaven but since the air had gotten chillier he'd let his beard come in. It was thick and mostly grey with bits of black, the opposite of the hair on top of his head—which was still mostly black with bits of grey.

"I don't know if I can spend that much time around other people," Hatcher said finally.

Alice sighed. She'd half expected this answer. "So you can't be in a village for that many months and I can't be out in the woods for that many months. What are we going to do, Hatch?"

The simplest solution would be to let him roam free while she settled down somewhere, but Alice wasn't that keen on the idea. She didn't worry that Hatcher wouldn't return to her—he would, no matter how far he roamed—but rather worried about his mental state if he was off on his own for that long. He might forget how to be a man altogether if Alice wasn't there to remind him.

If that's what's best for him shouldn't you let him be? Isn't it self-ish for you to keep him as a man when he's got a wild thing's heart?

She didn't know where that thought came from but she pushed it away just as quick as it had bubbled up. Maybe it was selfish for her to want Hatcher to be a man, but she was going to try all the same. She loved him, and love wasn't always patient and kind and selfless. It wasn't always the warm glow of tenderness.

Love was, she was learning, sometimes grasping and greedy. Sometimes it was a fierce and hollow burning at the base of her throat, a bright hard thing that made her choke and stutter. Sometimes it frightened her just as much as it pleased her.

Alice didn't want to live without Hatcher. If he always stayed a wolf then she would have to. If he went away from her for the duration of the winter he probably wouldn't bother being a man in all that time and might even forget how to change back when he returned to her. Therefore, she had to come up with a solution that would keep both of them happy.

It wasn't as insurmountable as defeating a goblin or a pale enchantress or stopping the Jabberwock from slaughtering everyone in sight, but it felt like it.

That girl. The Jabberwock.

"It was something to do with the Jabberwock," Alice murmured.

"What was?" Hatcher asked.

"My dream. I dreamed about a little girl named Elizabeth. And I helped her, somehow, and it had something to do with the Jabberwock. Except I don't think it was really a dream."

"But what does that have to do with me living in a village for the winter?"

"It doesn't. I was just thinking about it again. Never mind." Alice stood and dusted off her trousers. "There's no point worrying about it just now. Maybe a solution will present itself."

Hatcher shrugged. "Sometimes they do. And sometimes you have to hack and smash about until you make one that suits."

That, Alice thought, *is the trouble. The hacking and the smashing.*

They put out the fire, collected their things in their rucksacks and started off. They'd rarely seen another person in the forest in all the days that Alice and Hatcher had been walking since they left the cursed village where the White Queen had stolen the children (but Alice had gotten them back, she'd gotten almost all of them back and so she needn't feel ill when she thought about that place).

This made sense when they'd been walking in the burned blight that stretched from the City almost to that village, but they'd passed through many seemingly normal and un-cursed places since then. Alice thought they would have seen men out hunting or healing women gathering herbs or even scampering children out trying to outrun their household chores.

But it was never so. It was always only Alice and Hatcher and the wind and the scurrying little animals and the lumbering large ones. On one occasion they had seen a shaggy brown bear in a clearing—it was a huge thing, twice the size of Hatcher and thick with its winter fat.

Alice had seen a bear only once before then, in the City, and that had been a sad thin creature, dancing in the street for the whim of its keeper. She'd marveled at the size and power of the bear in the woods, but her awe had been cut short when she realized Hatcher was watching it and growling through his bottom teeth. If she hadn't grabbed his face and forced him to look away she was certain he would have transformed into a wolf right then and attacked it. That was the first time she truly realized that Hatcher was just a hairsbreadth away from forgetting he was a man altogether.

Yes, it was a problem. And the approaching winter was a problem. And Alice didn't know what to do about it, unless they came upon a handy cottage in the woods where Hatcher could come and go freely.

Cottages in the woods aren't necessarily the best solution, either, though. Those little houses are the secret-keepers for witches and haunts and other beings not readily accepted by close-minded villagers.

Then she thought, *Just like you and Hatcher, then.*

All she was doing was thinking in circles so she decided not to think about it. Hatcher loped along beside her, his grey eyes giving away nothing. He quietly took her hand and squeezed it.

She resolved not to worry for the rest of the day. Perhaps when she woke up tomorrow she'd find that her brain had done all the work for her in her sleep and their troubles would have a simple solution, after all.

Then it started to snow.

It didn't seem like anything to be concerned about, not at first. Alice actually had felt a little bubble of delight when she saw the first flurries swirling down, a remnant of that childhood joy associated with Christmas and snow. There was something so pretty about a few flakes of snow, like being touched by an enchanted sky.

Then her adult-self realized that a few flakes meant more to come, and soon enough that brief joyous feeling was thoroughly squelched by anxiety that built higher with each passing moment. Pretty drifting crystals soon became a torrent of white that blew into their faces and made it impossible to see. Alice squinted, hugged her cloak tight around her body, and took steps that became increasingly difficult as the snow piled up around her ankles faster than she would have believed possible. It was wet and heavy and it sucked at her boots and managed to sneak under the hem of her trousers and soak the tops of her socks.

Hatcher's hair and beard were quickly coated, making him resemble a snow-creature from a northern tale. Alice had heard tales of those creatures from one of her nurserymaids. They walked like men but were actually half beast, and covered all over with white fur. They had huge fangs and claws and were fiercely protective of their mountains.

Alice and Hatcher weren't on a mountain (*and thank goodness for that, we have enough trouble as it is*) but Alice could readily believe that one of those snow-creatures might loom before them at any moment.

After some time (Alice wasn't certain how long, because her view of the sun was entirely wiped out by the blizzard) Hatcher tugged on her arm. She halted and immediately felt snow piling up on her hat and the shoulders of her cloak.

"What is it?" she said. The wind seemed to whip her voice away into the gale.

Hatcher leaned close so she could hear him. "I think I ought to run ahead and see if there's any place we can rest for the night."

When he said "run ahead" he meant as a wolf, for he would move more swiftly and easily that way.

Alice stared at him. "You're mad."

"Well, yes, I am," he said. There was no grin, no hint of mischief. He was only stating the facts.

"That's not what I mean," Alice said. She wiped her face with fingers that were stiff with cold despite being covered in wool mittens. "I mean if you run ahead you'll never find me again."

"I'll always find you, Alice." Again, it was a simple statement of fact. Whatever Hatcher had to do he would find her again, even if it meant tearing himself to pieces to do it.

"Well, all right. I know you will," she said, and she did. She believed he would always return to her no matter the circumstances. "But what about your things? I'll have to carry everything, which means I'll go even slower than I am now. Maybe we should just try to make some sort of shelter and wait until this blows through."

Hatcher shook his head. Snow flew out of his hair and joined its fellows. "We don't know how long this will last. Look, I'll run ahead a ways and see if there's any village or structure that we can use, and then I'll come right back to you as soon as possible. I think it would be best if we don't wander aimlessly. If I don't find anything within an hour's walk we can try building a shelter then."

This was a very long speech for Hatcher, and that more than anything else told Alice that he was worried. Still, she wasn't fond of the idea that they separate for any length of time. It would be too easy to lose each other in the storm.

"What if you get hurt and I can't find you again?" she asked.

"I'll come back to you," he said. "No matter what."

She didn't like it, but then she didn't like the idea of trying to survive while exposed in this storm, either. She pressed her lips together and finally nodded.

"There's one thing, though, one very important thing you have to remember," he said. "Don't stop moving."

"You mean like we are now?"

"I mean it, Alice. If you stop moving in cold like this you'll die. Promise me that you won't stop, no matter how tired you get."

"I promise," she said. She could already feel her body cooling while they stood and talked, and she recognized the danger of prolonged stopping.

Hatcher took off his cloak, stuffed it in his pack and handed the pack to her. Then he stripped down to his skin, handing her each item of clothing to put in the pack. It made Alice freeze just to look at him. His teeth were chattering even before he got to his smalls.

Then he grinned at her and a second later there was a wolf standing before her instead of a man.

"Hurry," she said. "Hurry and come back."

He bounded away into the snow, a grey-and-black shadow that was swallowed up by a white gale.

Alice took the straps of her pack off her left shoulder so that it was only slung from the right, and then replaced those straps with Hatcher's pack. The two packs knocked together as she walked, but there wasn't a lot she could do about it. They needed the supplies in Hatcher's bag and he would certainly need his clothes when he returned.

The awkward weight made her pace, already glacial from breaking a trail in the snow, even slower. Ice crusted on her eyelashes and the bits of her hair that stuck out from under her cap. Every time she inhaled, her throat and lungs felt burned by cold (*that's a funny thought, Alice, how can cold burn?*) and then she would cough wildly, her chest seizing and contorting.

When she glanced behind her she saw her footsteps filling up with snow, wiping away the proof of her passage almost before she could blink.

Don't stop moving. You promised Hatcher you wouldn't.

"Hurry back," she said, or maybe she didn't. She might have imagined speaking.

She couldn't see anything around her except snow. There were no trees and no rocks and no path and no sky and no ground, only snow and cold and her trudging feet—feet that were barely lifting off the ground anymore, just sliding a few inches forward at a time like a snail, except she wasn't leaving a trail behind her.

How will Hatcher find me if there's no trail?

"He won't come from behind you, silly, but ahead of you," she said. Her teeth clattered together. She couldn't feel her cheeks anymore. Her voice sounded like it was coming from the top of a far-distant mountain instead of from inside her own chest.

Alice was hungry, but she was afraid to pause even for a moment to dig something out of her pack. Her fingers wouldn't bend any longer, either, so she wasn't sure how she would grasp anything.

She was so cold. She'd never been so cold, not even in the White Queen's castle. Her brain felt sluggish and so did her body. She wasn't certain she was even moving forward anymore. She might be walking in circles. There was no way to tell.

Her body decided enough was enough. Her feet ceased their endless shuffle. Her legs stiffened. Alice fell face forward into the snow.

It was almost warm, having the snow all around her and covering her up like a blanket.

You promised Hatcher you would keep moving.

But I just want to rest awhile.

You promised.

She tried to press her hands into the snow to lever herself back up again, but they only sank into the fresh pile.

You have to get up. You have to move again or you'll die out here, and then what will Hatcher say?

The packs had fallen to each side of her body when she collapsed and the straps were twisted and tangled on her arms. It was impossible to stand with the packs hanging at such awkward angles but her hands were far too stiff to pry them off. The snow blanketed her head as she made tiny pathetic movements that were meant to get her up and moving again. She only succeeded in making some very oddly shaped snow angels.

Alice started to laugh, and she knew the laugh was the insane laughter of the nearly dead but she couldn't stop herself. She was going to die here, buried in snow. After everything—after the Rabbit and the hospital and the Caterpillar and the Walrus and the Jabberwock, after all the perils of the waste and the giants that wanted to make her into a meal, after defeating Magicians with far more power and malice than she could ever have—she was going to die in a blizzard, alone and far from home.

Sorry, Hatcher, she thought, because her mouth was still laughing—the only part of her that was moving any longer.

After a while Alice began to think that she heard someone else laughing, too—a high, sweet sound, like that a child makes when running and playing outdoors.

But that can't be. No child could survive out here.

Still, she made herself clamp her lips together—this didn't work so well, as the laughter stopped but her teeth chattered like knocking boulders inside her skull. The other laughter continued even when Alice's ceased. It was even closer than it had been a moment before.

She lifted her face out of the snow and blinked several times. At first all she could see was more snow—snow that flew into her eyes and stung and made her eyes water—but slowly something else came into focus.

There was a boy.

A laughing boy.

He stood only a few feet away from her. At first she thought he wasn't really there, because he was so pale that he practically blended in with the snow. His hair was short and white and looked very fine, more like the downy fuzz on a baby duck than human hair. His skin was nearly translucent, the blue veins in his jaw visible.

She didn't know how old he might be—younger than school age, maybe, but only just. His cheeks still had the softness of babyhood but the rest of him looked slim and sturdy.

He didn't seem to be affected by the snow, though he wore a white coat with shiny silver fastenings. But the wind and the blowing white crystals diverted around him, didn't settle on his downy hair or his delicate ears or his white, white eyelashes.

Even that wasn't the strangest thing about him. The strangest thing was the color of his eyes—a strange sort of pinkish red, a hue so unusual that Alice thought she imagined it. They seemed to float in the air, unattached to his pale face against the pale background.

Those pinkish-red eyes laughed at her, and his very pink mouth laughed at her, and the indignity of a strange child laughing at her expiring in the snow energized Alice in a way nothing else had.

She clambered to her feet—she wasn't certain how she managed it, as she couldn't feel any of her limbs and she half thought she might have left one of her legs in the snowbank—and stared at the boy.

He'd stopped laughing while she struggled up from her prone position, but now his very rosy mouth split into a wide smile again and that high, sweet laughter rang out.

The boy turned and ran a few feet away from Alice before pausing again. He threw a glance over his shoulder that could only be interpreted as an invitation, those strange eyes crinkled at the corners.

He started off again and Alice noticed then that his white-furred boots didn't sink into the snow the way hers did. The boy darted lightly along the surface without leaving a mark.

I'd better hurry or I'll lose him in this gale, she thought.

The appearance of the boy had given her a jolt of energy, but the packs were still tangled up on her arms and she shook them away in frustration.

Part of her cried out, *Don't do that! Your clothes and food and matches and weapons are in those bags. Hatcher's axe is in there. What is Hatcher without his axe? What will you eat if you can't make a fire or toast or tea?*

But the other part of her, the part that was fixated on the boy, ignored this warning. She stumbled forward, hurrying as quickly as she could, her legs and arms as stiff as a nutcracker's.

The boy had to come from somewhere—somewhere close by, somewhere with a roof and a fireplace. Almost as soon as she thought this she caught a faint whiff of woodsmoke, and then had a glimpse of an enormous black shape in the near distance.

It disappeared again, hidden by the storm, and Alice tried to run toward it but her body wouldn't let her run, it was shutting down again, and she'd lost track of the pale boy in the snow.

She gritted her teeth in frustration, for now she had no packs and no boy and no shelter and no Hatcher. If this was all that was going to happen she ought to have just stayed in the snow and let it pile up on top of her. Maybe she would be preserved in the cold and when spring came she could thaw out and bloom afresh, just like the buds on the trees.

The laugh rang out again, though Alice didn't see the boy. She chased the sound through the snow though she couldn't see anything except the storm. The boy's laugh was the only rope she had to grasp.

Then suddenly the enormous black shape was there again, rising before her like the beanstalk in that story about the boy who stole a goose from a giant.

Alice swiped the snow away from her face so she could look properly. It was a house, a gigantic house plopped right in the middle of the forest as if some huge hand had placed it there.

She couldn't get a clear view of it, only a sense of black turrets and gabled peaks and flickering light at the windows. It rather looked like her worst idea of a haunted house, and experience told her that even if it wasn't haunted it would very likely be full of magic or Magicians, and not the benevolent kind.

Still, it wasn't as though she had much choice. She could enter the possibly dangerous house or she could freeze to death out in the storm.

But how will Hatcher find me? And if this house was here when he darted off then why didn't he find it and return to me? It's not that far from where he left me.

She didn't have the answer to the first question but she did have a shrewd suspicion about the second. The house hadn't been there when Hatcher passed by. It had been put there just for her.

Alice thought, rather tiredly, that it was likely something to do with her being a Magician herself (though a very poor one, to be sure). She'd had enough of people trying to lure her and trap her and hurt her for something she couldn't help.

Her entire body shook with tremors of cold. She had to decide—stay out in the storm or go into the house.

In the end there wasn't really a choice.

Alice stepped onto the porch. It wrapped around the whole building, and while it didn't protect her from the wind it was a relief to have the roof to keep the snow off her head.

Perhaps I could just shelter out here and avoid whatever's lurking inside.

She tried to stamp her feet and shake some of the encrusted snow from her cloak, but she could barely bend her knees and elbows. Alice had never lived in an excessively cold place but even she knew this must be an ominous sign. She couldn't possibly stay out in this weather. If she did she was likely to lose a limb.

Alice shuffled across the porch. The door was made of some heavy dark wood and it was enormous—twice as tall as she was and she was a very tall woman, and about five times as wide. It was an absurd door even for a large house—the sort of thing that ought to front a government building, or perhaps a castle.

It can't possibly be a good thing that the door is this size, she thought. *There's likely to be bears living inside.*

Well, perhaps as long as I don't sleep in their beds or eat their porridge I'll be all right. And that boy lives here, doesn't he? He led me here. Maybe the bears don't eat humans, after all.

She knew her thoughts weren't making sense any longer, but it was hard to think straight while freezing to death. Alice knocked on the door, or rather she attempted to make her poor frozen hand bang against the wood but it came out like a faint and feeble heartbeat.

I'll never make anyone hear like that. And where has that boy gone? Why wasn't he waiting for me on the porch?

There was nothing for it. She was going to have to try the door, no matter how impolite it might seem to the residents.

This was easier said than done, though. The door didn't have a knob but a bright silver handle that went up and down. She bent over to peer at it and saw that inside the handle there was a button to be depressed. She imagined this was what released the door but Alice couldn't make her fingers curl around the handle, never mind exert enough pressure to push the button.

She stared at her hands. Had she lost the use of them altogether? Were they so frozen they could never be healed?

Don't panic, Alice. You only need to get warm. And once you get inside you'll be able to do that. Don't panic.

But it was becoming very difficult not to panic, because no matter how much she wanted her hands to work they wouldn't.

She let out a cracked cry that might have been a sob if only she were warm enough for tears to flow.

Why can't I . . . why can't I?

Alice couldn't even sense the metal beneath her fingers. It was like there was nothing there.

My hands. I've lost my hands.

Now her vision was disappearing. Shadows crept around the edges of her sight, leaking ink stains that seeped in and covered everything.

A moment later she found herself slumped on her knees, neck lolling forward. She felt a little sick to her stomach and she didn't have any idea how she'd gotten there.

I must have fainted, she thought vaguely.

This door was going to defeat her, she realized. She was too undone by the cold to open it herself, and nobody inside would be able to hear her scrabbling over the screaming wind.

She moved her head back—slowly, so slowly, because her skull felt like a heavy iron bar was pressing down on it—so that she could see the door again.

It was open.

Did I do magic? She didn't remember doing it, and she wasn't very good at it to begin with. But it was possible that the force of her will had accomplished what her body hadn't been able to do.

The door wasn't wide open in welcome. There were no smiling faces there, no gentle hands to assist her inside. That made Alice think that perhaps she *had* managed it by magic, else there would surely be someone peering out at her. It didn't make sense that someone would come and open the door and then walk away and leave her there.

But it was open, that was the important thing—just a fraction of an inch, enough for Alice to fall forward and push it the rest of the way.

She couldn't stand. She knew she ought to, ought to face whatever was inside—for good or ill—on her feet. All she could manage was to lurch forward on her hands and knees.

There was a deep, plush carpet lining the hall behind the door. Alice could see it, see her mittened hands sinking into it—it was the color of wine, or perhaps the color of blood—but she couldn't feel it. Her hands were two useless blocks at the ends of her wrists.

Once she was fairly certain all of her parts were inside the house, she glanced behind and kicked at the door with her boot. It closed with a smooth, almost unnatural motion and though Alice couldn't hear anything except the storm raging outside she was sure that the hinges wouldn't make a sound, would be insulted by even the tiniest squeak.

The closed door blocked out almost all of the noise outside except the screaming wind. Alice heard her own ragged breath, the scrape of her knees on the carpet, the crunch of her ice-covered hair against her forehead.

Glass lamps were set at intervals along the hall and inside them were flickering candles, their light concealing more than they revealed. There were deep pools of shadow beyond the place where Alice paused, on her hands and knees like a child, unable to stand or move forward another inch.

She must have fainted again, because the next thing she knew her nose was mashed into the blood-colored carpet. It had been some time that she lay there, for the ice and snow on her clothes and face had turned to water. Her forehead was wet and so were her fingers where the melted snow seeped through. In fact, her hands were stinging.

No, they weren't stinging. They were burning, and the burning was so terrible that it made her cry out. She pushed up to her knees and pulled off her mittens with her teeth, sure that her fingers were on fire, but they weren't. They were very pale and also splotchy with red, but they hurt like nothing Alice had ever felt before, hurt inside under the skin. She tried to rub them together, to put them under her knees, but anything she tried only made them burn more.

"*It hurts, it hurts*," she whimpered, and tears streamed down her cheeks.

The more they burned the more her hands could move and flex, and once that thought registered she realized that the pain was because they had been nearly frozen and now they were warming. Knowing what the cause was didn't make it any easier to endure, though, and it was some more time before she was able to calm herself.

She slowly stood up, wobbling a bit as her legs were still stiff. All her heavy layers felt like they were now impeding her, so she took off her cloak and hat and hung them on a peg near the door. There were no other cloaks or hats, no umbrella in the umbrella stand, no wet boots on the mat. But somebody lived in the house. Alice was certain of that.

Her stomach rumbled and that's when she remembered that she'd dropped the packs full of food out in the storm.

"Stupid," she muttered, but there was nothing for it now. The packs would be buried by the storm. She hoped Hatcher would forgive her for losing his axe.

So she was hungry. She'd been hungry before and no doubt would be again, but there was no amount of hunger that could make her eat any food that she found in this house. Alice had seen enough enchantments and heard enough fairy stories to know that there was nothing more foolish than taking food from someone she did not know. The smallest crumb of bread passing her lips might be enough to keep her trapped there forever, or to poison her, or to make her fall into an enchanted sleep.

And then Hatcher will have to come and wake me with a kiss. She laughed aloud at the thought. There was no one less likely to fit a story-idea of a prince than her wild and bloody Hatcher.

Even if she had no intention of eating any food she still wanted to stay inside the house until the storm passed. She was worried about Hatcher, but she thought that if he came back this way he would surely see the house and know where she'd gone. He did seem to know how to find her no matter how long they were separated.

It might have been his wolf's nose or wolf's ears or it might have been the way their hearts were tied together with invisible strings that only he knew how to follow. It might have been a kind of magic of his own, for all that he was no true Magician. He had a little touch of Sight, but Alice didn't know how often he used it, or how often it occurred to him to interpret the strange images in his head as seeing the future.

Alice took a good look around the hall. It was perhaps twelve or fifteen feet long. There were three doors, one on each side about halfway down and one directly in front of her at the far-thest end.

One door leads to certain death, she thought, but it wasn't really a thought—more like a memory from a story she might have heard once. If she chose one door and didn't like what she found there would she be able to come out and choose another, or would she be trapped?

Alice crept toward one of the doors. She didn't know exactly why she was trying to be silent now—surely if there were any-body living in the house they would have heard her crying over her poor abused hands—except that she wanted to listen at each door before going in and her instinct was to make certain no one inside would know what she was about.

It wasn't a polite thing, to listen at doors, and politeness had been ground into Alice as a child. Her mother had always told her to "be a good girl" and "mind your manners." It was the hardest habit to break, even when ignoring it would keep her safe.

She carefully examined the first door on her right. It was made of wood that had been painted white, and it shone like a sharp tooth in the gloom. It was as tall as the front door, though not as wide. There was a brass doorknob but no keyhole to peer through, which made Alice wrinkle her nose in annoyance. Things would be so much easier if she could only see what might be waiting on the other side.

Why should anything ever be simple or easy? This was a very tired thought, the thought of a person who'd spent a long time struggling and didn't want to struggle anymore, who wanted a few hours of the day to be free from peril or hunger or difficulty.

Alice leaned close to the door, carefully placing her right ear against the wood. There wasn't any noise coming from behind the door. That didn't mean it was safe, though. There could be a man with a knife waiting silently to butcher her as soon as she entered.

Don't be a goose, Alice, why would anyone do that? Wouldn't it have been easier to slit your throat while you were passed out in the hall?

She felt the logic of this, but logic didn't apply when she was tired and alone and yes, a little frightened. The house had a strange and unsettled atmosphere, an expectant waiting. Alice didn't know what it wanted from her.

It wouldn't have been quite so frightening if she only had spent more time learning how to become a proper Magician. She imagined herself shooting fire out of her hands or turning an enemy to a puddle of goo with a fierce look, but she had no idea how to go about actually doing such a thing.

Well, perhaps not the second thing, she thought as she crossed the hall to the second door. *It would be very unpleasant to turn someone into a puddle, all their soft insides and stiff bones melted into a stew. A very unpalatable stew.*

Being a Magician had brought Alice mostly grief from those who wanted her power in some way. She still didn't really have any idea how to make it work consistently. Mostly she'd done some small things

(*well, not the Jabberwock, that wasn't a small thing*)

by wishing. What Alice needed was a teacher, a teacher who could help her find that wellspring of magic inside and harness it to her will. But every Magician she'd met thus far had been mad or corrupt or both and therefore not the sort of instructor Alice would have chosen for herself.

She pressed her ear against the second door, which looked exactly like the first door except that it had a silver doorknob instead of a brass one. Alice wondered if this mattered, if it indicated some arcane force at work or signaled what might be on the other side. Perhaps the knob was different only because they'd run out of brass.

At first she thought there was nothing behind this door either, then she caught a whisper of a sound. There was a kind of papery rustling, something almost like the sound of Papa turning the newspaper at the breakfast table or the *whish* of Mama's petticoats as she adjusted her skirts.

She hadn't thought of her parents like that in years—just a memory, without bitterness—and it made her sway on the spot, caught in a momentary loop of herself, happy and smiling and spooning too much jam from the pot onto her toast.

The rustling increased in volume, seemed to come closer to the door, and Alice imagined that it wasn't a person at all, but a giant moth with translucent wings. It was flying closer to the door now. Perhaps it was reaching out with one of its antennae, pressing it against the door, feeling for the vibrations of some nosy someone on the other side.

The rustling ceased.

Alice thought she should move away then but she couldn't. She strained, trying to determine just what was making the sound.

Something hissed, a long, sibilant noise that was nothing like a moth or a silent Papa turning the pages of the newspaper or like Mama's petticoats. It was a cry of alarm, or perhaps the cunning recognition of prey.

Alice didn't wait for whatever it was to exit the room. She darted toward the farthest door at the end, heart pounding.

I wish I was invisible, I wish you wouldn't see me.

The door behind her opened. She knew this not because she heard it but because the quality of the air shifted. She knew this because she sensed the presence behind her, a thing that peered into the corridor with hungry eyes.

It hissed again, and her thoughts became frantic crowded things, tripping over each other.

I wish I was invisible I wish you wouldn't see me hear me smell me you don't know that I'm here you can't I'm turning into a shadow a formless thing and you can't catch me you'll never catch me

She halted in front of the door. She should open it and go inside, because then there would at least be some sort of protection between her and whatever was behind her.

You can't see me hear me smell me you don't know I'm here

Alice knew she ought to look. She ought not to be a scurrying mouse, not when she'd been a fierce and fearsome killer once.

You made the Caterpillar pay. Do you remember that? Do you remember that girl, the one who slashed his throat without a regret?

But the dream-memory she'd had that morning—the one of the small girl who was hunted by a white bird—was still clinging to her edges, and so was the little girl Alice had been, the golden-haired doll who sat so prettily and ate so daintily at the table with her mama and her papa.

You're not that little girl anymore, that girl is gone, she's just a memory in amber and maybe not even that. Maybe she never existed but you exist now and you have to be here. You have to save yourself.

You have to save yourself.

Alice turned her head to the left, so slowly, like she was an automaton winding down. Her teeth bit into her bottom lip, and her breath was stuffed up inside her chest so she wouldn't make a sound.

At first all she saw was white—a pale glowing white like the snow outside, like the pale-faced boy in the white coat whose laugh had led her here. Her brain thought, *It's just a very pale person like him, it's all right to look more, it won't be anything that means you harm.*

She turned her shoulders, all the while thinking, *You can't see me hear me smell me you don't know I'm here*, because if the charm had worked thus far she was sure it was only because she hadn't loosened it from her grip.

The pale glowing thing was a hand, a hand that looked terribly like one that had haunted her—the hand of a goblin in the woods as he reached out, long fingers that brushed over her hair, a goblin that had wanted to put Alice's head on the wall because he loved her so much.

The fingers of this hand were long and slender and tipped with very sharp nails that one might call claws. The hand was attached to a thin arm that was shrouded in loose and crumbling skin, skin that flaked and rustled like paper in the fireplace.

The arm joined an elongated body loosely covered in a grey tunic. The tunic was littered with flaking bits of skin like fallen dragon scales and fell almost to the floor but didn't conceal the overlong feet, feet that were not quite human, feet that crouched on the balls and had toes that ended in curling white nails.

The feet were so hideous that she gave a little shudder and closed her eyes but she forced herself to open them again so she could see its face. She'd been afraid to look, afraid that if she met its eyes that it would see through her disguise.

She shouldn't have looked.

It wasn't a human head, it wasn't something that could even pretend to be human. The jaw was long, unhinged like a snake's, and a questing tongue darted out from its lipless mouth. The tongue was a strange faded grey, not like anything Alice had ever seen in nature. There was no nose, either, just two flaring nostrils.

The eyes were overlarge and seemed to stretch back from its face, like it could see in front and on the sides too (*and that's cheating, how is anything ever supposed to escape if it can see all around and maybe behind itself too*) and they looked so much like a reptile's eyes that she thought they ought to be yellow or green like others she'd seen but these were pink, pinkish red like those of the boy who had stood and laughed outside in the snow, but that boy had been demonstrably a boy and this was not anything like a boy or a man or a girl or a woman. This was not a person.

It had, though, something like a person's ears, but as strangely elongated as the rest of its body, ears that weren't soft and round and shell-like but stretched from nearly the top of the head to the bend of its jaw.

All these strange and disparate pieces were covered in the same papery, flaking skin as the rest of it, and Alice's brain couldn't make sense of this strange creature no matter how hard she tried, and its eyes made her shudder, which she shouldn't have done though she couldn't help it.

The creature was suddenly behind her. She didn't see how it moved in less than a breath, less even than a thought of a breath, and she willed her heart to beat more softly else it hear the very rush of her blood in her veins.

Its nostrils widened and she heard the quick sharp inhalations, its head bobbing up and down and side to side as it sought proof of her presence.

You can't see me hear me smell me you don't know I'm here.

She whispered the charm inside her brain and her heart over and over but she could hear the force leaking out of it, hear her strong intent withering as this terrible monster sniffed the air so close to her, so close that she could smell its papery skin, a smell like a faded sachet tucked into an old trunk of clothes, a trunk that hadn't been opened for years.

Alice could have killed the thing, if only she had any kind of weapon, but she'd dropped her weapons in the snow and she didn't know how to cast a spell that meant anything, didn't know how to strangle it with her mind or make it explode from the inside out. She didn't know how to do anything, really, except stumble around and survive by the skin of her teeth.

She was a useless little girl, really. She'd always been.

The spell wavered, and she felt herself becoming solid and visible again and she redoubled her effort but she had been seen, she knew it. The creature hissed, like it had seen her flickering in the shadows, a guttering candle that was blown out a moment later.

It lifted one of those horrible hands tipped with horrible

claws. It was going to slash out at her, or even just reach out to touch her and she couldn't bear the thought of either. She would have to run or fight. There was no more hiding.

Her hand fumbled for the doorknob behind her—it didn't matter anymore what was on the other side of the door, it couldn't possibly be worse than what was in front of her.

(Oh, but it could. You know that better than anybody. There could be horrors you've never imagined.)

The creature's eyes shot to the knob. It could see that moving even if it couldn't see Alice. Her hands were sweaty (*just a short time ago they were so cold you couldn't even bend your fingers and now they're so sweaty you can't grasp the door everything about you is always wrong, Alice*) and she couldn't get it to uncatch and it was all over because even if she could get the door open the creature could only follow her inside she was a fool such an absolute fool.

"Alice?" A man's voice. Hatcher's voice.

"Alice, are you in there?" And then the sound of a fist pounding on a door. It wasn't the front door, though. It was one of the side doors, the one opposite where the creature had emerged. And he didn't sound completely like himself, either. He sounded kind of slurry and sleepy, like he'd just woken from a nap. Or was drunk.

But Hatcher never drank spirits. Not ever. And he was hardly ever sleepy. So maybe it was a trick to lure her, and not really Hatcher at all.

"Alice? Alice? Open the door, Alice."

The creature hissed loudly and

(jumped? leapt? flew?)

to the other door, and Alice finally got the knob behind her to turn and she hesitated only a second, because it might be a trick but it might really be Hatcher, and if it was Hatcher then there was something wrong with him and she shouldn't leave him alone with this shedding-paper-snake monster, leave him alone with its fangs and claws, but she remembered then that Hatcher had fangs and claws of his own and she didn't.

Alice pushed the door open and stumbled through and at the last second she lost the spell entirely. The creature saw her, she could feel it seeing her, and it screamed a terrible sound, a sound that made Alice clamp down on the tip of her tongue in terror and her mouth filled with blood.

She slammed the door shut and felt the creature crash into the other side, heard its claws scraping the wood as it scrabbled for the handle. Alice ran her hands all along the seam of the door because it was pitch dark in the room she'd entered, so dark she couldn't see the door that she faced, and she knew there had to be a lock somewhere, in her parents' house every door had a lock

(so they could keep their secrets if they wanted to and they did seem to want to because she'd found so many doors closed to her and they'd never given her a key)

and then she felt it, the cold metal of a bolt and she grasped it and shot it through while the creature screamed and she swallowed her own blood, the taste of fear burning on her tongue.

And somehow, despite the screaming creature and the roaring of her own blood in her ears she could hear Hatcher calling her, "Alice? Alice? Are you there? Open the door, Alice."

She remembered the time that she stayed in an abandoned cottage in some woods when they first left the City, and all night long a creature knocked on the doors and windows and called out to her in the voice of her friend Dor, her friend who had died

(a friend who was not really a friend at all in the end but the creature didn't know that, it only plucked out the memory of little Dor from my memory like it was choosing the best berry from a fruit bowl)

and because of that Alice couldn't help being suspicious about hearing Hatcher's voice in this house. It seemed far too likely that it wasn't Hatcher at all.

She pressed her hands against the door and felt the monster's fury pulsing through the wood, the repeated attempts to destroy the obstacle in its way, but the door held firm. It didn't even rattle in its hinges. Whatever it was made from was proof against even the residents of the house.

Alice turned around then, opening her eyes wide in a vain attempt to try to see more clearly into the room she'd entered. There were no windows that she could see, or else they were covered so thoroughly that the sun was blacked out.

(Not that there's so much sun right now with the storm, but at least there's a little light outside or maybe there isn't because I don't know how long I've been inside here and the sun goes down earlier in the winter.)

She should make some light. Sometimes she could do that, if she concentrated hard enough, though the magic place inside her often seemed to shift around, like it was trying to hide from her.

Alice held out her palm flat and tried not to feel foolish. Whenever she'd done magic in the past it had seemed to spring out of her without conscious thought, the product of the need that she had in the moment. Whenever she tried to make something happen otherwise she always felt very silly, a performer fumbling about onstage while the audience grew restless.

I need some light, she thought.

For a second there was a little flare over her palm, like the brief flash of a firefly, and then it was gone.

"That won't do," she said.

Her voice echoed all around the space and came back to her—*That won't do That won't do That won't do*. Wherever she was the space was very large, and she thought of a ballroom or perhaps an oversized dining room with high ceilings.

She thought she also heard more of that papery rustling and she stilled, because the only thing worse than the creature outside screaming for her was the thought of facing one just like it in the dark.

The echo of her voice faded away. (*Where do those voices go when they disappear? Do they leave the room through cracks in the floor and live on elsewhere, or are they always seeking other lost voices, a place where they all speak and harmonize together?*) Alice listened hard, felt the muscles tighten around her spine, tasted the stickiness of her blood in her mouth.

There was no other noise, no sense of something breathing or moving. She must have imagined the rustling, her fear making her conjure lurking enemies.

It's not just your fear, though. You know this house is full of enemies. You knew when you followed that impossible boy through the storm, but you had no choice, because it was either come here or die in the snow.

"Light, I need a light," she muttered, and even though she

spoke only loud enough to be heard by herself her words echoed back at her again.

Light I need a light I need a light a light

Something rustled, and Alice was certain she'd heard it that time. It wasn't her imagination.

One of those creatures is in here with me.

She needed the light more than ever, and wished she could just have a candle and a match like a regular person and that she didn't have to somehow reach inside herself and pull out a ball of light using a power she didn't fully understand.

Life is never what you want it to be, Alice, only what it is. And you need to see what's in here with you so MAKE A LIGHT.

And just like that there was a light hovering over her palm, a light that seemed to wax and wane like the moon but a light nonetheless. She pushed away all her fears and worries and focused only on that little glowing ball. She held her hand aloft so she could see around the room.

If there was a creature in the room with her it wasn't attacking like the one outside. Still, she wanted to know precisely where it was in relation to her in the event it changed its mind.

Her sense that she was in a large empty room had been good. The room was perhaps fifty or so feet across, a long rectangle, and she stood at the farthest side from the other end.

There were three doors lined up on that side and the moment she saw them she couldn't help thinking, *More doors more choices more chances to encounter something I don't want to encounter or fall into a pit or get eaten up by a monster. Why must every place I go be a mystery that I have no interest in solving?*

As she sent the light around she saw only a marble floor

coated in a thick layer of dust. There were no windows, no furniture and more importantly, no occupants. Yet the papery rustling continued and the vast and echoing nature of the room
made it impossible to determine where it was coming from. Was
she simply hearing the monster outside, the one that had stopped
screaming? Was it now standing at the door, breathing and rustling, calculating the best way to reach her?

No, it's in here, Alice thought, and then she realized the only
possible place the noise could be coming from. As soon as she
realized this the light floating above her hand flickered madly,
the physical manifestation of her terror.

Just look, she told herself. *It's better to be certain.*

She sent the light drifting upward, slowly, almost lazily, like
a floating balloon detached from the string that kept it in a
child's hand.

Alice expected to see one of the creatures perched on a ledge
like a bird of prey, or else hanging upside down from its long
feet like a bat.

She did not expect to see the eggs.

"Eggs" was the word she used, not because they looked like
eggs but because it was the only thing that helped her make
sense of them at first glance.

There were dozens of them, all attached to the ceiling by a
long cord, except the cord wasn't a cord but something living,
something pink and pulsing, and the ceiling wasn't a ceiling
either but a vast field of flesh shot through with channels that
ran with blood.

The eggs swung gently below, many horrible cradles, and the

exterior of each was translucent and coated with thick mucus. Beneath this Alice could see strange pale shapes shifting, and whenever one of them shifted the rustling-paper noise drifted down to her.

They're not really like eggs at all, more like a butterfly's chrysalis, she thought, knowing that the proper name for them wasn't in the least important, but this was the thing her brain had latched on so that she wouldn't start screaming and screaming because that monster out there in the hall wasn't the only one, there was a whole generation of them growing here and somehow the house was feeding them.

I have to get out of this house. Storm or no storm, I have to get away.

But the only exit she knew of was behind her and it was blocked by the creature.

And maybe Hatcher was somewhere in the house, too (though she wasn't certain of this, not certain at all, but it seemed a thing she'd have to confirm) and if he was then she had to find him because she couldn't leave him in this house of monsters.

Whatever you're going to do you need to come up with a better weapon than wishing, because your magic isn't anything to write home about. If Cheshire saw you now he'd laugh and laugh.

She didn't know why she suddenly thought of Cheshire, whom she hadn't considered in any way since last she heard his irritating voice—and that had been some time ago. Perhaps it was something to do with the dream she'd had that morning (a dream that now seemed so long ago that it might not have happened at all). Or perhaps it was because whenever she'd been in peril he somehow always knew and was there to offer advice, though whether that advice was actually helpful was an open question.

So I have no Cheshire and no Hatcher and no Red Queen's crown to help me. I have only myself and I am not going to die here.

Thinking it made her calmer, freed her to consider how she ought to proceed. She was in no immediate danger from the egg-swings and the monster was on the other side of the door, seemingly unable to break it down.

Alice needed to get out of this place and try working back to the room with Hatcher's voice in it (she only thought of it as Hatcher's voice because she wasn't sure it was actually Hatcher, though the voice was attached to something or someone making it, it surely wasn't floating without a body).

She started across the room, stirring up the dust with her boots. It was so thick that her bootheels didn't ring, and Alice thought it was a good thing because she wasn't entirely certain the creatures above wouldn't wake up at any moment and burst out of the sacs that held them.

Of course, when she reached the other side she would have the Problem of the Doors, and that was no small problem because it was very clear that choosing the wrong door in this house would absolutely lead to certain death.

They might all lead to certain death, you know, and you've escaped from certain death before, so your odds are probably better than the average person's.

This was a very comforting thought, one that made her feel more sturdy than she had a moment before. She'd survived before. She'd survive again.

Halfway to the doors she sneezed.

There was just too much dust swirling in the room. Her nose had been twitching side to side like a nervous rabbit's as she tried to hold it in, but at a certain point she couldn't do it any longer.

The sneeze burst out of her, an insanely loud and comic thing that forced her to bend over and AAAAHH-CHOOOO like a clown sniffing a flower in a sideshow. If she'd been watching from the audience she would have laughed and clapped along with everyone else, but she wasn't in the audience, she was part of the entertainment and she knew that her sneeze was the worst thing that could happen at that moment.

Alice stilled, hunched over her knees, unwilling to even breathe loudly. She lowered the brightness of her light and covered it with her other palm, so that all she could see was the faint glow leaking out from between her fingers.

The rustling above increased as all of the creatures inside their eggs twisted and shifted. The noise was like the flapping of many tiny wings, a ripple that went across the entire ceiling and quickly reached a crescendo.

Then, just as suddenly as it began, the noise stopped.

Alice waited, because it might be a trick, a trap to lull her into a sense of complacency. But the rustling had mostly gone away, limited to only the occasional noise that made Alice think of a sleeper turning over in her bed.

She slid one foot forward, so very carefully, wincing at the slight scrape of her boots. It was barely noticeable, really, but to her it sounded like an explosion.

You're almost making more noise trying to be quiet. Just walk the way you did before.

Alice forced herself to stand up straight, to stride forward (*strong and forthright but still careful, yes, I am being very careful*). The doors drew closer, or she drew closer to the doors. Sometimes it was difficult to determine these things, and Alice had learned that not everything was as it seemed. She might not be walking forward at all, but marching in place while the room shrank.

No, it's you moving and not the doors, don't let your mind play tricks.

She was nearly there. Perhaps thirty steps would do it.

Her heart was beating so hard it hurt and she wanted to gasp but was afraid of the noise it would make so she pressed her lips tight together so as not to make a sound.

Don't make a noise, little mouse, don't let the cat hear you see you smell you or it will pounce.

Hatcher had told her once not to be a mouse, not to let anyone make her one, but it was hard to be the courageous and fierce Alice all the time. Sometimes the curled-up part of her that had been hurt wanted to hide instead of fight.

It wasn't easy to be brave all the time, and it was also, Alice reflected, perfectly all right not to be. The important thing was to keep doing her best.

It was hard not to think of the creatures swaying above in their cradles, hard not to imagine one of them tearing through its prison and leaping to the floor just in time to stop her from exiting the room.

Maybe twenty steps now. That's hardly anything at all. You'll be out of here safely before you know it.

She thought she heard a wet ripping noise, the sound of something with teeth tearing through flesh, and she hesitated.

There's nothing, it's all in your mind, just get out of this room because if a monster is about to fall from the ceiling then it's better for you to be out than in.

She opened her stride, heedless of any sounds she might make, any attention she might attract. There might or might not be a screeching creature about to fall, newly born, but whatever the case she didn't want to know about it. It wasn't any concern of Alice's because she wasn't going to be here when it happened.

Less than ten steps now. You'll have to just choose a door at random, no time for listening and being cautious.

A wet splotch fell to the floor directly before her and she halted. She thought about looking more closely at it, putting the light up to it, and then decided not. That glob of whatever it was

(birthing fluid, it was birthing fluid, something is emerging just above it, about to mewl its first cry into the world)

could only mean Bad Things and so Alice must leave, she shouldn't stop or look up or do anything other than keep moving forward.

Five steps now, you're nearly there.

She went directly for the middle door, her hand outstretched.

More drops of fluid fell behind her, making thick wet sounds that were nothing like water, but Alice was leaving. She was going to be out of the room before the creature was born.

Her right hand grasped the handle, her left hand held the light aloft and she knew that it would make her easier to find, but she didn't care. She didn't want to be left alone in the dark with a monster.

The door wouldn't open.

She tugged at the handle twice, lifted it up and down.

A high thin cry came from above, and more tearing.

Don't panic. Just try another door.

Fluid poured from above now. It sounded like a deluge, like the worst rainstorm Alice had ever heard and she still didn't want to look, didn't want to direct the light toward the monster being born and so she hoped that there was only one emerging and not all of them.

She moved toward the right-hand-side door, knowing before she reached it that it wouldn't be open either, knowing that this room was a trap closing around her, but she had to try. She had to be certain.

The thin cry filled out, became something like a howl of triumph and Alice wasn't sure because her blood was filling her ears, but she thought that there was an answering howl from all of the other creatures, like the first one was waking the rest.

I'm going to be trapped in this room with all the monsters, she thought as she darted to the left-hand-side door, the one that was also locked because she had done exactly the wrong thing, she'd done the wrong thing from the time she'd seen that pale boy with the strange eyes in the snow. She should have just stayed there and froze. Freezing was probably better than getting torn to shreds by a freshly minted flock of hungry monsters.

She turned around then and flattened her back against the wall, because at least then they could come at her from only three sides instead of four. The little ball of light rose up closer to the ceiling, because it seemed a wise thing to know exactly what she was in for.

Only one of the creatures had actually broken its chrysalis. This was the one that was pouring globs of thick mucus onto the dust-coated floor. The others were roiling inside the egg-swings, their forms indistinct but clearly moving.

The one that had broken through screeched when Alice's light approached the ceiling. One of its wings was partially free of the membrane, and its head was entirely out, but the remainder of its body seemed to be still trapped in the fluid.

I still have time, she thought. *It can't get out that easily. I still have time to figure out how to break through this door.*

It would be a very useful time to suddenly manifest real power, to make the doors fly off their hinges or to produce waves of flame to burn all the creatures before they emerged.

It would be very useful, but Alice didn't have the least idea how to do such things, and she certainly couldn't do them when she was scared, and she would happily have used any kind of weapon available but there was nothing that she could see, not even a broken stick of furniture. She was in a big empty room and the only way out was back through the hall where the first creature lurked.

Think, Alice, think, think.

No one is coming to save you now.

Alice remembered the first time she'd really felt her magic, when she put on the Red Queen's crown and she'd saved all the lost children. Her power had filled her up then, had burned through her so easily. And even though she'd given up the crown she'd been certain that she'd be able to find that magic again, that it would bloom through her as simple as the sunrise. It had seemed, in that moment, like it would.

But once the thrill of defeating the White Queen faded away she'd been unable to find the spark again. Her magic receded into a small and half-forgotten thing, but it was not because the power was actually small. It was only that she didn't really know how to use it.

Remember when you killed the White Queen? You slashed your hand and off went her head.

(But that was because of the Red Queen, not me.)

And that, Alice thought, was the real trouble. She wasn't certain that in that moment, giddy with easy power, she was the one who'd done the spellcasting.

I think you ought to try, though. I really think you ought to.

The reason she really thought she ought to was because the creature was half in and half out of its prison, and it certainly was aware of her presence because it was looking right at her and screaming and the screams were making her ears hurt, the screams were penetrating inside her head and snaking around in her blood and making her brain swell against her skull.

Alice pushed her fingers against her ears trying to block out the screaming because the noise was half of the problem. It was so noisy she couldn't think, and she realized that this was part of the way the creature subdued its prey. It would keep screeching so that she would stay in place and wait to be devoured, rather than doing something tiresome like running away and forcing it to chase.

Think, think! You aren't just some ordinary Alice. You're the Alice that defeated the Jabberwock, the Alice that killed the Caterpillar.

But it was so hard to think, so hard to cast a spell or even to make a wish.

I wish all this noise would stop.

The creature's screaming halted, but only for a moment. It was almost a hiccup, and Alice could imagine its bewilderment. But then the sound started again, seemingly louder and more terrible than before.

I WISH this NOISE would STOP, Alice thought.

And it did.

The monster's screaming blinked out like a snuffed candle.

Alice looked up.

Her little ball of light had continued to burn despite Alice's lack of attention. That was a very good sign, she realized. She hadn't been fully engaged with it, yet her magic had perpetuated the light without her conscious knowledge.

Now that the creature had stopped screaming she felt herself much calmer. The light illuminated its confused face—*could such a monster feel confusion? It certainly seemed to*—as it opened and closed its mouth and found that it couldn't do anything to subdue her. It was the same sort of creature as the one she'd encountered outside the door, except this was a newborn version, slick with fluid, its features somehow younger though not in the least less terrifying.

Alice laughed, though it wasn't quite the merry ringing of the boy in the snow. It was the laugh of a gravedigger, someone standing very close to death. She'd managed to make the monster stop screaming, but now she felt terribly wrung out, and it was probably because she was exhausted and starving and had nearly frozen to death, and she thought that if she wasn't all of those things she might be able to dredge up the energy to turn the monster into a grasshopper or a cuddly kitten, or perhaps to make the whole house wink out of existence. But she didn't have that sort of energy at all and she thought it was better just to leave before the monster managed to wrest itself from its chrysalis.

Then there came another sound of something thick and wet falling to the dust-coated floor, and Alice saw one of the other egg-swings had torn open. Soon the new creature that broke through would start its own scream and she'd be straight back to the beginning again, like a pilgrim unable to find the center of a labyrinth.

She needed to stop worrying about weapons to defeat the monsters and think about the door.

She didn't want to turn her back on the room—that seemed deeply foolish, even Alice knew that one should never expose the back of one's neck to a predator—so she groped behind her for the door handle. It was not a regular knob but a straight handle like the one on the front door.

She pushed it down again, vaguely hoping for a different result than the first time, but still nothing. If the door was anything like the one she'd used to enter the room there would be a bolt somewhere on the frame on the other side. All Alice needed to do was find a way to undo the bolt from this side.

Surely you can do this even if you are tired and unsure and unmoored. Surely you can manage to move the bolt with your mind or some such thing.

The rainfall-patter had begun again. That meant the second creature's head was nearly out. Soon it would scream. Soon Alice wouldn't be able to do anything except hold her head and wait for them to come for her.

The first creature had worked its second wing out of the

chrysalis and flapped them madly, its mouth open even though it couldn't make a noise. Alice thought that in a moment the rest of its body would slide out but it seemed its legs were still encased in the fluid inside the membrane.

Open, door. Open, lock.

A faint, almost pathetic sound reached her. It sounded very much like a rusty bolt moving, but only shifting a tiny bit—the length of an eyelash, perhaps.

(Alice, don't you want to live? Don't you want to see Hatcher again?)

It's a strange thing to be chided by oneself, Alice thought, especially since the tone adopted sounded an awful lot like her mother's when Mama was annoyed with her.

(Don't think about Mama now! Don't think about those other things now! You must get out of this room! You must save yourself!)

Yes, she must save herself. Save herself as she had done before, as she had saved Hatcher and everyone in the Old City when she turned the Jabberwock into a butterfly.

There was an ominous squelching noise from above, something that sounded very much like a creature finally wriggling free of its egg. Alice didn't want to look. She didn't want to see her death flying to her.

She turned her back on the room, and the light above winked out. Now she was alone with the sounds, the sound of monsters wresting free from their prisons, the sound of wings in the still air.

Alice pressed her hands against the door.

It's coming for me now.

It's coming.

I don't want to die.

OPEN, LOCK!

She heard the bolt fly free. In the same instant there was a rush of air against the back of her neck. Alice grasped the handle and the door flew open.

She stumbled through the door and slammed it shut behind her, throwing the bolt just as the creature crashed into the place where she'd been standing a moment before. Alice heard a faint, frustrated hissing coming from the back of its throat—the only noise it could make now that Alice had muted its cry.

She leaned her head against the door, breathless, her face covered in sweat.

Alice, when will you learn not to wait until the last moment? When will you learn to use your magic properly?

This last was a silly question to ask even of herself, for the only person she knew who would admit to being a Magician and who wanted to teach her lived in a rose-covered cottage far away. She'd run from that person, as she'd run from everything in the City, both Old and New. She'd run because she wanted a life free from shadows and pain, and because she wanted that for Hatcher, too.

But you can't escape from shadows or pain. You only find new ones. It's better, I think, not to try to escape them at all but to accept that they will be there, and to remember that good things happen, too, even if you can't always see them.

(But in the meantime, you need to get out of this house of haunts, even if it does mean going out into that terrible storm again.)

The creature slammed its body into the door then, making it rattle in its hinges. Alice backed away, staring at the door like it was a box that held something horrible, something that might burst forth at any moment like an unwanted gift.

But the door held firm, just as the other had when she entered the ballroom. She noticed then that she was in a space lit by the same faint and flickering lamps as the front hallway, and turned slowly to see what terrors were in store for her now.

She was in a kind of antechamber, a very small space with a low ceiling. Behind her was the door into the ballroom and on either side a lamp. In front of her was yet another door.

Alice reached for the doorknob, then paused, shaking her head. Her hand dropped away and became a fist at her side.

No, she thought. *I have had ENOUGH of doors and ENOUGH of games and ENOUGH of being afraid. I'm not going to be a plaything for a monster or anyone else, anyone who might be watching and laughing while I struggle.*

OPEN, DOOR!

The door flew open as if caught by a hard wind, and Alice felt a rush of something leaving her.

Well, you know you can do something if you get angry, at least. Although I don't think it's a reliable way to go about things.

The anger simmered just under the surface, made her stride forward ready to attack.

There was nothing except a stairway.

Alice felt herself deflate a little, felt the fury recede into the background. But the thought that had occurred to her a moment before—the thought that there might be someone watching her fumble through the house, someone who might be throwing obstacles in her way—that thought became surer. Of course there was some hand designing all of this. There always was.

And the only kind of hand that could do this was a Magician's.

Somewhere in this house, a Magician waited for Alice.

The stairway before her curled upward like the stripe on a candy stick, and as her eyes followed its course she thought that the house must be taller than she first thought, for the stairs seemed to go farther than her initial impression of the house would allow.

Or perhaps it's only another trick, an illusion to make you think you must climb and climb until you are too exhausted to fight.

The very instant that she thought this the stairway shimmered like something seen in the distance when it is very hot out, a kind of hazy warping of the air. A moment later the vision resolved itself, and Alice saw a stairway still curved like a peppermint stripe, but one that rose only to the next floor, where it met a long landing.

And you didn't even need to be angry to see that, Alice. Your magic is there, if only you would let it be instead of fighting it all the time.

Was that what she did? Alice wondered as she climbed the curving staircase. Did her magic struggle because she struggled, searching for it and trying to draw it forth only when she wanted it?

Yes, you are like an engineer trying to tame a river with a dam, or to reroute the water only where he wishes it to go. Water will always push through the cracks and find its own path.

She knew then that despite what magic had done for her that she had always fought it, always tried to keep it in a place where she could control it. The only time she hadn't was when she'd worn the Red Queen's crown, and it had been easy enough afterward to decide that the ease with which her power flowed had been due to that external force, and that it wasn't really her at all.

You've been scared to be a Magician, Alice. Deep down, underneath where nobody can see—not even Hatcher, who sees everything—you've been afraid.

She'd been afraid of her power, afraid to be something she'd always been taught was wicked and wrong. It didn't matter that the people who taught her that were small in heart and mind, that those same people had sent her away from them when she'd become an inconvenience. It had been her first lesson about magic, and the first thing you learn always stays with you whether you want it or not.

Her second lesson had been that people who did not have her power would want it, and that they would do anything to get it.

That lesson, too, had made its mark.

And so even when she'd felt the wonder of her own magic flowing freely Alice shut it away again, locked it behind a door where she could keep it—and herself—safe.

While she thought all these things her feet moved of their own accord, taking her to the next floor, and her hand brushed against the banister as she climbed. She noticed (in a distant, vague sort of way) that the banister seemed to pulse like a vein beneath her fingers, as if blood flowed through the house like a living thing.

When she stepped onto the landing she felt that same pulsing in the floor beneath her boots, and she glanced down, half expecting to see the boards shifting. But they appeared still and quiet.

Another illusion. They only seem like they are quiescent, but you know better. You can feel it.

She stepped forward cautiously, thinking hands might reach through and grab her ankles. There was an uncomfortable sucking sort of feeling as she walked, a sense that her boot soles were planting deeper than they appeared to be.

It's not those monsters that are the problem, you know. It's the house itself. Somehow the house is a live thing, something watching and waiting, something testing and judging. It's trying to frighten you, to trick you. But to what end?

The landing was shaped like an "L," starting from the point where Alice stood at the top of the stairs, wrapping around the wall to the left before stopping at the following corner. The walls that lined the landing were smooth and white, no doors or windows that could be seen by human eyes.

But there are doors here nonetheless. Doors that I can feel even if I can't see them. Doors the house is trying to hide from me.

The other two walls were lined with enormous glass windows that showed the still-blowing blizzard outside.

Just to remind me, Alice thought with a sour twist of her mouth, *that I can take my chances with the house or the storm.*

She turned the corner of the landing, ignoring her sense that there were openings in the wall before that. Those were not doors for Alice. She wasn't interested in playing games for the house, or whatever entity was controlling it. Her only thought now was to discover the house's heart, or its brain.

It can amount to the same thing sometimes, when the heart leads the brain instead of the other way around. That's your own difficulty, very often.

Halfway down the second part of the landing Alice stopped. She rested her hand against the wall—smooth, unassuming, white.

Nothing to see here, she thought, *but there is something on the other side all the same.*

The tips of her fingers glowed as she pushed against the wall, and a rectangle of it slid away, smoothly swinging open as if it hung on greased hinges. Alice felt a momentary satisfaction, for her magic had come easily and naturally, and she hadn't been deceived by any trick.

But as her eyes adjusted to the gloom behind the door, she wished she hadn't found this one, that she'd never known what was here at all.

Alice's feet moved of their own accord, taking her closer, and here in this room there was no deception of wooden floors at all. The ground beneath her was soft and pink and pulsing, the twin of the ceiling in the ballroom below. It was, in fact, the room directly above the ballroom, for it was as long and wide though not nearly as high.

She did not want to stay in this room. She wanted to run, but there was nowhere for her to run except back out to the snow, and she saw now how neatly this had all been arranged, and how helpless she'd been to avoid it.

All throughout the room there were people, men and women and sometimes—Alice's heart clutched at the sight of them— even children. They were encased in pods made of some kind of clear film filled with a jelly-like substance. She could see each pod pulsating gently. From each pod ran something like a cord or vein that connected to the floor, and Alice realized that these people were feeding the eggs of the monsters below.

At first she thought to rush about, to try to find some way to break open the pods and save the people inside. But as she knelt beside the first pod and looked closer she saw this wasn't like the White Queen drawing energy from living children. There was no cord of magic that she could cut.

The person in the pod was already partially decomposed, the flesh of his abdomen eaten away, revealing half-gone organs beneath. He had no eyes and no tongue and the skin under the jaw had begun to peel away, showing white bone beneath.

Alice turned her head away, shuddering. There was nothing she could do here, no valiant rescue to be made. These people were already dead, their living flesh preserved to feed the creatures below.

But to what end? She stood, scanning the massive room. *Is the house breeding these monsters to set upon the world?*

She heard someone laughing behind her then, a high-pitched squeal full of merry joy. Alice spun on her heel and saw the boy standing in the doorway, his white hair and strange eyes glowing in the snow-light that came through the windows.

"Did you do this?" Alice asked, anger bubbling up under her skin.

"Don't you like my creations, Magician? Won't it be a wonder to see all my beautiful children flying throughout the world?"

"Children," Alice said, as if the word were something filthy upon her tongue. "Those things below are your children?"

She could imagine them flying, yes. Imagine them flying in a flock and sweeping down upon each settlement they saw like locusts at the feed, destroying the human population inch by inch until there was nothing left but the terrible, triumphant screams of those things that should not be.

The boy laughed again, and his laugh was like the cry of the monster below—a knife-edged thing that pierced Alice's ears and brain and heart and made her stumble forward, clutching her head with both hands.

He's not really a little boy, Alice thought. *It's only the form he takes. He's some kind of monster himself.*

"Yes, they are my children, and like all good parents I have wanted to give them the best possible start in life. They age too quickly, you see. My firstborn—you met him below, I think, in the hallway—he's lost his power far too soon. He is like an old man, ancient and bent, and he cannot fly any longer. And he was only born a month ago. That won't do, you see. How can my beautiful children go forth to conquer the world if they die so soon?"

Alice tried to think, but it was as if the boy's laughter was still ringing in her ears. The boy was coming to the heart of it, the reason she'd been led here, and she knew she needed to think, to destroy him, to escape. The laughter was inside her, though, terrible bells that wouldn't cease their chime.

The boy laughed again, and it rolled over the echo of the first laugh and made Alice's eyes feel like they were swelling inside her skull.

I can't think with this noise Make it quiet make it quiet quiet quiet QUIET

Silence swept up in the wake of the laughter, rolled behind it like a wave. Alice felt her mind clearing as it did, felt the pain and pressure inside her head ease. It wasn't because the boy had checked his mirth, though.

It was because she'd pushed back against his power, made it harder for it to affect her. She let her hands fall away from her head and straightened, savoring the feeling of emptiness.

The boy laughed, but the laugh didn't go anywhere, didn't chase around inside her. It stopped at her ears, the way it was supposed to—irritating instead of debilitating.

I still don't understand how I stopped it, though. There has to be a better way to do magic than this.

The boy was talking again, clearly delighted to explain his plan and how Alice had fallen into his trap.

". . . and then I realized I needed a Magician's power to sustain them, a Magician's blood to feed them."

"Of course you did," Alice said wearily, but the boy did not seem to hear her.

"And so when I sensed you approaching in the forest I knew just what to do. A storm is an easy thing to make, and it's even easier to drive a fool into my net."

He smirked at her, because he thought she was the fool in question. But Alice wasn't stupid. She'd only been tired and cold, and need might make one act foolish but it didn't make them a fool forever.

It was always the same story, always the same need. A person who had no power wanted some. A person who had some power wanted more. If you were a Magician, like Alice, then your magic was like a flaring candle that drew others to you. Alice needed to learn how not only to use her power properly but to keep her light hidden.

She sighed. *So many things to learn. But now is not the time for learning. It's the time for doing.*

The boy was still talking. He didn't seem to grow tired of hearing the sound of his own voice.

". . . would have liked to have that half-wolf creature that runs beside you but he skirted away from me before I had the house in place."

"So the house wasn't here before, then?" Alice asked. She'd suspected this.

"Of course not," the boy said. "I can take it wherever I like. It's part of me, after all."

Part of him, Alice thought. *Yes, the house is alive, just as I felt.*

"And Hatcher isn't here? That wasn't his voice downstairs?"

"I thought you might be deceived by that," the boy said, his smile cruel.

He reminded Alice of a boy in a book she'd read once, a book about a boy who stayed young forever and never cared what happened to anyone else as long as he was pleased. Alice hadn't liked that book.

"No," the boy continued. "I don't have your pet wolf, but it's only a matter of time, isn't it? He'll come back for you. I heard your desperate declarations to one another in the snow."

"Yes. He will come back for me. But the important thing is that I know he isn't here."

"Why?" the boy sneered. "So that you know your love isn't caught in my net?"

"No," Alice said. "Because I know he won't be caught in mine."

She didn't think too hard on what she was doing or how to

do it—she simply flung out her hand to one side and thought, *Break*.

The wall cracked in two from end to end, folding in on itself.

The boy cried out and slapped his hand to his face. A moment later his fingers came away bloody. There was a long cut in his left cheek that ran from under his earlobe to the bottom of his nose.

Alice didn't wait for him to fight back. She threw her hand out to the opposite wall and thought, *Break*. That wall also cracked in two, and so did the boy's other cheek. The ceiling above creaked ominously. Plaster dust showered down.

Don't wait, Alice. Don't wait for him to use his power on you. Break. Break. Break. Everything that makes up this house shall break and crumble and bleed and die.

The house rumbled then, the floor shifting beneath Alice's feet. Another split formed, this time in the floor, and the boy screamed then, a high terrible scream like the monsters he'd created but it did not trouble Alice, for she was immune to his tricks now.

Break, Alice thought, and the boy screamed again but this time it was a cry of anguish. He grabbed at his white, white hair with his white fingers, and Alice saw blood running away from his scalp and over his pale face and tumbling in waterfalls (*bloodfalls?*) to his white clothing.

The boy dropped his hands to his sides and tightened them into scarlet-coated fists. Alice saw the intent on his face, the promise of revenge, but she wasn't giving him any chances for revenge.

BREAK NOW, she thought. She threw her arms forward, pushing all the magic she had behind her will.

The boy fell to his knees, mouth open, but no sound issued forth. His red eyes burned into Alice, burned in hatred and fear.

Then his red eyes were no more. They exploded out of the sockets.

His mouth drew open, wider and wider, too wide to possibly be real, and then the jaw fell away from the rest of the skull, tearing the skin around it like paper.

His nose crumpled and caved into what remained of his face and then the ears shriveled into dried-up husks. The boy's legs split from his ankles and his arms split from his wrists, tearing an open seam that ran up to his torso before the limbs fell away.

Alice watched in horror, for though the boy had been terrible this was also a terrible thing she had done—something far worse than she could have imagined.

The house rocked beneath her, and only then did she realize she'd made the whole thing crumble but the trouble was that she was still inside it.

Oh, Alice, she thought, and ran.

The creatures in their egg-sacs began to scream together, and the sound pierced through the floor and made Alice stagger. There were too many of them, and there was too much, and she was tired now from breaking the boy who'd thought he could break her.

She stumbled to the doorway and onto the landing, past the people whose flesh had fed the monsters, past what remained of the boy who thought himself so clever and cruel. Her hands pressed against her ears in the vain hope that she could block the screams, but it did nothing.

I'll never get out of this house before it collapses, she thought as the house leaned to one side. All around her the walls were cracking and breaking and bits of the ceiling fell away. The windows that lined the front portion of the house shattered, glass crashing to the floor below. A tremendous gust of wind and snow rushed in.

The cold helped clear her mind, if only for a moment.

There's no need to try to work your way out of this labyrinth of a house, and there's no time anyway.

One of the boards beneath Alice's boot cracked. Soon the landing would collapse.

The creatures' screaming reached a fever pitch.

No, there isn't any time.

She ran for the window.

Don't think about what you're about to do.

She ran, trying not to consider what might happen to a human body if it crashed to the ground after falling a full story.

I'll break my legs. I'll break my arms.

(or I could die)

I'll definitely die if I stay in this house. I'll be crushed beneath the weight of the collapsing walls.

And indeed Alice heard the crunch of splintering wood and the thud of falling plaster behind her, but she did not look. She kept her eyes focused on the window and the opening made by the shattered panes and she sped up so that she wouldn't have time to stop and think.

Alice pushed off the landing with her left foot, leaping forward with her right, and tucked her arms in so they wouldn't catch on the frame. A jagged bit of glass swiped across her right cheek just before she cleared the window, and she had a moment to wonder if it would scar and give her a mark to match the one on her left cheek.

Even if it does, it's my scar. I earned it. I saved myself.

Her body was free from the house and in midair. For one wonderful moment it seemed that she was floating, suspended in a gust of wind.

Then Alice was falling, falling, falling with a terrible quickness but all she could see was white, for the snow was still blowing in every direction. She tried to turn her body in midair so she could land on her side instead of her legs but she didn't have any real sense of which way was up or down when all she could see was snow.

The falling ended sooner than expected, for a moment later Alice crashed into a snowbank, sinking about a foot into the soft, wet powder. All the breath went out of her body in a rush. She struggled for a bit, flailing to find purchase in the snow, and finally managed to roll over and sit up and dust the snow off her face.

Good thing this snow was here, though my cloak is inside that doomed house, she thought, and just then the storm abruptly ceased. The clouds rolled away like they were being chased by a hunter, and a thin pale sun emerged.

There was a tremendous crashing behind her, and Alice twisted around to see the house folding in on itself as the upper floors broke and pushed into the lower ones. After a few minutes it looked like a giant had stepped on it.

Alice tried to stand in the snow, but she couldn't find her balance and she realized this was because the snow was melting away beneath her feet. She stumbled forward, trying to find solid ground as water pooled and then rushed around her ankles. It soaked through her pants and into her boots.

She couldn't escape the water (and her socks were already wet through) so she planted her feet in the muddy ground and let it rush around her like a river. Some of it was soaking into the ground but there was far too much quantity for all the water to do this.

Something moved in the corner of her eye and Alice turned just in time to see the packs she'd abandoned in the snow floating past. She sloshed forward and plucked them out of the water. Any provisions inside would be ruined but the other things would dry.

And I haven't lost Hatcher's axe. That's the most important thing.

A faint, mewling cry came from the remains of the terrible house. Alice gave the ruins a hard stare. *Surely nothing could have survived that.*

A white hand, strange and long fingered and tipped with claws, pushed out of the rubble.

No, Alice thought. *Let it all burn. None of it can live.*

The house, despite being soaked through with water, immediately became a bonfire so hot that Alice had to back away lest her face be burned.

The white hand in the rubble curled its fingers and sank away into the flames.

A great plume of black smoke, polluted and stinking, rose into the sky.

A shaggy grey wolf appeared at her side, and then the wolf was Hatcher.

He looked at the burning house, and then at Alice. "Did you do this?"

"Yes," Alice said.

He tilted his head to one side, giving her his quizzical-dog look. "That was a silly thing to do, Alice. You could have sheltered there from the storm. Though I suppose making a giant bonfire out of it is just as good, if you were very cold."

Alice laughed, and then suddenly found herself sobbing into Hatcher's shoulder. He patted her back like she was a child.

"It's all right," he said. "I came back. I told you I would come back."

"Yes," Alice said, wiping her eyes. "And I'm glad that you did. But I'm also glad to know that I didn't need you to. I saved myself."

"You've always saved yourself, Alice. I don't know why you should be surprised by this."

But she was surprised, though she probably oughtn't have been. She'd stabbed the Rabbit in the eye, after all. She'd run from him and held herself together even when everyone thought she was broken.

"You're right," she said. "I didn't know."

"Well, you can tell me about the house as we go. I've found a good place for you, a place where you can stay the winter. It's not far," Hatcher said.

It wasn't very far, though it took longer than it should have since everything was wet and muddy and that made the walking more of a hard slog than it should have been.

"But why did you take so long, then?" Alice asked.

"I got confused in the storm," Hatcher said. "I ran right past this place. When I decided to circle back to you I found it."

Soon enough they were at a snug little cottage in a clearing, a cottage made of stone. The last of the summer flowers had been placed in bright boxes at the windows, and Alice saw the remains of a kitchen garden at the side.

The front door opened before they reached it, and a slender, green-eyed woman stood there. Alice wasn't sure how old she was, for though her hair was long and silver her face was young. She was certain, however, that this woman was a Magician, as sure as Alice was herself.

She didn't feel the same quailing fear she'd always felt in the presence of other Magicians, though. There was no predatory seeking, no desire for more. There was only a warmth that welcomed Alice.

"I've done very well, haven't I?" Hatcher said as the woman smiled at them and held out her hands to Alice.

"Yes," Alice said as she put her hands in the other woman's grasp. Their power touched, light recognizing light.

Yes, this will be a good place to spend the winter, and to learn what I do not know, so that when I call my magic it will heed me.

"You've done very well, Hatcher," Alice said, and thought, *and so have I.*

When I First Came to Town

Alice was asleep, but Hatcher was awake.

The weak winter sun filtered through the window and made the yellow of her hair gleam like spun gold, or at least that was what Hatcher thought when he saw it. He reached out to touch it. Her hair was baby-fine and smooth and just long enough to brush against her cheekbones.

Her scarred cheek lay against the pillow. The skin of her face and neck was golden brown from these months out in the open, but below her shoulders she was pale as milk. His hand ran from her hair down to the slim, strong arms, brushed against her hip bone, stroked up over her stomach and then between her breasts until it reached the hollow of her throat. His hand rested there for a moment, feeling the pulse of her blood, feeling the life and warmth that was Alice.

She was a miracle to him, and he knew he didn't tell her this often enough. He never thought he'd be anything but a blood-soaked blade after Hattie died, after he changed from Nicholas to Hatcher. But Alice made him human again. Alice loved him, even when he didn't deserve it.

I should have been there for her in that terrible house, he thought. It was hard not to think this way, even though he knew his Alice was capable—hadn't she destroyed the damned boy on her own? Hadn't she burned down the structure and all the monsters within? But he still thought he should always be there, always be ready to stand in front of her and keep her from harm.

This, he knew, was because he hadn't been able to keep his wife or his daughter from harm, so long ago. When he thought about that time, the things that happened and what he did afterward— everything inside him would start swirling and writhing and his brain would fill with blood and shadows and sometimes it was hard to see, hard to know anything except the way he felt when his axe was in his hand and he was hacking, hacking, hacking at the flesh and bone that gave way beneath his fury.

Alice was the only thing that ever cut through the contortions inside him. She was the only person who made him feel like he could still be good—not just the mad Hatcher, but Nicholas, somewhere deep down.

Not that he'd been such a good man when he was Nicholas.

No, and not even a man, either, he thought. *Nothing but a boy, a boy who strutted like a rooster and thought he could never lose until he lost everything.*

"But I'm not that boy anymore," Hatcher said. "I know better now."

"What do you know, Hatch?" Alice asked.

Her eyes were still closed, her voice a murmur.

Don't think on those days now. There are better days ahead, days with Alice.

His hand moved from the pulse at her throat to the swell at the top of her breast, hesitating there. He leaned in close to her mouth so he could breathe her in.

"I know that I love you," he said. "Even when I'm a wild thing, a wolf running in the woods, you're my only star, the star that brings me back home."

Her eyes opened then, soft and welcoming. "Hatcher. Yes."

She took away his shadows for a while. After a time she slept again, though wrapped up in his arms, all her skin touching his skin so that he knew for certain she wasn't a dream.

Hatcher didn't sleep. He stared at the wooden beams that ran across the room of the cottage, listened to the witch who'd given them her hospitality tying bunches of dried herbs in the next room.

He knew she was doing this because he could hear the rasp of twine against the stems, just like he could hear the squirrel chittering in the tree outside and the scrape of a bear's claws on the ground a half mile away. He was not the same man he'd been before the White Queen

(Jenny she was Jenny she was your daughter your only child turned into a monster because you didn't watch over her the way a father should because you were too busy being a Big Man in Town)

turned him into a wolf, a wolf that was supposed to come at her call, but she couldn't call anymore because Alice had taken off her head.

Now he was sometimes a man and sometimes a wolf, and even when he was a man it was hard to shake the wolf off entirely.

There was always a part of him that was out in the night, running until all the terrible things he'd done fell away into nothing.

Hatcher knew he should let those terrible things go, let the foolish boy he'd been fade into the ghost he ought to be. But maybe that was a foolish thought, too, to think that he could leave his past like lost luggage, something forgotten in a train station.

I can't forget. Maybe I shouldn't. Maybe I don't deserve to.

But everyone deserves happiness, don't they? Even me.

Maybe happiness doesn't mean you're absolved, though. Maybe happiness doesn't mean you're allowed to forget.

And there were good times, too. Or at least what passed for good times in that stinking stew.

Back when you were Nicholas, and you were going to be the greatest fighter in the Old City.

"Where do you think you're going now, useless boy?" Bess said.

She didn't say it, though; she screeched it out in that way that made Nicholas shudder and slam the door behind him without answering. It was a moot question anyhow—she knew where he was going and who he was going to do it with, but if he said it out loud she'd only use it as an excuse to have another screaming match and he wasn't in the mood.

Soon he would have enough from his winnings to leave the old hag's house anyway. *Just a few more fights*, he promised himself, though he'd also promised himself a sharp new pair of leather boots. It wouldn't do to go around in the same pair he'd been wearing for the last three years, the soles peeling away and the laces broken beyond repair.

He fingered the shiny silver buttons of his new waistcoat and tried not to feel guilty over the purchase. What was so wrong with wanting to look smart instead of threadbare? When he'd come home wearing the garment Bess had nearly burned his ears off, shouting about the cost of feeding him for so many years and how the least he could do was contribute instead of fancying himself up like a peacock.

A peacock, he thought with contempt as he made his way through the maze of streets and alleys toward the fighting club. *I'm no peacock. Peacocks are those rich sharps up in the New City, the ones with carriages and walking sticks and oil in their hair. I'm no peacock.*

As he walked he heard his name being called by the various denizens of the neighborhood, shopkeepers and whores and gamblers and gangsters, all of them as familiar to him as his own hand. He'd grown up here, on these streets and with these people, a part of the filth that stained the Old City.

And I'll always be filth, and proud of it. Nicholas would never be anything else, and he didn't aspire to be. He only wanted to be free, and money meant freedom—the freedom to have his own roof and come and go as he pleased, the freedom to buy what he wanted when he wanted it.

He wanted new clothes and whiskey that hadn't been watered down and a steak on his table every night, a real one, not scraps from the cheapest joint at the butcher's.

To get to the fighting club he had to cross into the red streets. This was the part of the Old City where every inch was ruled by one gang boss or another, and they fought each other for supremacy. Some blocks changed hands two or three times a day, as the tides of battle turned or a third party came in to take advantage of the chaos.

Those who lived in the red streets kept their heads down and paid their tithes to whoever was in power that day. Life wasn't any better or worse under one or another, and it wasn't as if leaving was an option. The men who controlled the New City never allowed the garbage of the Old City to dirty their cobblestones, and there was only so much space in the Old City with the New City circling it like a shining silver prison. Besides, what good was it to move from one street to another street? There would only be another gang.

Nicholas didn't care whether he walked in the red streets or not. He'd already gained enough of a reputation as a fighter that few would cross him, and he'd made it clear that he wouldn't be bought by any gang. Putting himself under the thumb of a boss wasn't his idea of freedom.

The fighting club was tucked in the basement of a whorehouse. To someone not from the Old City this might seem a strange place for a club until one realized that more than half the buildings in the red streets were whorehouses. The sight of half-dressed women, their lips smiling scarlet underneath hard eyes, was so common that Nicholas barely noticed it.

He hurried down the stone steps to the wooden door below. He knocked twice and a rough voice asked, "What do you want?"

"It's Nicholas," he said.

The door swung open. Pike, the doorman, grunted at Nicholas as he walked in.

"Boss wants to see you," Pike said.

Nicholas checked his stride, but only just. Usually when the boss, a man called Dagger Dan with a warped ear and three missing teeth, wanted to see you it meant nothing good for you.

Dagger Dan was called so not because he was especially fond of knives (which might be presumed, with a nickname like that) but because his fists were so sharp in the ring that his opponents felt like they were being stabbed repeatedly. It was well-known that Dan used those fists liberally when one of the boys—Dan called everyone a boy, even the ancient men who hung around the club playing cribbage when they couldn't fight any longer—was called in to see him.

But Nicholas hadn't committed any offense—at least, none that he could think of. Offenses ranged from poor fighting (which brought in less money at the pits), throwing a fight without the express consent of Dagger Dan, cheating Dan out of his share of the fighter's take (Dan took a percentage, since he arranged the fights) and so on.

In general, if you made Dan less money than he thought you ought to, whether by accident or guile, you were called into his office and given a taste of why you should strongly reconsider your actions in the future.

Since Nicholas had no such stain on his soul he simply nodded at Pike and proceeded into the club with almost no trepidation whatsoever.

Pike sat in a kind of anteroom just inside the doorway. There was nothing here except a wooden stool for him to perch on and a hook for his coat and hat. The anteroom was always filled with smoke, for Pike puffed away continuously, rolling the next cigarette before the one that dangled from his lip was burned through.

An open doorway led from Pike's station into the main floor

of the club. There were three rings for practice fights—always occupied by fighters and frequently surrounded by the less ambitious among them placing bets on their favorites. Heavy sacks filled with sand were set at intervals for those who wanted to practice punching while the rings were full. Everywhere was the smell of stale sweat and blood and beer—most fighters drank beer between fights, since the water was frequently of questionable cleanliness. The remainder of the room was taken up by tables populated with older fighters, most of whom spent their time playing games that didn't require their fists.

I'll never be one of them, Nicholas thought. *When I'm done fighting I'm going to be somebody, not an old man clinging to the last best days of my life.*

A few of the fighters called out to Nicholas as he passed, and he called back in a cheery voice that didn't betray any of the (very small) amount of anxiety churning in the bottom of his stomach. Most of the men were at their own work, slugging away at the sandbags or sparring in the practice rings.

The vast majority of a fighter's training happened outside the club, though, since the single best quality any fighter needed was the ability to stay in the ring as long as possible. There were no rules in a fighting pit except that if a fighter knocked down his opponent and the opponent stayed down for more than thirty seconds the one who hit him was declared the winner. So most fighters trained up their endurance, some of them hiking around the Old City several miles a day to increase their lung capacity and therefore their ability to stay in the ring long enough to deliver the final blow.

Nicholas himself would run in a loop early in the morning,

in the small hours when all the criminals went to sleep but before the decent folk got up to set out fruit in their stalls or deliver the milk. His old boots would ring against the cobblestones as he circled around the streets he knew so well, three or four or sometimes five times, until his chest felt ready to burst open and his legs were on fire. Then he would return to the small bedroom in Bess' house. He'd curl his hands in fists with the knuckles on the floor and brace on his toes and then press his body up and down as many times as he could, until he was exhausted or Bess called him to breakfast.

Dan's office was on the far side of the room. A thug called Harp sat outside the office day and night, his massive size straining the chair that he perched on. Harp was well over six and a half feet, easily the largest man Nicholas had ever seen. There was no fat anywhere on his body, no hint of softness from the sharp cheekbones to the scarred fists. He wasn't the smartest fellow in the Old City by a long shot, but he was unswervingly loyal to Dan and always willing to mete out punishment with fervor.

Harp nodded at Nicholas. "Dan wants to see you."

Nicholas gave Harp his coolest nod in return, so supremely unconcerned it might have had frost on it. Harp reached out one of his enormous fists and banged on the office door once.

"Enter," Dan's voice called.

Nicholas pushed open the door. Only at that moment would he allow himself to admit that his heart beat faster than he liked. It wasn't that he was frightened of Dan, exactly. It was only the uncertainty of the moment, and underneath it a burgeoning sense of outrage that he might have been falsely accused of some wrongdoing.

"You wanted to see me?"

"Sit, boy," Dan said, gesturing at the wooden chair that he kept for visitors.

Dan didn't have a desk. A desk, he once had told Nicholas, would only get in the way if he had to be "active," as he put it. There was a large safe in the corner of the room where Dan kept cash and account books and, it was rumoured, the occasional stash of opium.

Nicholas was certain Dan wasn't a full-time opium trader, just a dabbler who occasionally took advantage of opportunities that came his way. The fight boss would need permission from one of the bigger gangs just to lay hands on a larger quantity of product, and Nicholas didn't think Dan was keen to be pressured by a hand higher than his own. Dan liked to be the one who did the pressing.

Other than the safe there was a large chair for Dan himself to sit in while he contemplated the state of his business. This wasn't a plain hard wooden affair like the guest chair. This was an opulent stuffed thing, red shot through with swirls of gold thread, something better suited for the parlor of a nobleman—or perhaps a prostitute's sitting room. Now that Nicholas considered this, he realized this was exactly where the chair had come from in the first place.

The walls of the office were papered with fight notices, many of them featuring Dagger Dan himself, although if Dan especially favored a fighter then one of those notices might make their way into these hallowed halls.

Dan himself wasn't especially large—he wasn't as tall as Nicholas, who topped up at six feet and at seventeen years old was still growing. But the older man had an outsize personality, a presence that made him seem bigger than he was. He was whippet lean, his body a slender knot of muscles tied to bone. His hair was red and mostly gone from his head and his eyes were blue and harder than diamonds, though at the moment they were thoughtful.

Nicholas sat in the wooden chair, which had been placed directly across from Dan's. He breathed out a tiny sigh of relief. If Dan had intended to interrogate or beat him then the chair would be in the center of the room, all the better to intimidate. Dan liked to walk around behind a fighter when he wanted to throw another man off guard, make him worry about where the blow was coming and when. The change of furniture position meant that Dan only wanted to talk to Nicholas, though he still had no notion of what the topic might be.

He waited. Whatever his inward feelings, Nicholas had realized from a very young age that showing his emotions was not productive. The more people knew about you, the more they'd try to take advantage. It had been hard work to learn how to keep his face smooth and noncommittal, perhaps mildly interested. He would never show if he was angry or sad or scared—especially scared, as a hint of blood in the air would make all the predators swarm.

Dan leaned back in his chair, crossed his ankle over the opposite knee—a king at his leisure. Nicholas sat easily in his chair—not slumped, not insouciant, not in any way disrespectful—but made certain that Dan saw he wasn't troubled by this meeting.

"I like you, boy," Dan said abruptly.

"Thank you," Nicholas said. He was surprised by this, because

Dan had never seemed to notice him especially, nothing beyond the usual "Well done, boy" that he gave out to every fighter who didn't lose.

"I've been watching you. You keep your head down, do your work and do it well." Dan's eyes strayed to the shiny silver buttons on Nicholas' waistcoat. "Have a bit of weakness for the flash, but who doesn't? It's better than some weaknesses. You don't drink more than you ought or come in with your eyes red-rimmed from the pipe. And you've won every fight since you joined the club."

Nicholas nodded. He wasn't certain where Dan was going with all of this, but it was best to keep his mouth shut until the destination was clear.

"I've had an . . . opportunity, you might say, come my way. And I've been thinking hard on who I should give this opportunity to. There are plenty of fighters out in that club that have more experience than you. There are a few that are as tall as you are, but have more bulk on them and might stand a better chance against this particular opponent because of that. But I like you. I like the way you dig in, the way you won't let yourself stay down if you're knocked down. And I think you might be fast and agile enough to stay out of this man's reach long enough to win."

Nicholas knew very well that was his prompt, so he said, "Who is this fighter?"

Dan's mouth quirked up for just a second, an almost-smile. "The Grinder."

The Grinder. Nicholas tried hard to school his face, but he knew that a flicker of shock showed there.

"You're surprised," Dan said, and this time he really did smile. "As well you might be. A fighter of his stature doesn't usually brawl with pit boys like you or me."

Nicholas noticed that Dan had put them on the same footing, and that surprised him as much as anything else.

"The Grinder doesn't fight in pits anymore, as well you know. He fights in a ring for the nobs of the New City. The trouble is, he's just too good at what he does. Any fighter that goes up against him gets ground up like meat under those paws, and you know that's where he got his name from. It's not so interesting anymore for those rich boys to watch a fight when they know the outcome. Which means that more and more of the nobs are finding that they'd rather watch fights elsewhere, or spend their money on something besides gambling."

"So the takes are shrinking," Nicholas said.

Dan laid his finger on the side of his nose. "You've got the way of it. The Grinder has ground up every respectable fighter in the circuit and the few he hasn't don't want anything to do with him. They don't want their careers ruined in one round. Grinder's . . . agent came to me, offering good money for a strong fighter who might be able to go up against him, give the nobs the kind of bloody show they want."

It was a funny thing, but Nicholas was certain Dan had been about to say "Grinder's owner" instead of "Grinder's agent." He wondered who this man might be, and then thought it was better not to know what kind of person held such a fearsome leash.

"What do you say, boy? It's a guaranteed number plus a piece of the take, as usual."

"How much?" Nicholas asked.

Dan named a figure that Nicholas couldn't have earned if he had a hundred fights that year. He was fairly certain his face didn't change but his heart was hammering. *So much money.*

Nicholas sat back and clasped his hands together, trying to give the occasion the kind of due process it deserved. He shouldn't jump at the chance just because he was about to make more money than he could ever make in his life. He shouldn't be so willing to throw his body away just because this was the thing he'd been waiting for, the shiny gold ring at the top of the mountain, and all he had to do to pluck it off was fight.

But look who you're fighting, you fool.

The Grinder. A man so fearsome that his name was whispered in the pits like the legend of some bogeyman, a killer who would come for you sleeping or awake.

When Nicholas was younger (and had managed to sneak some money out of Bess' purse for the occasion) he'd seen the Grinder fight. This had been in the pits, of course—Nicholas would never have been permitted to enter the New City.

The Grinder had seemed as big as a mountain to young Nicholas, his shoulders as broad as some men were tall. His thighs strained against the seams of his pants and Nicholas had half expected those tremendous muscles to burst through the cloth. The Grinder's arms looked like massive tree trunks and at the end of them were those already legendary fists, fists that pulverized the Grinder's opponents better than any butcher's hammer.

The Grinder had been up against another fighter whose nickname was Bull, a man whose own size and ferocity were just as

fabled. The match had been billed as a fight of the century, glad-
iatorial combat between two of the greatest fighters of the age.

Bull had never stood a chance.

He managed to land a punch or two as they danced around
each other. The Grinder was surprisingly light on his feet for
such a big man, and he dodged the worst of Bull's initial flurry
easily. It looked like the appetizer course to a long, delicious
meal, one in which each fighter would show their best before one
eventually prevailed.

But it wasn't like that at all. Bull got in reach of the Grinder's
meat hooks, and the Grinder hit him so hard that Bull flew into
the wall of the pit. While Bull stood there, dazed and shaking
his head, Grinder attacked.

The Grinder left him alive. That was all the good that could
be said for Bull.

It was all over in less than ten minutes.

Nicholas had watched in horror as three men ran into the pit
to drag Bull away while the Grinder raised his bloody fists in
celebration.

They said Bull never fought again after that day, and that it was
months before he could chew anything harder than thin gruel.

*And this is the man that Dan wants you to fight. He lied to you,
Nicholas. He doesn't like you at all. If he did he wouldn't ask you to
get in the ring with that monster.*

Still . . . Dan was right about one thing. Nicholas was fast,
maybe fast enough to avoid getting snagged and held in place by
the Grinder's fists. But was he strong enough to knock the other
man out? For that was what it would take to win, Nicholas was
sure of it. It wouldn't just be a matter of knocking him down for

thirty seconds. Nicholas would have to make very certain that the Grinder went down and stayed down.

"You've decided," Dan said.

Nicholas, whose mind had been far away, blinked at Dan. "I suppose I have," he said slowly.

"You're already thinking on what you have to do to win. I knew I was right to choose you," Dan said, clapping his hand on Nicholas' shoulder.

Maybe he was a fool. Maybe he'd die at the Grinder's hands. But Nicholas knew he'd never have a chance like this again. He couldn't say no.

"Yes," he said.

Dan had an apartment in the brothel above, with a separate entrance from the customers'. He asked Nicholas to leave his grandmother's house and live there, at least for the duration.

"That way I can ensure you're getting fed properly," he said with an avuncular smile. "Can't have my prize fighter passing out from hunger before the match even starts."

This was what he said, but Nicholas had a strong feeling that instead it was a way for Dan to keep his fighting dog on a short leash. Once he made the commitment to the match Dan would be in for a large payoff himself—Nicholas was no fool, he knew Dan would make even more than he would—and he might be in for a fair bit of pain or monetary loss should Nicholas lose heart at the last minute and run away.

Nicholas didn't like the idea of living with Dagger Dan. It was too much like being caged, and it ran counter to every instinct he had to run wild and free. Still, Dan was offering him a chance to leave the streets where he was born, the streets where he would never be anything more than Bess Carbey's troublesome grandson. He wanted to make a name of his own, and this was the first step. Once he'd made his money from the fight he'd have the means to be out from under Dan's thumb.

If he didn't get killed by the Grinder first.

Nicholas knew Bess would rail at him if he tried to pack up and leave in the daytime, so he waited until he heard the soft snore coming from her bedroom. If he knew how to write he might have left a note—Bess could read, and make sums, too, but Nicholas had never wanted to learn writing and she grew tired of trying to teach him. He could read well enough to get by, and that was all that mattered to him.

Besides, he thought, *she'll probably be glad to see the back of me. I've never been anything but a trial to her since the day my mother left me on her doorstep.*

He put the few things he owned into a small rucksack and climbed out his window, stealing away into the night.

Dan had very strict ideas on what a fighter should eat, and those ideas ran contrary to Nicholas' notion of good food. He didn't mind eggs, but he liked them cooked instead of raw, which was how Dan wanted Nicholas to consume them.

The first time Dan placed a mug filled with four raw eggs in front of him Nicholas had stared at the fight boss.

"Drink it," Dan said. "Build your muscles up. You've just been sparring."

"You couldn't fry them up with some potatoes?" Nicholas said, staring into the mug at the unappetizing mess of yolk and white. "What about a sausage?"

Nicholas had eaten very few sausages in his life, as meat was more costly than fish and Bess often couldn't afford it, which meant that a fish-and-chip fry-up was the standard fare. However, since he'd started making his own money he ate as much meat as he could. Never steaks or anything of that nature—but he could have a sausage or occasionally a meat pie. He didn't even care if it was fatty or filled with gristle, either. Fish fry-ups were for poor folk, in Nicholas' mind, and he didn't want them anymore if he could avoid them.

Of course, he didn't want raw eggs, either, but Dan gave him such a fierce stare that Nicholas picked up the mug and swallowed them as quickly as possible, ignoring the way the back of his throat seized and his stomach threatened to toss all of the eggs back out again.

"Good boy," Dan said, grinning. He swiped Nicholas' sweaty hair with a rough hand. "Now we can see about that sausage. Don't think I've forgotten what it's like to be a young man and hungry all the time."

Dan fried up three sausages then and there and placed them on the table in front of Nicholas with a big hunk of bread and a knob of butter.

Butter was something else Nicholas had rarely eaten, and he slathered a good deal more than necessary on his bread.

Maybe, he thought, *it isn't such a bad thing to be under someone else's eye.*

Nicholas wasn't any kind of fool, though. He knew very well that if he didn't win the fight against the Grinder, or at least make a good showing, Dan would toss him out on his ear.

Worse, if the Grinder made Nicholas look inept or injured Nicholas' body beyond repair then he would have no recourse for the future. No one would want a broken-down fighter who'd been mashed up by the Grinder.

And if he won . . . well, he tried not to make those kinds of promises to himself. Nicholas knew all too well that things never seemed to go exactly as one planned, and that in the Old City promises were just words that were trampled beneath fate's boots. But it was difficult, sometimes, not to dream, not to imagine himself in fine clothes (and sometimes with a fine woman on his arm) strutting through the streets of the Old City. Everyone would know his name and men would want to stand him drinks in every pub and young boys would want to touch his hands, the hands that had defeated the undefeatable, the hands that had beaten the Grinder down.

But there was much to be done before that day could come, and Nicholas wasn't the type to shirk his work if there was something he wanted. Oh, he'd run out on any number of chores that Bess wanted him to do but that was different. There was nothing at the end of her list of chores except more chores, and maybe falling into bed dead exhausted at the end of the day.

This—the work and training he needed to do to win the fight—this was something else altogether. He knew that at the end of the tunnel there could be great reward, greater than he could possibly imagine.

So he woke at dawn every day and ran the streets, ran for two or three hours at a stretch sometimes, dodging the carts and sellers and the increasing crowds. Then he'd return to Dan's apartment, where he'd drink his mug of raw eggs (he never got used to the taste and texture, either, and vowed privately to never come near a raw egg again once this fight was over) and then eat a proper breakfast of toast and very strong tea.

Every day after breakfast Dan would have him down in the ring, sparring for two hours with anyone willing to show up that early in the morning.

Of course all of the fighters knew that Dan had chosen Nicholas for the special task of fighting the Grinder, and there was a fair bit of grumbling about it. Some of the fighters thought it patently unfair that a youth such as Nicholas had been given a chance that many of the older members had never been given. Many of them were certain that Nicholas hadn't a chance in hell of beating such a fearsome fighter.

"You only need to look at his size," Roger Davies said loudly one morning as Nicholas sparred in the ring. "Sure, he's tall as the devil himself, but he hasn't got any meat on him. No matter how Dan brags about the boy's speed it won't help him if he gets caught by that monster. He'll break in two."

Nicholas' practice partner was Mick Frost, a fighter a few years older and several pounds heavier. Dan had Nicholas practicing with bigger fighters, as logic dictated he would need that sort of practice to defeat the Grinder. Dan himself was in the office at that moment, berating another member for a poor showing in the pits the night before.

Roger Davies would never have dared criticize Nicholas so

loudly if Dan had been in the room. Dan had made it quite clear that Nicholas was his boy and that everyone else in the club could keep their opinions to themselves.

Nicholas and Mick had paused long enough to get a dipper of water from the bucket that hung over the edge of one corner of the ring. Dan had been making a special effort to get clean water for Nicholas in the club. Nicholas gave Roger Davies a hard stare as he took a drink and then passed the dipper to Mick.

"Don't trouble yourself with him," Mick said in an undertone. "He was never any great shakes at fighting in his own time, and he can't stand it that someone else is going to have glory he could only dream of."

"I'm not troubled," Nicholas said, turning his back on Roger Davies in a deliberate cut. "Besides, there's no glory unless I win. So let's get back to it before Dan comes out and finds us resting."

Mick gave him a nod and they went back to it. Roger Davies kept on, his voice rising above the sound of fists striking flesh.

"Not certain why Dan didn't put old Frosty here in with the Grinder. He's not as big as Bull, but he's no lightweight. He'd have a better chance than that bean sprout."

"Shut your gob, Rog," said his companion. This was another of the old cribbage boys, a duffer called William Pattenson. His voice sounded uneasy.

Nicholas tried to ignore their chatter and focus on his work. He dodged away from Mick's swing for his jaw and ducked in under the bigger man's reach, delivering two quick blows to the body that made Mick grunt and blow out his breath in a hard exhale.

"Who are you to tell me to shut my gob, Will? I'll speak what I want and who I want to speak it to, and I say that skinny boy is no match for the Grinder. I'll lay odds that he'll be knocked out in less than a minute."

He's only a green-eyed old fool, Nicholas told himself, ignoring the rising tide of anger that welled up inside. *Keep your mind on the match in front of you or else Mick will make you pay for it.*

Besides, he knew that everything Roger said would be shouted by the crowd at the fight, and with interest. Once the audience saw the size difference between him and the Grinder they'd laugh themselves silly. If he couldn't handle the jeering of one old man then he'd never be able to get through the fight.

Mick kicked out with his left foot, catching Nicholas unawares, and made him stumble. As Nicholas tripped forward Mick jabbed him with an elbow. Nicholas threw his body up, trying to right his ship, but before he could Mick landed a solid blow to Nicholas' stomach. In a real fight Mick would have pressed his advantage, landing a flurry of blows while Nicholas was doubled over. Since it was a training match he backed off for a moment, letting Nicholas catch his breath.

"Ha!" Roger Davies shouted. "See what I mean, Will? There's nothing to that boy at all, and there never will be. The Grinder will crush his bones to powder."

Nicholas straightened up, shaking his head. He couldn't afford to let the old man get to him, but that was exactly what was happening. He was distracted, off his game. It wasn't worth it. They were only words, stupid words coming out of the mouth of a stupid man.

Nicholas nodded his thanks to Mick and they returned to circling one another.

"Don't think Dagger Dan will come to collect your body once the Grinder's finished with you, boy! A man like Dan hasn't got time for losers."

There weren't very many people in the club at that hour—a few other fighters practicing on sacks of sand, and three tables of old duffers at their games. Everyone in the room was now deathly quiet. Nicholas felt their eyes on him, wondering what he would do in the face of such an insult.

Loser. Nicholas was no loser. He'd won every bout he'd fought in to date.

But the word dug into his skin the way nothing else had, burrowed underneath and got into his blood. Nicholas swung out hard at Mick's jaw—much harder than he meant to—and caught the other man by surprise. Club rules meant punching at half strength in practice fights, or at least making an effort not to seriously injure their training partners. Mick staggered back and Nicholas could practically see the stars in his eyes.

He dropped his fists and went to Mick, putting his hand on his shoulder.

"I'm sorry," he murmured, low enough for just the two of them to hear. "I didn't mean to hit you so hard."

Mick gave him a dazed look, his eyes going in every direction. Then he seemed to come back to himself, shaking his head back and forth like a wet dog.

He patted Nicholas' arm. "He got you riled up, good and proper. I know who that punch was meant for."

"I shouldn't have—" Nicholas began.

"Nothing a man can do about it when he sees red," Mick said. "Sometimes that takes over no matter how you might want it to be different."

Nicholas nodded, though he still felt bad about it. It wasn't right to take his spleen out on the fighter who'd been good enough to help him train. He glanced over Mick's shoulder at Roger Davies, who was being subjected to a furious whispered diatribe from Will.

"Don't you waste your energy on him," Mick warned. "Dan will have your hide if you break your hand on that fool's jaw."

It was tempting. It was so tempting. Nicholas could see it happening in his mind's eye, see himself vaulting the ropes around the ring, see himself marching up to Roger Davies, see the old man's watery blue eyes widen in fear.

Somewhere, deep down inside him, he reveled in the thought of that fear.

He jerked his head back, feeling sick. Was that the kind of man he was, the kind who liked watching some helpless stick of a man being terrified?

No, he thought. *I won't be like some gangster scum. I'm not going to hurt somebody just for fun.*

"You're right," he said, loud enough for everyone to hear. "He isn't worth it."

Roger Davies' eyes did widen then, but in furious embarrassment. He stood up from the table, shaking off Will's whispered "No, don't!" and grasping hand.

"You think I'm nothing but a weak old man, eh? You think

you can take me down just because you're Dan's favorite today? You're nothing, and no matter how old I get I can still school some ignorant boy."

Nicholas felt his hands curling in tight fists again. He didn't have to stand here and take abuse from some has-been, old man or not. He wasn't ignorant, and he wasn't nothing.

Nothing but a burden and a heartbreak. That was what Bess had always said.

Nothing but poor scum. That was what the shopkeepers said when he was small. They'd follow him with their eyes and make sure that he didn't run off with their wares, even if he came with money in his pocket.

Nothing but another fighter, there's hundreds of them. That was what the people in the neighborhood said when he came home flush from his first fight.

Nothing but another man out for his own pleasure. That was what her eyes had said, the eyes of the first woman he'd ever had, one he'd paid a few coins for a hurried encounter in a back alley. Her eyes said she didn't get paid enough to fake enthusiasm. The experience had put him off whores for good, and thinking about it always made him feel vaguely ashamed.

Nothing. Nothing. Nothing.

That was what people said when they saw him. Even now he was nothing but meat for the Grinder's hooks, nothing but a pretender trying to be something he wasn't.

He was moving before Mick realized his intentions. Nicholas didn't exactly know what his own intentions were, come to that, but he knew he wasn't going to be insulted. He didn't have to be. He wasn't nothing.

"Let him be!" Mick shouted, grabbing at Nicholas' shoulders and pulling him back before he climbed out of the ring.

"I won't," Nicholas said through his teeth, shaking Mick off.

He really was seeing red now. His eyes seemed like they were filled with blood and his body wanted blood, too, wanted to feel it running under his hands, to see Roger Davies' smug face coated in it.

Nicholas vaulted over the ropes and something in his face made Roger Davies' smirk fade. He backed away from Nicholas, his hands up in a gesture of surrender.

"I . . . I didn't mean nothing by it," he said. His voice was quavering and thin. "It was just a joke. I didn't mean nothing by it."

Nicholas had his right hand up to strike, but the pathetic, pleading tone cut through the red haze.

What am I doing?

"What's all this then?" Dagger Dan's voice cut through the room.

Roger Davies' face suddenly looked small and frail instead of smug. His eyes watered and Nicholas wondered if the old man was actually going to cry. Roger would never be able to hold his head up in the club again if he did.

Nicholas dropped his hand, turning away from Roger Davies, pretending not to see the tears—the tears he'd put in the old man's eyes.

"Nothing," he said. "It's absolutely nothing."

The fight was only a week away the first time he saw her.

All Nicholas had been doing for the last two months was

eating, sleeping and training. No amount of raw-egg drinks had made him bulky—his body just wasn't built that way. He wasn't as thin as he had been, though.

His body had become a long taut wire, sleek and strong like a cat's. And all that practice had made him as fast and vicious as a cat, too. None of the fighters in the club could land more than a glancing blow on him, and even the doubters had started to say that maybe Dan had chosen right, that Nicholas might actually have a chance.

It was midafternoon, and the club was as full as it got. Every ring had fighters waiting for their chance to spar, and all of the sandbags were in use. There were plenty of hangers-on, men who belonged to the club but had no intention of practicing, and instead spent their time playing games at the tables or betting on the outcomes of those games or simply standing around talking and watching the fighters practice.

Nicholas finished his second sparring session of the day. Dan stood at the edge of the ring watching, and Nicholas saw the pleased gleam in his eyes.

"Good work today, boy," Dan said as Nicholas went for a dipper of water. "Time for some tea, eh?"

Nicholas nodded. He felt jittery, full of energy. He'd done such a good job of building up his endurance that he could practice for six or more hours a day. Dan had a rotating cast of fighters who'd jump into the ring with him whenever one man started to flag, and Nicholas could beat them all no matter how many opponents he faced.

He bounced up and down on his toes. "I could go another round, boss."

Dan laughed. "You could. I bet you could chew through steel right now. But there's no need to wear you out before the fight. In fact, I think we'll cut back to two hours a day. That way you'll be fit and full of energy before the match."

Nicholas reluctantly climbed out of the ring. He was hungry, but he would rather have fought a little longer. It felt like something was sparking in his blood, something that made him want to run around in circles until he was exhausted. Maybe he would go for a run later, when Dan was busy with other things.

Dan clapped his hand on Nicholas' shoulder. "If you've still got fire in your blood after tea I suggest you go and visit one of the ladies upstairs. They'll wear you out enough to sleep."

"Mm," Nicholas said. He wasn't about to explain his aversion to prostitutes.

"No point living like a monk, boy," Dan said.

Dan himself visited "the ladies" several times a week. Nicholas had occasionally been put in the awkward position of hearing his boss grunting and groaning since Dan's apartment shared a wall with the whorehouse.

"I admire your work ethic, but it's healthy for a young man to let loose now and then."

Nicholas was spared the trouble of responding. A large party had just filed through the smoke-filled anteroom. Silence rolled through the room in the wake of the group's entry, and one by one every man in the club stopped what they were doing to stare at the newcomers.

There were six men in the group. That would have been enough to make everyone gawp, but there were three women with them as well.

No woman, as far as Nicholas knew, had ever crossed the sacred boundary of the club door. Pike was under strict instruction to keep them out, as Dan believed that fight clubs were for fighting and if a man wanted a woman, then he could go to a place for that purpose. Dan liked to keep his world ordered and sectioned.

Five of the men had the look Nicholas associated with common gangsters—stupid eyes and an aura of violence. They were all dressed better than any fighter in the club, in brightly colored waistcoats over cotton shirts and striped trousers with large leather belts. Cotton was far more expensive than wool, and a cotton shirt was a sign that one could afford to buy cloth in a shop instead of being forced to weave it. Nicholas had many memories of Bess at the loom, sighing as she spun out the wool.

Every man had a red cap on his head, clearly a sign of their affiliation with their leader.

And there was no doubt whatsoever who was the leader.

It wasn't simply that he was the man in front, or that his waistcoat was slightly better quality than the others, or that he wore a bright red coat over it. He didn't have a cap, either, and his leather boots shone with the kind of gleam that only comes when one can afford servants to polish them.

He was taller than his fellows, though not as tall as Nicholas, and his eyes were blue-green and flat as a snake's.

There was a sense of barely leashed violence about him and something else, something Nicholas couldn't quite put his finger on but made the hairs at the back of his neck stand up.

"Magic" was the word that flitted across his brain but he stuffed that away before anyone could see it on his face. Magic wasn't a thing that was allowed anywhere in the City. His own grandmother had a touch of the Sight, and Nicholas liked to pretend that he didn't know anything about it. He wasn't afraid of much, but only a fool wasn't scared of magic.

Two of the women wore the same red caps as the men and silk gowns that left nothing to the imagination. They gave several of the fighters the kind of long, slow assessments that made men think about scented skin and tangled sheets.

Nicholas almost laughed out loud at the hanging tongues. *None of you will ever be able to afford their rates, my lads.*

He could see the women's charms, in a distant sort of way, but they weren't the kind to appeal to him.

Then he saw the third girl, and everything inside him shifted. He felt like he had tumbled from a high cliff and crashed to earth, and he drew in a stunned breath before he forgot how to breathe altogether.

Compared to the other girls she wasn't anything to speak of. She was very small, her head only just at the shoulder of the leader. Her hair was plain and brown but it looked soft, soft like the pelt of a rabbit. She wasn't wearing the same sort of dress as the other women but a relatively respectable gingham, even if it was cut a little lower than strictly polite.

Nicholas saw all of these things and registered them as if from a distance. There were only two features of the girl that he really noticed.

One was that she had the biggest, saddest blue eyes he'd ever seen.

And the second was that around her wrist was a string, and

the other end of that string was held by the leader of the little gang—the man in the red coat.

Nicholas felt Dan shift beside him and glanced at the other man. Nicholas was surprised to catch a flicker of unease on the fight boss's face. It was there and gone before Nicholas was certain he'd actually seen it.

"Rabbit," Dan said, giving the other man a nod.

"Dagger Dan," Rabbit said. When he spoke it was like the air filled with frost.

"What brings you to my club?" Dan asked. He didn't puff up his chest or cross his arms but the words had the same effect.

Rabbit's mouth twitched, an almost-smile that made Nicholas think of sharp teeth.

Rabbit's the wrong name for him. He ought to be called Wolf.

Nicholas saw several of the men near the group edge away, like deer scenting a predator.

Rabbit stepped toward Dan, his tread so light that the soles of his boots didn't even click on the hard wood of the floor. The sad-eyed girl stayed still at first, her gaze somewhere far away. Then Rabbit gave the string a cruel jerk and the girl stumbled forward to stand at his elbow, the two of them less than a foot from Nicholas and Dan.

Nicholas felt a haze of anger bubbling up as he noticed blood welling at the girl's wrist. The string that bound her was so tight that it cut into her skin.

Everyone else in the club had cleared away from the four of them. Nicholas saw a few of the old duffers discreetly slipping out behind Rabbit's gang.

Like little rabbits themselves, scampering away, Nicholas thought. Roger Davies was one of them, his face tucked inside his collar like he hoped no one would recognize him.

"I came to have a look at the . . . fighter you've put up against my Grinder," Rabbit said.

The way he say "fighter" made it sound like he was actually saying "rubbish." It was fairly clear that Rabbit didn't think anyone Dan had could be worth Grinder's time.

But he's happy to take any money he makes off the fight, no matter what quality of fighter is on the other side.

"Well, here he is," Dan said, gesturing at Nicholas. "You've had your look."

Rabbit gave Nicholas a long once-over, the kind of look that a man gives when surveying a potential lover. He smirked at Dagger Dan when he was finished, a smirk that told everyone in the club that Nicholas wasn't any threat at all.

It was an insult in every way, but Nicholas found he didn't care much what this man thought. He cared about the girl, the girl who never looked above Rabbit's elbow. He didn't know a thing about her—not even her name—but he wanted more than anything to take that sad look out of her eyes.

"Perhaps I could see a demonstration of the boy's skill?" Rabbit said, his tone all silk and wine. "It's only fair, after all. Everyone here knows about the Grinder's skill."

"I can do that," Nicholas said. He didn't care about Rabbit or his opinion. He wanted the girl to look up at him, to see what he was worth.

When he spoke she did glance up, just for a second, like she'd been startled out of walking sleep. Then her face dropped again just as quickly.

Well, what do you expect? You're hardly at your best right now, bare-chested and covered in drying sweat. If she's any kind of decent girl . . .

But that was his most foolish thought yet. Of course she wasn't a decent girl. She was a prostitute, just like the others. And it was pretty clear whom she belonged to.

Dagger Dan slashed his hand down in Nicholas' direction, as if the gesture would keep him from speaking again.

"You'll see his demonstration at the match," Dan said. "He's not a show pony to perform on demand."

Rabbit stepped closer, but Dan didn't look away or move an inch. He glared at the other man.

"I think you would do well to remember who invited you to participate in this match," Rabbit said.

"I think you would do well to remember that this isn't Heathtown," Dan said through his teeth. "And no matter what you are there, you aren't that here. These aren't your streets, Rabbit. And this isn't your place. It's mine."

Something flickered in Rabbit's eyes. Nicholas thought for a wild moment that the other man might lunge at Dan, might slash him across the throat with a knife. He hadn't seen a knife on Rabbit anywhere but that didn't mean one didn't exist.

He was, in fact, quite certain one did exist. He knew it, could even see it in his mind—a long, thin silver knife, almost too long to be called a knife at all.

More like a sword. Where has he hidden it? Nicholas wondered, scanning Rabbit all over, looking for a telltale bulge in the smooth line of the man's coat. The knife would have to be easy to reach. It wasn't in Rabbit's belt, plain for all to see.

No, he's not that sort. He's the kind to sneak, the kind who stabs you in the dark before you have a chance to turn around.

It wasn't in the man's trousers, which were worn tighter than was strictly fashionable. If a knife were in there everyone would know.

That meant it was in the lining of his coat, or maybe in his boot, though the boot seemed less likely.

There's a second blade in the right boot, he thought, and suddenly he didn't have to wonder. He simply knew, with the same certainty that told him Dan would make him drink raw eggs in the morning. *There's one in the coat and one in the boot. He'll take it out of the left side of his coat with his right hand. No matter how fast he is it will take an extra second because he has to cross his body.*

Nicholas shifted, ready to block any attack.

Rabbit's blue-green gaze caught Nicholas, and the flicker of violence there intensified. The other man had seen Nicholas' movement.

Nicholas lifted his chin and stared back at the other man. He wasn't frightened of some gangster so small he had to bully a little girl to feel better about himself.

I know what to do. When he reaches for it I'll grab his wrist. He's at a disadvantage in a fight, though he doesn't seem to realize it yet. He's forgotten about that little girl tied to him. It won't be easy for him to move.

There was a strong probability that the men standing behind Rabbit would jump into the fray immediately, but Nicholas

hoped if it came to that then other club members would see fit
to jump in as well. He couldn't worry about the thugs who
loomed behind Rabbit. His only priority was making sure Rabbit didn't kill Dan.

And that the girl doesn't get hurt.

Everyone in the club seemed to be holding their breath. Rabbit and Nicholas stared at each other long enough for Rabbit's
gaze to shift from violence to a kind of reluctant respect. Underneath it there was something else, too—interest.

Nicholas wasn't afraid of Rabbit, but he didn't want to be
interesting to him, either. Rabbit wasn't some benevolent boss
like Dan. He wouldn't let Nicholas be free.

There was a palpable change in the air, a kind of easing.
Nicholas realized then that the air around him had seemed as
though it were sparking, like the sense that one got when a storm
was coming and could feel the lightning even though it was
far off.

That was Rabbit's magic, he thought. *He really does have
magic.*

"That's enough of that," Dan said, shouldering Nicholas back
so he stood a step behind.

Dan wasn't angry anymore, though. Nicholas could tell. He
thought it might be that Dan was pleased with him, that he'd
made a good showing to Rabbit.

"Unless you've come to practice in the ring there's no place
for you here," Dan said. "And we don't allow women on the
premises."

Rabbit laughed. It was a horrible laugh, a laugh that had
never held mirth. Nicholas felt it grating under his skin. He saw

the girl tied to the Rabbit's wrist shuddering. He wished he could slice that string and see her away from Rabbit, see her sad blue eyes realize freedom.

"I'll make you happy and go, then, Dan," Rabbit said. He waved a hand behind him, and all the men and women who'd entered with him turned toward the exit and filed out. He stayed for a moment longer, giving Nicholas a thoughtful look. "I've seen what I came to see."

Nicholas wondered at that look, and he saw Dan did, too. Then his wonder evaporated as he saw Rabbit tug at the blue-eyed girl's string. He heard her little cry of distress, just a tiny puff of air with a mouse squeak inside it, and he had a crazy idea that he would fight Rabbit anyway. He thought, in that moment, that he would do anything to keep her from making that noise ever again.

Then Rabbit was gone, disappeared into the smoke of Pike's anteroom and on into the night.

A babble of talk broke out immediately. Dan said something to him, but Nicholas didn't hear the words. He heard only the girl, that cry of pain, and the roar in his head that told him to go after them and kill Rabbit before she suffered for one more second.

"Boy, are you listening?" Dan said, shaking his arm.

"What?" Nicholas asked.

It seemed that he'd gone to a faraway place, a place where there was no Dan and no club and no Grinder and no fight and no Rabbit, a place where there was only him and the blue-eyed girl whose name he didn't even know.

"Come away now," Dan said, steering Nicholas toward the exit.

"My clothes," Nicholas said belatedly. His shirt and waistcoat were still in a neatly folded pile at the side of the ring.

"I'll have someone bring them up," he said, and murmured to Pike on the way out.

His grip on Nicholas' arm wasn't exactly rough, but it was the kind that brooked no argument. Nicholas didn't want to argue in any case. Now that it was all over he felt drained. He didn't even want to eat, only to put his head down on his pillow and sleep for days.

It was strange, because he'd felt like he could fight for hours just before Rabbit had come into the club. It was like the man had drained away Nicholas' energy.

Dan unlocked the apartment door and pulled Nicholas in behind him. Nicholas collapsed immediately in a chair at the table.

Dan rustled around in one of the cabinets and pulled out a bottle. He put two glasses on the table and poured a very generous measure of whiskey in each.

"Drink," he said, putting the second glass in front of Nicholas.

Nicholas didn't like whiskey. He knew that most men would mock him for this, but the taste of it made him gag and he avoided it whenever possible.

"No, I don't—"

"Drink it," Dan said.

Nicholas was too tired to fight him. He lifted the glass and drank it as quickly as possible so he wouldn't have to taste it.

Lovely warmth flooded into his chest and a moment later he sat up straighter, feeling revived.

"That's better," Dan said. He sat down across from Nicholas and gave him a stern look. "Now, boy, why didn't you tell me you had magic?"

Nicholas stared at him, stupefied. "I don't."

"Don't lie to me," Dan said, and there as a warning underneath the words. "I felt it. Everyone in the place felt it. Thought any moment there would be a clap of thunder. Every hair on my body stood up, and I could see a fair few of the lads wanted to run."

"That was him." Nicholas gestured at something nebulous in the air. "That was the Rabbit. He has magic and it was everywhere. What kind of a name for a man is that, anyway? Rabbit? Makes him sound like something that hides and runs."

"He's not the sort to hide and run, but I think you figured that out already," Dan said. "Yes, it's well-known that Rabbit has some magic. It's just as well-known that he's always seeking more. He likes to be cloaked in power, does our Rabbit. And you showed yours to him as plain as your eyes are grey."

"But I didn't," Nicholas said. "I don't have magic. We don't have it in our . . ."

He was about to say "family," and then he remembered that Bess had a touch of the Sight. He also remembered how certain he'd been that Rabbit had two knives, and how he could even picture them in his mind, and how clear it had been, how Nicholas could see what Rabbit would do next.

Was that magic? Do I have the Sight, too?

"Remembered something, have you?" Dan asked.

His face was twisted up in something that Nicholas thought at first was anger before realizing it was worry. Dan was worried—for him.

"I don't think it's magic like you're thinking of," Nicholas said slowly. "I don't think I can cast spells and whatnot. But my grandmother has a touch of the Sight, and just when we were downstairs I felt very sure that I could see what Rabbit was going to do next, and how he was going to do it. I didn't think anything of it at the time. I only thought I was seeing what would happen next the way I do in a fight sometimes, the way you can sense which direction the next blow will fall."

"You've done this in fights?" Dan asked.

"Well, not on purpose, like. It just sort of happens. But I thought that every fighter did it, and that it was just the way you learn to read the other fighter's cues, the tensing of his muscles or the shifting of his weight. And you know where he'll strike and so it's easy to dodge."

Dan frowned. "It's true that a good fighter learns those sorts of instincts. And I have always thought yours were exceptional, especially for a young fighter. But perhaps it wasn't instinct at all."

Nicholas felt the first twinge of panic. "You won't turn me in, will you?"

Dan had been staring into his whiskey glass like it was a crystal ball. Now he glanced up at Nicholas and gave a sharp bark of a laugh.

"Turn you in? Whatever for? Do you take me for a fool?"

"Oh. Well, it's only that magic is illegal in the City. Everyone knows that." Nicholas felt very foolish at that moment, very young.

"Rules and laws are for the New City," Dan said. "Remember that. They make the laws, but they don't come here to enforce them. It's illegal to whore, too, and to murder, and to steal, but all of those things and more happen here every day and those posh bastards never look down their noses long enough to take notice. I don't care that you've got some magic, boy. I only care that Rabbit knows about it now."

"Do you think he'll call off the fight?" Nicholas asked.

"No," Dan said. "He's got too much money in this. And anyway, he might think he's got a better chance to make more now that he knows what you're made of. A boy with some kind of magic might actually have a chance against the Grinder."

"I thought you *did* think I had a chance," Nicholas said, stung.

"I did think that, though my reasons were different. I didn't know about the Sight," Dan said. "What I'm saying is now Rabbit thinks it too. The whole point of this match is to give the nobs a good show, isn't it? They're tired of seeing the Grinder wear every fighter to a nub in ten minutes or less. If Rabbit knows you've got some kind of spark in you then he'll have realized you're not like the usual fighter. You'll stand up to the Grinder and give the rich bastards what they want. That's what he came to find out, anyway, though he didn't expect to discover it just that way, I'd say."

"If he's got magic of his own then he'll know that I'm not like him," Nicholas said. "And anyway, isn't it like cheating to use the Sight during a fight?"

"Cheating?" Dan looked flabbergasted. "Is it cheating to use your natural-born gifts? The Grinder is the size of a mountain. That gives him an unfair advantage, but nobody says he's *cheating*. If you're faster than another lad, or your punches are sharper, do you say that you're cheating?"

"No," Nicholas said. He understood what Dan was saying—that he'd been born with this Sight and it was foolish not to use it if it would help him win. Still, he couldn't help feeling like it *was* cheating. There couldn't be many fighters with his sort of gift.

"I wish I'd known sooner," Dan muttered. "You didn't know you had it yourself, so you haven't been training it the way we trained the rest of your body. If I'd known . . . but we still have a week. There's still time to develop it as much as we can before the fight."

"What are you going to do, bring in a witch to guide me?" Nicholas said.

"I just might at that," Dan said seriously. "Though not a woman. We can't have a woman in the club distracting all the men. Besides, she'd make everyone ask questions, and I don't want them all to know about your Sight."

Nicholas frowned. "But you just told me that everyone in the club could feel what was happening when I looked at the Rabbit."

He didn't know why he kept thinking of the man as "the" Rabbit. Something about his name felt more like a title, Nicholas supposed.

"I can put the word around that it was only Rabbit's magic," Dan said dismissively. "You know how it is. People see things, feel things, but after a while the memory fades and a well-placed word can change it, make someone certain they'd seen something they never had."

"If you say so," Nicholas said.

"I know so," Dan said. "And I think I know just the person to help out with your special skills. The only thing is he's a little, erm, *noticeable*."

"More noticeable than a woman in the club?" Nicholas asked.

"Yes. We'll have to keep his visits to very early in the morning or late at night, and clear the club of anyone but you and . . ." Dan paused, thinking. "Mick would be best, because he won't blab to the others. And he's been a good partner for you. And Pike, of course, but he'll never talk. All this assuming the bloody little bastard will come at all, that is."

"Who is it?"

"He calls himself Cheshire," Dan said. "Try not to stare."

Nicholas was trying very hard not to stare. He was trying harder than he'd ever tried at anything in his life, but there were so many things about the little man to stare *at*.

For starters, he wore the most flamboyant purple coat that Nicholas had ever seen. Even in a place where every gangster wore bright colors and flashy metals this man would stand out. He was also very small, much smaller than average, but something about him—an aura?—gave the sense that he was much larger.

He had bright green eyes, eyes that seemed unearthly, eyes that winked like jewels.

And his *manner* . . . well, Nicholas wasn't certain how to describe it. It was as if Cheshire wasn't entirely tethered to this world, that his body was present but his mind and soul went away somewhere else part of the time.

Nicholas stood uncertainly before the little man, flanked by Mick on one side and Dan on the other. Cheshire looked Nicholas up and down, gazed closely at Nicholas' eyes for a few very uncomfortable moments, then nodded and turned to Dan.

"There's something about him. Oh, yes, there is something about him," Cheshire said, rocking back and forth on his feet and speaking in a very dreamy tone. "I'd like to have his story, when it's all written out. I think it will be quite a tale."

"But can you help the boy?" Dan asked. Nicholas heard the bite of impatience, barely suppressed, in his voice.

Cheshire shrugged. "Who can say? I can help him if he wants to be helped, but perhaps he doesn't want to. He's not quite comfortable with all this, you know. He didn't know he had fairy dust sprinkled on him, that he was one of the blessed."

The way Cheshire said "blessed" was not a compliment. It was something sweet and sour at the same time, a juicy apple with a worm inside.

"Or perhaps it's only that he's not quite comfortable with *me*," Cheshire said, opening his eyes wide.

His smile stretched across his face and it somehow had too many teeth.

Nicholas felt he ought to say something to this, but it wasn't his nature to tell polite lies, so he didn't speak.

Cheshire laughed then, and his laugh careened crazily around the mostly empty room. "Oh, I like him, even if he doesn't like me, even if his future is painted red like my roses."

At that Nicholas started, and he saw a strange flash. Himself, holding an axe, and his breath was hot and all around him was a field of blood.

Dan blew out an irritated breath. "Can you teach him how to use the Sight or not?"

"Nobody can teach unless the student wants to learn," Cheshire said. "Do you want to learn, bloody Nicholas?"

"Yes," he said.

Cheshire leaned forward and shook his finger at Nicholas. "Thought you weren't a liar."

Dan looked from Nicholas to Cheshire and back again. "What's all this about lying? You want to win the fight, don't you, boy?"

"Yes."

"But he doesn't want to cheat," Cheshire said. "He thinks it's cheating."

Nicholas didn't know how Cheshire knew this, but the fact that the little man did made him uncomfortable. Was this what Magicians could do? Could Cheshire read his mind?

Cheshire laughed again. "I'm not seeing into your thoughts, silly boy, but into your face. You have such an *honest* face. A face that tells everything a person could want to know if they only look right."

He leaned forward then, his hand on one side of his mouth, and whispered, "But don't worry. Most people don't know how to look right."

That, Nicholas felt, was no comfort at all. Something about Cheshire made him feel like a book that the other man was thumbing through, picking out his favorite bits to read.

"Not this cheating business again," Dan said, exasperated. "I told you, boy. It's a gift, and you'd be a fool to waste that gift."

Cheshire gave Nicholas a sly, sideways glance. "Perhaps he'd rather be ground up in the ring. He'll be broken and mutilated, but at least he'd have his noble pride."

Nicholas felt his blood rising in his face. "It's not about my pride," he muttered.

"Do you want to win or not?" Dan asked. "If you do, then you'll do whatever it takes."

Whatever it takes, Nicholas thought. Would it truly be crossing some criminal line to use the Sight—what Sight he had?

Then he thought of the girl, the blue-eyed girl tied to Rabbit's wrist. Maybe, just maybe, if he won the match he could . . . but that was foolishness, and something for another day. He'd have to win first.

Winning was the thing. Without it then his dreams were just that—phantoms that existed only in his mind.

"All right," he said. "I'll try."

Dan clapped him on the shoulder, and it began.

Cheshire wasn't a very helpful teacher, Nicholas discovered. He stood on the side of the ring and watched Nicholas and Mick spar for several moments without saying a word, his jewel-bright eyes following their motion like darting birds.

At first Nicholas was self-conscious about the new audience, and second-guessed every thought that bubbled up, wondering, *Is that the Sight? Or did I just read Mick's little movement?* It distracted him so much that Mick got the advantage of him several times.

After a bit Dan called a halt to the proceedings. He scowled at Nicholas. "What's the matter with you, boy? You're acting like a greenhorn out there."

Nicholas swiped his forehead with his wrist and looked uneasily from Cheshire to Dan. "Sorry."

"I think," Cheshire said, "that we are going the wrong way about the thing. And everyone knows that the right way to go about a thing is to follow the right path."

Mick, Dan and Nicholas stared at the little man, who took no notice of their obvious confusion.

"Dan is a fighter, and so he thinks the answer is in your hands. But it isn't there. And you are suspicious, Nicholas, so you think the answer is up here." Cheshire tapped the side of his head. "But Sight doesn't come from your body or your mind. It starts in your belly and flowers in your heart. Your heart is as tightly closed as your fists."

"Well, you're not telling him what to do," Dan said angrily.

Cheshire gave Dan a mild look. "I don't believe it's my place to tell him what to do, as you put it. I can only guide, and it's not my fault if he doesn't follow me on the path."

"Can't see that you're doing any guiding to speak of, either," Dan said. "You're just standing there and somehow you've got the boy all mixed up. Yesterday he was as perfect a fighter as ever was, and today he looks like a newborn."

"The only person who can mix up Nicholas is Nicholas himself. I'm not responsible for those silver fish darting around in his head."

That's what they feel like, too, Nicholas thought. Fish wriggling inside his brain, flashing from idea to idea.

"I brought you here to help him!" Dan exploded. "He's going to get killed if you don't."

"That," Cheshire said very clearly, "is none of my affair. And don't get above yourself, Dagger Dan. I'm only here because of my own interest. If this play stops being interesting I can just as easily find another one to watch."

It was strange, for Cheshire's tone was mild as milk, but Nicholas was certain there was a threat buried inside it.

Dan appeared chastened, and that shocked Nicholas more than anything, for he'd never seen such an expression on Dan's face before.

Cheshire clapped his hands together twice. "Take a walk with me, boy Nicholas. I think we ought to have a word or two out under the sky, such as it is. Sometimes you can't see the sky here in the Old City, only the plumes of smoke and the crooked buildings, their faces bent over us like unfriendly giants."

Nicholas looked at Dan, who nodded his assent and then abruptly went into his office, slamming the door.

"Guess I'll get myself some breakfast then," Mick said, rubbing the back of his head.

Nicholas dried his upper body with a rag and then put his shirt and waistcoat back on. Cheshire stood by the club entrance, whistling an odd little song. Half the notes were off-key, but Nicholas had an idea that this was purposeful. Something about it touched a chord of memory inside him, a hazy thought of a dark-haired woman rocking him back and forth.

Not Bess, though. Bess never had dark hair like that since I knew her.

His mother? He'd never seen her, or didn't remember seeing her. She'd left him with Bess before he could walk or talk. Whenever Bess spoke of her it was always anger mixed with sadness, and she'd cut him off before he could ask too many questions. He'd learned not to bother asking them. It didn't matter anyhow. She'd never returned for him, not even to make sure he was still alive.

He'd walked to the door while he was thinking all these things, only half aware of what he was doing. Cheshire was watching him again. Nicholas thought he saw a brief flash of pity, but decided he must have imagined it. Cheshire didn't seem like the kind who had a pitying heart.

The little man procured a wood walking stick from Pike's care. The stick was lacquered so it shone even in the dim light, and the top of it had been carved into an intricate rose. He spun the stick around like a baton twirler in the circus and then pointed it toward the door.

"Off we go then, young Nicholas, out into the world to see what we shall see," he said.

Nicholas followed him without a word. It had been a long time since he'd felt so unsure of himself, but something about Cheshire made him a tongue-tied schoolboy.

Cheshire seemed content to stroll along in silence. This was the hour when Nicholas usually had his run. He liked the quiet time when all the denizens of the night had retired—all the gangsters and the whores under covers until late afternoon, when they emerged like moths from their cocoons. Some of the sellers were setting up their carts, putting out fruit and fish and meat.

The warm scent of bread drifted from a nearby bakery, and Nicholas' stomach rumbled so loudly that Cheshire heard it and sent an exaggerated double take at Nicholas' midsection.

"It appears I have undertaken to feed you since I took you from your lair," Cheshire said.

"Oh, no, don't bother about it," Nicholas said. "I'll eat when I go back. Dan says I'm always hungry, anyway."

"And so you are, for you are a growing boy and growing boys have so many wants," Cheshire said. He'd lapsed into that half-dreamy tone again. "Yes, boys need so many things. Thick slabs of bread and thick slabs of butter and thick slabs of meat on a plate. Shiny silver buttons and silk shirts and pretty girls tied on a string."

Nicholas halted, and Cheshire stopped immediately, almost as if he'd expected Nicholas to do just this.

"What was that?" Nicholas said sharply. "What was that about a girl on a string? Do you know her?"

"Yes, a girl on a string. Tied like a balloon to Rabbit's wrist so that she won't float away into the sky."

"Do you know her name? Why does Rabbit keep her like that?" Nicholas asked.

Cheshire's expression refocused, and he raised an eyebrow at Nicholas. "Why so interested, my lad? She's not for you. She belongs to Rabbit, and that one will never let anything go until he's used . . . it . . . all . . . up."

He drew this last bit out, emphasizing each word.

"Besides, it's not as though she was beautiful," Cheshire said.

Nicholas should have known he was being baited. He realized that after. But in that moment he couldn't help himself, couldn't help saying, "I think she's the prettiest girl I've ever seen."

Cheshire pushed a finger into Nicholas' arm. "I had you marked as a knight from the moment I saw you. She slayed you with those mournful eyes. Going to rescue her from the tower, are you? Going to whisk her away to a better life?"

Nicholas knew when he was being mocked. "And what if I am?"

"How do you think you'll free her from her dragon? Do you think Rabbit will hand her over if you only ask politely?"

"No, I—" Nicholas started, then stopped. He had no earthly idea how he might do such a thing, how he might convince Rabbit that the sad, pretty girl belonged with him.

"Rabbit will never give you anything for free," Cheshire said. "And if you want it and he knows you want it, he'll make certain it costs more than you ever thought you'd be willing to pay. What would you give him for that girl, bloody Nicholas? Are you prepared to pay?"

Nicholas shook his head, suddenly angry. "What's it to you, then? Why do you care?"

Cheshire looked away, giving his shoulders an elaborate shrug. "It's nothing to me. I was only giving you a bit of friendly advice. It makes no difference to me if you succeed or fail, and since you'll probably _fail I should have saved my breath."

"Well, you're supposed to be giving me advice about how to use the Sight," Nicholas said. "That's what Dan hired you for, isn't it?"

"_Hired_ me?" Cheshire said. "There was no _hiring_, boy. Dan asked a favor of me, with the knowledge that I would one day ask a favor in return. It speaks volumes about how he feels about you that he was prepared to give that favor, not knowing what I might ask for."

Nicholas felt a warm glow inside. Dan cared about him. He wasn't just another fighter. That glow was immediately dashed by Cheshire's next words.

"Of course, it might simply speak volumes about how much he has at stake in this fight. If it happens that you're not much to write home about, as they say, then Rabbit will come and visit Dagger Dan again. And this time the visit won't have such a pleasant outcome."

Nicholas felt a sudden chill that had nothing to do with the air.

"If Dan promised you a favor then you have to help me, or else you can't ask for the favor back," Nicholas said.

"Well, I did only promise to come and have a look at you, and see if you were worth troubling about," Cheshire said. "So I could say that the terms were already fulfilled, really."

"That's—" *cheating*, was what Nicholas was about to say, only Cheshire turned those jewel-bright eyes on him and now they were blazing.

"Don't think you can dictate to me, boy," Cheshire said. "Don't mistake me for some silly oddity that you can dismiss. I've forgotten more than you'll ever know."

A cold wind blew, making Nicholas clasp his hands together and blow warm air on his fingers. He nodded. He couldn't have done anything else in that moment.

Cheshire smiled then, and the cold wind dropped away.

"Now that we have that settled. As I was saying, Dan asked me to come and have a look at you. I have done that. But I don't know what I can teach you that you don't already know. You were already using the Sight."

"But I don't know how I do it," Nicholas said. "It just comes over me."

"And that, my boy, is how all magic works. Whether it comes in a trickle or comes in a flood depends on you. If you're frightened of it, or push it away, then it will emerge when you least expect it to, in flashes and fits and starts. If you're relaxed and open then those visions will come steadily, and you'll learn to accept them as truth. But I can't teach you how to do that. That's something for you to determine."

Cheshire's shoulders moved a little, the tiniest of shrugs, as if to say, *What can one do? I don't make the rules.*

"So you can't really help me, not in the way that Dan thinks," Nicholas said. "But what should I tell him if he asks me what we talked about while we were walking out here?"

"Tell him the truth—that I gave you advice to help you control the Sight," Cheshire said. "You won't have to tell any lies if you don't want to, bloody Nicholas. Such a good and honest killer you are."

"I'm not a killer," Nicholas said, staring at him.

"Sure about that?" Cheshire asked, and he smiled that too-wide smile once more.

Nicholas was about to say he was sure, that it wasn't the sort of thing one could mistake about oneself. Then he remembered that strange flash—his hands blood-soaked and holding an axe, and bodies all around him.

"I see you aren't sure about that," Cheshire said, and nodded in satisfaction.

"Just what kind of Magician are you?" Nicholas asked. He felt confused, and irritated on top of it. "When Rabbit tried to do, well, whatever it was he tried to do in the club everyone could tell. Everyone. There was a feeling in the air, like lightning before a storm. But I don't think he can do half of what you do, and you do it all without anyone ever noticing."

"Well, who said I was nothing but a common Magician?" Cheshire said. "I am something that cannot be explained, something far, far more wonderful than Rabbit and his play-magics. There is nobody in all the City like me, dear darling bloody Hatcher."

"My name's not Hatcher," Nicholas said, but it rolled off his tongue like it belonged there.

"I'm sorry, I forgot. You like to be called Nicholas now."

A strange thing seemed to be happening. It was like Cheshire was gradually disappearing before Nicholas' eyes, bleeding out like ink-covered paper in water.

"Cheshire?" Nicholas said, but in the half breath it took to say the man's name he was gone. The only thing that remained was a kind of afterimage of his smile, floating in the air, and as Nicholas blinked that disappeared too.

"I almost forgot," Cheshire said, and his voice seemed to come from everywhere and nowhere at once. "You asked me a question that I never answered. I know it's very important to you."

"What is?" Nicholas asked.

"Her name." The voice was fading now, whipping away in the air.

Nicholas' heart leapt. "What's her name?"

Hattie. It wasn't a voice now, more like an idea that sort of drifted inside Nicholas' head. *Her name is Hattie.*

Nicholas had never been inside a carriage before. In point of fact a large number of the Old City streets weren't even wide enough to accommodate them, and the few conveyances in this part of the City tended to be taxis that ran along just a few roads.

The carriage was waiting in line at a checkpoint between the Old City and the New. It wasn't completely true that there was no way between the two parts of the City. Commerce and people did flow between the two, although it was strictly regulated and didn't flow so much as trickle. Anyone who wanted to pass between the two Cities needed a stamped letter of permission from a City Father.

Since the City Fathers lived in the New City this wasn't exactly an easy object to attain if one lived in the Old City, and that was how the City Fathers liked it. They weren't interested in making it simple for the rabble to pollute their beautiful shining City.

The process first started with applying at one's local police station, and "apply" was well-known to mean "bribe." If you gave the correct amount of money to the correct person (and this was by no means guaranteed, as the correct amount of money and the correct person seemed to change as frequently as the sunrise) then your application was passed on to the Old City governor. There was one, it was said, though Nicholas hardly believed it. No one had ever seen such a person. No one even seemed to know where he lived.

The governor would read over the application (which, of course, came with its own packet of money to compensate the illustrious person for their time) and if one's cause was deemed worthy enough to be seen by a City Father then it would be passed on.

The City Father was the final arbiter of one's cause. If this most important individual deemed one's application was valid then a stamped letter of permission for a specific purpose and length of time would wend its way back to the police station at the Old City, where of course the applicant would have to pay over an "acceptance fee" to retrieve this precious piece of paper.

If the acceptance fee wasn't to the presiding officer's liking then the letter would be withheld until the individual came up with the correct amount—again. Sometimes the letter might be auctioned off to someone else, if the applicant wasn't able to pay.

And of course, if one was from the New City and wanted to pass into the Old City one didn't need any such letter. They only needed to obtain a silver chit from the guardhouse as they entered, and simply show it to the guard when they chose to return to their clean, safe home.

Many young men from the New City liked to taste danger on the streets of the Old City, to roll with the whores who flashed their wares in a way that no respectable girl of the New City ever did. If they were robbed by gangsters or had their watches picked from their pockets then what of it? Their fathers always gave them more money to spend when they got home, and they would have an amusing tale to tell over cognac.

Sometimes young women from the New City would come, too, looking for the same sort of adventure as the young men. But of course the kinds of adventures that happen to young women are never the sort that you tell over cognac, and they usually leave scars.

Whenever Nicholas saw young ladies of this sort—giggling and thinking they could come into the Old City and have a round at the bar, flirt with some gangster and go home—he would try to warn them off. If they listened he made sure they got safely back to one of the checkpoints. If they didn't listen there was nothing he could do, really, except cover his ears against the screams he heard outside his window in the night.

There were only two official checkpoints into and out of the New City—one on the east side, and one on the west side. The east-side checkpoint was where they waited for their turn, the carriage rolling forward a few scant inches every few moments. The guards at the checkpoints were known to scrutinize every letter, checking and rechecking the stamps and seals to make certain there was no attempt at forgery.

Nicholas had heard tales of those who tried to forge letters. These tales were never told by the person who did the forging, because those persons were dragged away and never seen again. Stories like this were the reason that forgery was not commonly attempted.

The carriage had been sent by Rabbit, although it wasn't his seal on the door. That was the family seal of "some flash bastard," as Dan called him, and Nicholas took this to mean that while Rabbit might be the Grinder's patron that there was another patron above Rabbit himself.

This, Nicholas reflected, was very likely the person who was bankrolling this endeavor, and the reason why Rabbit had been so anxious to take Nicholas' measure. Whoever put up the money for the fight would want to see a good return, and a good return meant lots of betting on the match.

This betting was about more than just the winner of the match or even a round. Gamblers would bet on everything—who would throw the next three punches, whether or not they would land, if one of the fighters would get a broken bone or a lost tooth. And wealthy gamblers would throw away huge amounts of money on these minute outcomes.

A good long fight with the Grinder had never been seen, and therefore the possibility of all those small bets had been eliminated. For a while Grinder's fights had still made money, for people came just to see the carnage, and would toss their coins on bets to see how long the other fighter could withstand the beating. But soon enough it wasn't interesting to see Grinder mutilate another poor sod.

Nicholas understood from Dan that Rabbit—and his backer—had hyped this fight up in the New City like no fight had ever been before. Nicholas himself had been proclaimed "the only man alive who could make the Grinder go three rounds." He hoped like hell that he could dance out of Grinder's reach that long.

He felt like he hadn't slept properly since the day he saw Hattie. Every night he dreamed of her, dreamed of seeing that sad face lit up in a smile, dreamed of dancing with her in a quiet room where he could hold her close. He'd wake up aching all over, his body and mind desperate for this impossible dream, and he would toss and turn until the sun filtered through the tiny window.

Dan saw his haggard face every morning and assumed Nicholas was nervous about the fight, and spent lots of time clapping him on the shoulder and saying that he shouldn't worry.

But Nicholas wasn't nervous about the fight. He was only worried that she might be there to see him lose.

The carriage finally reached the checkpoint. Nicholas thought the soldiers would open the doors and ask about their business, but everything seemed to be quickly and quietly conducted by the driver. After a moment they moved on.

"I hate to give Rabbit any credit at all, but without the seal on the side of this door we'd have been there for a lot longer," Dan said, rapping the side of the carriage with his knuckles. "It's not usually this easy."

Nicholas didn't say anything. He moved the curtain aside so he could look out the window. He'd never seen the New City up close before.

He'd seen the shining buildings, of course. Once when he was small he'd climbed to the top of the wall that ringed the Old City. It had been the hour just before sunrise, and the soldiers who were supposed to patrol both sides of the wall were dozing on their feet. He'd slipped between two of them and scampered up, finding handholds in places where there didn't seem to be any. Then he'd curled into a seat, his arms wrapped around his knees, and waited for the sun to come up.

He'd seen the first touch of the sun on the roofs of the New City, roofs that were clean and neat and cared for. Little puffs of smoke emerged from chimneys as the morning meal was put on, and soon the scent of bread and bacon wafted up to him. His insides had gnawed with hunger, for Bess hadn't had much work lately and there wasn't enough food to go around—not nearly enough to satisfy a young boy.

People emerged from the houses, people that Nicholas recognized instantly as servants (they didn't have that snooty air that he associated with the wealthy). These servants would polish the front windows or bring a carriage around for their master or sweep the walk.

That impressed Nicholas more than anything—that in the New City everything was so clean that people even had the public sidewalk swept. Not that there was anything to sweep, really—no broken bottles or cigarette ends or empty fish wrappers or puddles of blood that needed to be cleaned before the day's business could begin.

Then one of the soldiers had looked up and seen him and shouted for him to get down from the wall. He did, and tried to dart away before the man could cuff him, but the soldier was faster than he looked and snagged the collar of Nicholas' shirt. He'd given Nicholas a black eye and a split lip, but Nicholas had gotten his revenge when he staggered forward and pretended to be dizzy, grabbing onto the soldier's leg. The man had pushed him away in disgust but Nicholas had already palmed two coins from the man's purse.

He'd run off then, eye swelling, lip bleeding freely, but he went straight to the baker and bought a whole loaf of bread for his own self and had eaten it in an alley before he went home to Bess. The other coin he'd saved for another day when there didn't seem to be much to eat in the house.

Nicholas had been six on that day.

Now he was almost eighteen, a man instead of a boy. But as he looked at the clean streets and gleaming doorknobs and the very fine people strolling about he still felt the same gnaw of hunger in his guts, and knew it had nothing to do with food.

It didn't seem so very much to ask, really, to be able to eat when you were hungry or to walk in the street without smelling the stink of dead things.

Those people out there, they know the Old City is a terrible place. It's so terrible that they won't even look at it if they can avoid it. But still they leave us there. Still they don't even try to help.

He turned his head away and shut the curtain.

The carriage went this way and that, and then slowed and halted. Nicholas heard the driver jump down from the box. The door opened before Nicholas had a chance to grasp the handle.

"Gentlemen," the driver said, indicating they should step out. Nicholas had to give him credit. When he said "gentlemen" it sounded like he meant it.

They were in an alley behind a very large brick building, but it wasn't an Old City alley. There was no stink of filth or leering prostitutes. It wasn't that much different from a regular street except that there was less light. One gas lamp burned above a white door with no sign on it.

Dan knocked on the door while Nicholas shifted nervously beside him. Now that they were here, now that the fight was upon him he felt all the jitters he'd been suppressing rise up.

Please don't let me make a fool of myself in front of everyone. If I have to lose, at least let me lose well.

He didn't know whom he was pleading to—maybe only himself—so his head jerked in surprise when he heard a response.

You only have to use what's within you.

"Chesh—" he started to say, but the door opened then and they were beckoned inside by a man that Nicholas thought of as New City tough. He had the look of a fighter—the broken nose, the scarred hands, but his clothes were clean and cared for and his face had the look of someone who ate meals on the regular.

"This Grinder's opponent?" the man asked, looking Nicholas up and down. He was shorter than Nicholas—there was nothing to that, most people were—and he did not appear impressed by the results of his survey.

"Yes," Dan said.

"Well, this way," the man said.

He led them down a long white hallway—Nicholas had never seen walls so white, they practically glowed—and deposited them in a small room with a lounge bed, a table and one wooden chair. On the table was a pitcher of beer and two glasses and a bowl filled with shiny fruit.

"I'll let you know when it's time," the man said, and left.

Dan collapsed into the chair and poured himself a very tall glass of beer. This was the first indication Nicholas had that Dan was as nervous as he was.

Nicholas took off his waistcoat and shirt and folded them into a neat pile, placing them on the arm of the lounge bed. He adjusted his leather belt, made sure it wasn't too tight or too loose, then bent down to double-check the laces of his boots. He tucked the ends of each lace inside the top of the boot.

Then he stood there, his hands held loosely at his sides, at a loss for what else to do. He didn't want to wait. He was ready to fight.

"Eat something," Dan said, taking an apple out of the bowl and crunching into it.

Nicholas shook his head. "I don't want it to come back up later."

Dan grunted, which Nicholas took for agreement. Nicholas paced around the room once, twice, three times. He breathed in through his nose and out through his mouth and tried very hard not to think about anything in particular.

It seemed like an eternity to Nicholas but it couldn't have been more than ten minutes before the man came back and said, "It's time."

How can it be time? I'm not ready, Nicholas thought, his brain suddenly running in every direction like a panicked crowd. *What was I thinking? What am I doing?*

Then another voice, the voice that had intruded outside the building, said, *Only do what you know how to do. Don't think of anything else.*

Yes, Nicholas thought, letting the blank panic recede. *I know how to do this. It doesn't matter if he is the Grinder. He's just another fighter.*

They followed the doorman down the long white hall again. A door opened on the opposite side of the hall and out came the Grinder.

Nicholas had seen him before. He knew the other fighter's size. But seeing him squeezed into that tiny hallway made him appear even larger, almost impossible in his height and breadth, an actual giant among men.

His shoulders actually brushed the sides of the hall, and the muscles in his back and shoulders rippled as he walked. His thighs really were twice the size of Nicholas', maybe three times the size.

And those hands. There was no real way to describe those hands. Nicholas knew that if Grinder held his palm up to Nicholas' face, the hand would cover him completely.

The Grinder didn't see them or didn't care and went straight for the last door at the end of the hall. Rabbit followed Grinder out. Hattie was still attached to his wrist. Her shoulders curled forward like she was carrying something heavy on her back. Nicholas saw fresh blood at the place where the string pulled tight around her skin.

Rabbit glanced back and gave an exaggerated double take, so clearly false that Nicholas felt moved to punch him in the face. He checked this impulse, though. He didn't think Dan would like it.

"If it isn't sweet Nicholas and Dagger Dan," Rabbit said.

Grinder halted, glancing back over his shoulder. He saw Nicholas and the corner of his mouth quirked up. Then he proceeded down the hall as if there wasn't anything to notice.

I'll make you notice me, Nicholas thought savagely. *By all that is cursed or holy I will make you notice me, you son of a bitch.*

Rabbit gave them a little shrug, perhaps meant to convey that he couldn't be responsible for Grinder's lack of manners. Then he, too, proceeded down the hall without another word.

"Don't mind about them," Dan said in a low voice.

"I'm not," Nicholas said.

And he wasn't. The sight of Hattie and then the Grinder had washed away everything except his purpose. He was a fighter, and he was there to win.

Grinder opened the door, and the sound of the crowd washed in. Nicholas let it roll over him once, and then he blocked it out. There was only one person he cared about now.

The door opened into an arena with seats built up like stairs all around a center stage so everyone in the room had a good look at the action. On the stage was a ring, a proper ring with ropes on it.

This was much different from the pits where Nicholas usually fought, which were often just open areas with a waist-high wall around them. Spectators would push and shove and climb over one another to see what was happening.

Here all the spectators sat on long wooden benches. Vendors walked up and down the stairs hawking grilled meat on sticks and large glasses of beer. Gambling tables were set up at intervals throughout the stands, making it easy for any member of the crowd to reach them and place a bet.

As Grinder entered the crowd cheered, but the cheer seemed half-hearted to Nicholas. This was followed by rumbles of excited chatter as they caught sight of Nicholas. The words he could catch as he passed by ranged from speculative to doubtful.

They don't matter. The only person that matters is the Grinder. Keep your mind where it ought to be.

Ahead of him Rabbit tugged Hattie into the front row of seats while Grinder climbed up into the ring. Dan tapped his shoulder and said, "Good luck, boy," before following Rabbit.

Nicholas noticed an especially well-dressed man lean over to speak close to Rabbit's ear.

That must be the real boss, Nicholas thought. He didn't have time to get a good look at the man or to think any more about it, though. He climbed into the ring after Grinder.

In the pits there were no real rules—anything was allowed except biting, which most men seemed to think was unfair and unbecoming of a fighter. There were no rounds or breaks—fighters simply hit each other until one of them couldn't stand up again. Dan had explained to Nicholas that the New City fights did follow a set of rules, although there was a fair amount of latitude in those rules.

The first thing was that there were actual rounds, of a sort. They didn't have set times, but when a fighter went down the round ended. He could be helped to his corner and the next round would start thirty seconds later. If a fighter couldn't reach the mark in the center of the ring under his own power within eight seconds then he would be declared the loser.

Kicking, gouging, butting with the head, biting and low blows were all potential offenses. Nicholas would never do any of the first four things, but a "low blow" was the sort of thing that seemed open to interpretation. In his own mind it meant any punch below the waist, but that may not be what the monitor thought.

"It's all down to the monitor, really," Dan had told him. "He decides what's unfair and what isn't. So watch yourself, and try not to have a foul called on you."

Too many fouls and a fighter could get disqualified out of the match. The last thing he wanted was to leave the ring in shame.

The monitor waved Nicholas and Grinder to the middle of the ring, where they both placed the toes of their boots against the mark scratched there.

Nicholas could almost look Grinder in the eye. They were both tall, but Grinder wasn't as tall as he seemed from a distance. It was just his bulk that made him appear larger.

The Grinder stared at Nicholas with dead eyes. There was no emotion there at all—no anticipation or excitement, not even boredom at being presented with another victim. There was nothing—nothing at all.

He's going to try to kill me, or the closest thing to it, Nicholas realized.

The monitor said, "All right, boys. You listen to me and we're all going to be just fine. If I say stop, you stop. If I say foul, it's a foul. This isn't the pits, this is a high-class establishment and we'll have no kicking or biting or wrestling down."

Nicholas nodded, but Grinder just stared at him. The bigger man had blue eyes and Nicholas thought they were colder than a frozen sea.

"Hands up," the monitor said. "Touch knuckles."

Nicholas tapped his fists against Grinder's. His own hands appeared pitifully small.

Then there was no more time to think, for the monitor said, "Begin."

The Grinder swung out one of those massive paws immediately, not bothering with the traditional opening of feint and retreat. Nicholas dodged out of the way just in time, though he heard the whistling of the other man's fist as it went past his ear.

He heard a rumble of surprise ripple through the crowd.

There would be no testing of the waters here, Nicholas realized as he danced away. The Grinder's method was to hit the other fighter hard and then keep hitting until his opponent was down on the ground wondering where all the circling birds had come from.

Grinder swung again with his right fist. Nicholas kept an eye on the left, expecting the follow-up jab that came a moment later. He dodged the first blow and snuck in around the second, landing three hard punches against the Grinder's jaw.

Those punches hardly seemed to do a thing except irritate the Grinder. Still, there was a moment of stunned silence, and then suddenly the crowd around the ring seemed to explode with activity. Nicholas couldn't look, couldn't do anything except dodge the next punch, but he sensed that by simply landing those hits he'd changed the expected trajectory of the fight.

His jaw is like iron, Nicholas thought. *Let's see how he takes a body blow.*

The Grinder seemed to prefer wide swinging roundhouses. It made sense, because smaller fighters would have to get inside that huge reach to try to land a hit. But Nicholas' reach was almost as long as Grinder's, and he was so much faster on his feet that Grinder couldn't catch him.

At least not yet, Nicholas thought. *There's a lot of fight left in him. I've got to make him tired. He's probably never fought for more than ten minutes at a stretch.*

The Grinder swung out again, aiming for Nicholas' head. Nicholas could see the punch coming long before it approached him. He backed up a few inches, let the hit whoosh by in front of his nose, then aimed several hard and fast hits under the Grinder's ribs.

The other man coughed and staggered back a few paces. Nicholas heard Dagger Dan shout, "That's it, boy! Don't be a gentleman. Get him while he's out of it!"

Nicholas went into the Grinder fast, hitting his body, pushing the bigger man up against the ropes. All around him the crowd was screaming.

I wonder if Hattie is watching, he thought, but that thought was his first mistake.

Grinder managed to get his left arm loose and knock Nicholas' head hard enough to make his neck snap sideways.

Nicholas' body moved before he even had a chance to think, *Get out of here!*

He skipped backward, shaking his head. His vision tilted crazily for a moment and then it righted itself, just in time to see the Grinder charging at him like an angry bull, his head down. The Grinder's head slammed into Nicholas' chest so hard that he thought one of his ribs cracked. All the breath went out of him as his back slammed against the ropes.

"Foul! Foul!"

Nicholas heard Dan's voice shouting, but he wasn't the only one. A loud chorus of "Foul! Foul!" went all around the stands.

"Foul!" the monitor shouted.

The Grinder backed away, grinning at Nicholas.

Nicholas slowly straightened. The Grinder had a foul on him, and that was a good thing, because if he committed four more then the Grinder would be out of the match and Nicholas declared the winner.

The trouble was that even though the foul had been called Nicholas still had taken the damage. That head-butt had the full force of Grinder's bulk behind it, and Nicholas could feel a worrisome ache in his lower right ribs. It made him feel like he had trouble catching his breath.

You don't have time to try to force him to foul out of the match. A couple more hits like that and Dan will be taking you to the hospital in a stretcher.

Nicholas put his fists up again and moved toward the center of the ring. *Let him come to me and see how he likes it.*

Grinder seemed to think that Nicholas was standing still because he was hurt or scared. His grin grew wider, a sick yellow-toothed smile filled with lots of teeth that seemed tiny in his enormous head.

The Grinder shuffled in Nicholas' direction. Nicholas stood his ground and let the other man swing away.

At the last moment Nicholas squatted to avoid the hit, then shot up again inside the Grinder's arm. He pummeled the larger man's body, hitting him over and over again in the triangle just below where the ribs met. It was like hitting a frozen slab of meat and Nicholas felt his knuckles tearing, but every hit made Grinder puff out a pained breath.

Nicholas knew if he punched the Grinder long enough in this exact place that the other man wouldn't be able to get enough air. Every blow kept the Grinder from drawing a full, deep breath.

The crowd was on its feet now, every man standing and screaming. Nicholas tried not to think about them, tried not to think about Hattie's sad blue eyes and how she might be looking up at him now, her face glowing. He just kept punching, punching, punching until the Grinder's eyes rolled in his head and he fell heavily to the ground on his bottom.

"Round!" the monitor shouted, coming forward to chivvy Nicholas away from his opponent.

He shouted into a deathly silence. Everyone in the crowd was staring, stunned, at the Grinder sitting on the floor of the ring. Grinder's face was grey and covered in sweat. Nicholas wondered whether the other man might be sick in front of everyone.

"Into your corners!" the monitor said.

Nicholas didn't know which corner belonged to him so he just backed up to the one farthest from the Grinder. His face and body were coated in sweat and his knuckles were crusted in blood.

Nicholas noticed the toff who pulled Rabbit's strings gesturing to two men a couple of rows away. They jumped up and ran down to the ring to help Grinder into his corner.

The monitor was counting off the seconds. Grinder had thirty seconds to get to his corner, but he had eight seconds to reach the mark in the center of the ring after that and he had to get there under his own steam.

As soon as the monitor started the eight-second count Nicholas moved back to the center and put his fists up and his boots on the mark.

The Grinder shook off the two men who'd been sent to help him. He stalked toward the center mark.

Nicholas realized two things then. First, the Grinder had no intention of finishing this as a fair fight. He'd been humiliated, knocked down by a boy half his size. There was nothing he wouldn't do to make sure that Nicholas lost.

Second, if Nicholas wanted to survive the next ten minutes he needed to give up any idea of fighting fair himself.

But Grinder has to make the first move, so that the crowd and the monitor can see you're just defending yourself.

Nicholas knew then what he had to do, and it was terrifying to consider. He'd have to take the blow that was coming and hope like hell that it didn't kill him.

He's going to kick out your legs and then try to get on top of you and pummel you into meat.

Nicholas didn't even have to contemplate whether or not this was true Sight. It was, he knew it was, and knowing what was coming next made him calmer, made it easier to think how he could get away before Grinder broke all the bones in his face.

The monitor had his hand up, ready to start the next round, but Grinder didn't stop at the mark with his fists ready the way he was supposed to. He knocked the monitor aside with a careless swipe of his arm. The monitor flew across the ring and slammed into the ropes.

"Foul! Foul!" was heard all over the arena again but Grinder didn't care, he wanted Nicholas' blood and Nicholas didn't need the Sight to tell that.

Grinder kicked Nicholas' left shin with a huge and heavy boot and Nicholas felt something break as his leg collapsed beneath him. His scream of pain was drowned out by the absolute pandemonium going on around them now—people yelling, stamping, running toward the ring.

*Don't think about the pain, don't think about it, they all know
what he is now and all you have to do is get away long enough to
keep from becoming a very public murder victim.*

Grinder shoved at Nicholas' shoulder, ready to knock him
over and pound Nicholas' face into putty. Nicholas used the
momentum to roll over onto his stomach. Then he pushed back
up to his feet even though his broken leg was screaming, and
jabbed the Grinder hard in the throat.

The Grinder made a choking sound and Nicholas didn't
hesitate. He slammed his fist into the other man's nose. Blood
spurted into Nicholas' face and he swiped it away with his wrist.
The Grinder howled and swung blindly at Nicholas, who dodged
out of the way, swaying a little as he landed on the injured leg.

The dodge had put Nicholas behind Grinder. He leapt onto
the Grinder's back and wrapped his right arm around the Grinder's throat. He had to stop this now, put the Grinder down. He
pulled his arm tight.

The Grinder grunted, tried to pry Nicholas' arm off but
Nicholas had a good hold. The other fighter staggered backward,
tried to buck Nicholas off, but Nicholas held on.

He had a sudden flash—Grinder falling to his back, crush-
ing Nicholas beneath his weight. Nicholas loosed his grip just in
time and fell away a second before the other man threw his body
backward. Grinder's landing made the whole ring shake. Nicholas rolled away, trying to get back to his feet before the Grinder
did, but Grinder snagged Nicholas' left wrist and twisted.

Nicholas screamed as he felt all the little bones in his wrist
shatter to dust.

How can I beat him now? How can I beat him with one good arm and one good leg?

He saw a flash out of the corner of his eye, a figure in a plain muslin dress. She was watching him, and her eyes were full of tears.

She's watching him beat me into nothing.

Nothing. Nothing. You're nothing.

A tide rose up in him then, a tide that washed everything red. He wasn't nothing. He wasn't nobody.

He yanked his wrist away from Grinder, who was still rolling on his back like a turtle on its shell. Nicholas managed to stagger to his feet while Grinder slowly lifted himself to a sitting position. The other man was too big and bulky to rise quickly, and the long fight was clearly sapping his energy.

Nicholas kicked him in the face. His boot caught under the other man's chin and snapped the Grinder's head back. The big man fell backward again and Nicholas stomped hard on the Grinder's left hand.

He heard the Grinder scream, but the scream came from somewhere long ago and far away, the blood was rushing in Nicholas' ears and there was nothing he wanted more than blood, wanted to see the Grinder's blood run all over the ring. He wanted an axe in his hand so he could grind the Grinder up, but he didn't have one, an axe would definitely not be allowed but he still had his boots and one good leg and so he smashed the Grinder's other hand to powder, too, because if the Grinder's hands were broken then there would be no more grinding, not ever.

Then somebody was pulling him away, shouting in his ear,

and the red in his eyes washed away. Dan was holding Nicholas in his corner and all the spectators had gone completely berserk, everywhere there was screaming and clapping and little white tickets being thrown in the air.

It was then he realized that he'd won, and that all those people were clapping for him.

Nicholas stared around at the arena, looking for only one person.

She was staring at him, her hands clasped together at her breast, her blue eyes wide with something like shock. Next to her stood the Rabbit, who didn't seem to notice Hattie at all. He was watching Nicholas, too, and his gaze was full of speculation.

Dan somehow managed to find a doctor in that crowd, or perhaps one had been kept on hand in the event that Nicholas was beaten stupid just like all of Grinder's other opponents. The doctor followed Nicholas and Dan out of the arena. A crowd had gathered around Grinder, who seemed to be passed out from the pain.

No doubt they're trying to figure out how to move him, Nicholas thought. The Grinder would need a lot more medical care than Nicholas would and it wouldn't be an easy thing to get the enormous man onto a stretcher.

Nicholas held his left wrist in his right hand and every step made him want to cry out, but he kept his head up because every man he passed wanted to slap his shoulder and tell him he'd done well and Nicholas wasn't about to humiliate himself in front of all those people.

As soon as they were inside the hallway and away from the crowd Nicholas slumped against the wall. Dan was there to prop him up.

"It's all right, boy. It's all right now. You can rest. You did well. You did better than well."

"I've seen some brutal fights in my time," the doctor said conversationally, "but I've never seen anyone give the Grinder a beating like that."

"He deserved it," Nicholas said. His voice sounded slurred, like his tongue was thick and swollen. "He was going to kill me."

"Yes, I think we all realized that," the doctor said. "Well done for not letting him."

Nicholas laughed, or tried to, but it was a choked-out thing that died away quickly. He was tired. He was so, so tired.

He remembered Dan lowering him to the lounging bed in the room they'd been in before the fight. Then later he remembered someone half dragging, half carrying him to the carriage. Somehow he got from the carriage to his own bed in Dan's apartment, and there wasn't anything else after that.

Two days later Nicholas was playing draughts with Lee Miller, one of the oldest duffers in the club. Nicholas' wrist and leg were wrapped tightly in plaster and tape. He was in constant pain but flatly refused to take the laudanum that Dan kept trying to press on him. Nicholas had seen the wide empty eyes of laudanum addicts and he wasn't about to become one of them.

Lee leapt over three of Nicholas' pieces in a row, cackling as he did so. "Gotta get up pretty early in the morning to beat me!"

Nicholas stared resignedly at the single black piece he had left on the board. "Guess my future isn't in draughts."

It was midmorning. There were only a few fighters around practicing, and even fewer old fellows at the tables. Dan was sequestered in his office, though he had passed by the table earlier. He'd clapped Nicholas on the shoulder and given him a broad grin, the way he always did now.

His take must have been even bigger than he imagined it would be, Nicholas thought. *I don't think I've ever seen Dan so happy.*

Dan had been fair, though—more than fair. Nicholas had seen a pretty good-sized take himself, though he'd asked Dan to hold on to it for him in the office safe. Nicholas didn't want to spend it on silly things, shiny things.

He had an idea that he might like to buy a little house somewhere, and make it nice.

He tried not to think about who might fill up the rooms with him, or how he might see her again.

Nicholas heard the outside door open and close and turned to see who was on their way into the club.

It was Rabbit, and he was alone this time except for Hattie. The girl wasn't tied to his wrist this time, though she stood just as close as if she were still attached. Her hands were folded in front of her and her eyes were downcast.

Nicholas got to his feet, grabbing the crutch he needed to get around until his leg healed. Rabbit halted in the center of the room, watching Nicholas make his careful way.

"Something I can help you with?" Nicholas asked.

"Yes, there is, as a matter of fact," Rabbit said. "Is there somewhere we can speak privately?"

Nicholas jerked his head back toward the office door. "Dan's office."

Rabbit pursed his lips. "My business isn't really with Dan, you see. It's with you."

Nicholas gave him a hard stare. "If you've come to collect on me because I took down your fighter you've got another think coming. He broke the rules before I did."

"Peace, boy. I've not come on Grinder's account. Everyone in that arena saw that you were only defending yourself."

"So what is it that you want then?"

Rabbit made a little gesture toward Dan's office door. "In private, if you please."

"It's Dan's office and Dan's club, so whatever you want to say to me will be heard by him," Nicholas said, leading the way.

"Well, I suppose he'd find out eventually in any case," Rabbit said. "Fine, fine, I will speak in front of your master."

"He's not my master," Nicholas said sharply. "No one's my master. I'm my own man."

"Are you now?" Rabbit said, and smiled.

That smile made Nicholas want to knock some of Rabbit's teeth out, so he knocked on Dan's door without responding. Harp gave him a sideways glance but didn't say anything.

"What?" Dan said.

Nicholas stuck his head in. "Rabbit's here and he wants a word in private."

Dan stared at Nicholas for a moment, then waved. "Send him in."

"He wants me, too."

Dan shrugged, as if to say it was all the same to him.

Nicholas filed in, followed by Rabbit and Hattie. There was only the one chair, and Nicholas' inclination was to have Hattie sit in it, but Rabbit took it and then Hattie stood behind him. Nicholas limped around to stand next to Dan.

"You want to sit, boy?" Dan asked in an undertone.

Nicholas hoped his face didn't appear as shocked as he felt. Nobody ever sat in that seat except Dan.

"No, I need to stretch out or I'll get stiff."

They turned their faces toward Rabbit in unison.

"What do you want, then?" Dan asked.

"Well, strictly speaking, I want to have a word with your boy," Rabbit said.

Dan narrowed his eyes. "What sort of word?"

"He impressed a lot of people with his performance against the Grinder, including me. I'd like to offer him a job."

"He doesn't need a job," Dan said. "He's a fighter. Besides, he earned enough off the other night to quit, if he has a mind to."

"I'm not speaking to you," Rabbit said mildly. "I'm talking to Nicholas."

Nicholas thought Dan would fire back at Rabbit—nobody talked to Dan that way—but the club boss only raised his hands in the air in surrender.

Rabbit gave Nicholas an expectant look.

"What sort of job?" Nicholas asked.

"Let's say it's not very far out of your current skill set. Occasionally there are people who come to me for things—loans, let's say, or other things of value. And occasionally these people have trouble repaying those loans, or they don't like to do it. Or sometimes there are those who steal from me or those under my protection. These are just examples of different kinds of circumstances," Rabbit said, waving a hand back and forth. "And in these particular circumstances you might go and have a chat with these people, and encourage them to change their ways."

"You want me to be an enforcer," Nicholas said.

"If that's the term you prefer, yes," Rabbit said.

"What kind of terms?" Dan asked. Dan was always looking at the bottom line.

Rabbit named wages that Nicholas couldn't have imagined in his wildest dreams.

It would be enough to help me set up, buy all the things I would need for my house. Between that and the fight money I'd be doing pretty well.

But I wouldn't be free. I'd be Rabbit's man, and I'd have to do what Rabbit said. What if I have to beat up somebody who's innocent just to prove a point of Rabbit's? Could I do that?

Nicholas looked from Rabbit to Dan to Hattie. Hattie was staring at the ground.

"Dan," Nicholas said, very quietly, very respectfully, "I wonder if I can have a word with Rabbit in private."

Dan gave him a long look. Nicholas wished he could explain, for the other man had been good to him, but there was something Nicholas needed to do. Or try to do, anyway. He'd never be able to live with himself if he didn't try.

After a minute Dan nodded and left the room without a word.

Rabbit gave Nicholas a delighted look. "Want to negotiate

without Dan leaning over your shoulder looking for a finder's fee, eh?"

"No," Nicholas said.

He didn't like Rabbit. He wished like hell that he could have made this deal with someone else, anyone else. But Rabbit was the only person who could give Nicholas what he wanted.

"Why does she always follow you around like a dog?" Nicholas asked, gesturing at Hattie.

"My little Hattie?" Rabbit asked. He reached back over his shoulder and Hattie obligingly put her hand in his without his even asking. "Oh, she was a prize that I won and I like to keep her close. Her father was a good man, a respectable man in Old City terms, but poor Papa liked to gamble too much. When my collectors came to collect from him Papa didn't have anything to give, not even a brass coin under his pillow. But he did have this pretty girl."

"Why did you tie her to you?" Nicholas could see the raw red marks where the string had bound her to Rabbit.

Rabbit had been stroking Hattie's hand, but now he gripped it hard enough to make her cry out. "Hattie had a bad habit. She kept trying to run away. So I was forced to leash her until she understood that I was her master. But she's good and broken in now, is my Hattie."

Nicholas felt a surge of anger and for a moment it was like he couldn't see anything except Rabbit's head spinning away from his shoulders and falling to the ground. Then the vision cleared, and he wasn't sure if it had been the Sight or his own wishful thinking.

"Why are you so interested, Nicholas? I've been told by many little birds that you never go and see the whores in the house upstairs, or ever take a woman at all. Those little birds seemed to think that your interests lie elsewhere." Rabbit gave Nicholas a crafty smile. "I know a place that has the prettiest boys you ever did see."

Nicholas didn't rise to the bait. Sodomy was illegal—at least in the New City. In the Old City anything was allowed. Nicholas didn't care if men wanted to sleep together and didn't see why it mattered, but it did bother him that some of the boys in those places were too young. Some of the girls in the house upstairs were too young, at that, and it made his heart ache even though he knew he couldn't do a thing about it.

"I want to make you an offer," Nicholas said.

"Do tell," Rabbit said, crossing his legs and leaning back. "What can you offer me besides your ferocity, Nicholas?"

"I can save you some money on those wages," Nicholas said. "I'm sure you can use it to buy yourself some more velvet coats and pretty top hats."

For a moment Rabbit's face went white, and Nicholas realized he'd accidentally hit Rabbit in his pride.

Stupid, stupid. You're going to blow the whole thing because you can't keep your smart mouth shut.

The tension in Rabbit's face relaxed suddenly and he gave a short, sharp laugh. "Go on, then. Tell me how you're going to keep me in style, Nicholas."

"I'll take your job, and three-quarters of the sum you offered. But I want Hattie."

Rabbit's eyebrows raised. "You want Hattie? What makes you think I'm so inclined to give her up?"

"She doesn't matter to you," Nicholas said. "You only wanted to break her. Now that you have you'll toss her in one of your houses and look for a new toy to play with. All I'm asking is that instead of tossing her you give her to me."

He hated that he was talking like this, hated that Hattie could hear him referring to her like a horse to be traded. His only hope was that Rabbit would agree, and that Nicholas could explain later that he'd never meant it at all, that he only wanted her to be free from him.

Rabbit gave Nicholas a speculative look. "You're right, sweet Nicholas. I am getting bored with her. But I don't see why I should give her up for such a small sum as you offered. Her father owed me quite a lot of money, you know."

Nicholas waited. He knew Rabbit would want to negotiate the figure down. That's why Nicholas hadn't offered himself so cheaply to start. He didn't want Rabbit to see how important this was. But he did want Rabbit to feel satisfied, like he was in control of the situation.

Rabbit abruptly released Hattie's hand. "Half the wages I offered, and you can have her."

Nicholas took a moment. He didn't want to appear too eager. "It's still a good wage. And I assume there will be opportunities for increases in the future."

Rabbit laughed, and it was the first genuine laugh Nicholas had ever heard out of him. It made the gang boss sound disturbingly human.

"Always the eye on the main chance, eh? That's the kind of

attitude I like," Rabbit said. He stood up then and dragged Hattie around to stand in front of Nicholas. "Well, she's all yours, and I wish you joy of her."

Nicholas stared down at the top of Hattie's head. She hadn't lifted her face once during the entire conversation. He wondered if she'd even heard any of it.

"I'll give you a fortnight, since you're hobbling around on that stick," Rabbit said. "Then you come to my place in Heathtown."

Nicholas nodded. "I'll be there."

Rabbit tipped his hat at Nicholas and sauntered out of the room, leaving Hattie behind.

Now that he had her Nicholas had no idea what to do with her. She stood as still as a statue, her hands folded in front of her, her eyes on Nicholas' boots.

He cleared his throat. "Listen. I didn't mean any of that stuff, about you being a toy and all. I want you to know that. It was only that I wanted Rabbit to let you go and I had to talk in a way that he would understand."

She didn't move, didn't raise her face to his, didn't say a word.

"You don't have to stay with me if you don't want to," he went on, though his heart longed for nothing else in the world. "You can go back to your parents or wherever you want. I don't want to force you to stay with me. I'm not like him."

"Why?"

The single word was so soft, so fragile that Nicholas almost imagined that he'd heard it.

"Why what? Why did I make him give you up?"

Her head moved just a fraction.

All the things he'd been feeling since he first saw her were stopped up inside him, tangling up and making his words seem useless.

"Because you looked so sad," he finally said. "Because I've never seen eyes as sad as yours. And because he treated you like nothing, tied you to him and made you bleed."

Hattie made a choked sound. "That was hardly the only part of me that he made bleed."

Nicholas didn't know what to say. He wanted to hold her close to him, to stroke her hair and tell her that it would be better, that no one would ever hurt her like that again. But he didn't want to touch her unless she looked at him. He wanted to know that she was allowing him to do it. He wanted her to know that he wouldn't take what he wanted from her like Rabbit had done.

"I know you don't have any reason to believe this," he said. "But I want you to know that I won't hurt you. I'll never, ever hurt you."

She did look up then, and he saw the tears streaked on her face. "How can you say that? Hurting is what men do. I saw what you did to that man at the match."

"He did a little hurting of his own," Nicholas said, glancing at his broken hand and leg. "But that was different. That was a fight. Any man who'd do something like that to a woman isn't a man."

"I want to believe you," she said. "I want to."

He did take her hand then, but so gently that it was like he was holding the most delicate piece of china. He put her hand against his heart. "I promise. I promise I will never, ever hurt you. I'll keep you safe. All I want is to see you smile."

She stared intently into his eyes for several moments. He felt that all he was and ever had been was laid open for her like a book, and she was reading the truth of his life there.

"You don't have to stay with me," he said again. "I would never make you stay."

"And that," she said, "is why I believe you."

And she smiled.

The
Mercy
Seat

The long winter was over. Every morning Alice found her eyes lingered longer on the horizon and what might be beyond it.

She had been safe in this cottage in the woods, and the generosity of the witch who lived there—for she was a witch, and her name was Olivia—had certainly kept her alive. It had even occasionally kept Hatcher alive, when he returned from his wild roaming to see her.

One night she had a dream, the same dream she'd had more times than she could remember. She stood on the edge of a long clear lake, its water glittering blue in the sunlight. On the opposite side of the lake were high mountains with rocky crags, and the highest peaks were covered in snow.

But down here in the valley everything was green, and there was a field of wildflowers spread out in riotous color. Behind Alice was a snug little house made of fieldstone, and when she turned she saw Hatcher standing in the doorway. In his arms was a black-haired babe.

When she woke her face was covered in tears she'd cried while she slept.

Alice knew two things then. First, it was time to leave the sanctuary of the cottage in the wood.

And the second thing she knew was that her baby would be born at the end of summer.

Hatcher was not there when Alice said goodbye to Olivia. He hadn't returned to the cottage for several days, but this wasn't an unusual thing. She might be inclined to worry more if she hadn't felt so secure in the vision she'd had in her sleep. Alice knew Hatcher would be with her in the little house by the lake, surrounded by fields of wildflowers.

Alice wore new trousers and a new shirt, both of them sewed carefully by herself throughout the long cold days. She was inordinately proud of the clothes she'd made, as no one had ever bothered to teach her how to do these tasks when she was young, and it was a fine thing to feel that she could be self-sufficient, to spin and weave and sew.

Olivia had also showed her how to tend plants, even in winter, so that one could keep small bits of herbs or vegetables that could be grown in pots indoors. She'd explained how to set by the summer crop in jars, and how to salt and dry meat so that you'd have enough until spring.

All these things had naturally been done in her own house

when Alice was young, but they were done by servants, barely noticed by the pampered youngest daughter of the master.

Now there were no servants, and Alice wouldn't have wanted them anyway. She liked to do things with her own hands, to feel the glow of accomplishment when a job was well done.

Olivia had, of course, taught her more than just the care and feeding of a household. She'd taught Alice how to use her magic, how to accept what it could and could not do, how to make it come when she called and lie quiet when she didn't need it.

Much of what she taught Alice had seemed like knowledge Alice already had, only it was hidden under the surface of her skin, waiting for her to peer underneath.

Alice carried one large rucksack with all the things she and Hatcher would need—his clothes and axe included. One thing she'd learned from the debacle in the snow was that it was very difficult for her to carry two packs in heavy weather. Hatcher spent more than half his time as a wolf anyhow, and Alice was stuck lugging an extra pack while he roamed around the woods.

Alice loaded her pack on her shoulders and turned to Olivia, who stood in the doorway clasping her hands together.

"I don't know how to thank you," Alice said.

"There is no need for thanks," Olivia said. "I was glad for you. Your company made the winter easier to endure."

Alice wanted to ask Olivia why she stayed here in this lonely place. She'd wanted to ask this many times, but always decided it was too intrusive a question. If Olivia wanted her to know she would have told Alice, and Olivia never had, so Alice held her tongue now. Besides, if Olivia hadn't chosen to stay in this lonely place she wouldn't have been here when Alice needed her.

Alice went to the other woman then, and embraced her. They held each other for a long time, both trying to say many things without words, and some of those thoughts must have been conveyed, for when they separated each woman turned aside to discreetly mop the tears away from her eyes.

"Thank you," Alice said, and Olivia nodded.

Alice was out the door and partway through the clearing when Olivia called her.

"Alice!"

She turned back, wondering what had put that sudden frantic note in the witch's voice. Olivia rushed from the doorway to grasp Alice's hands.

"Alice, there is danger ahead for you. I can feel it."

Alice nodded. "Yes, I know it, too. Only I don't think it's the kind of danger that can be avoided. There's a place I'm trying to get to, and something bad is directly in its path."

"I can't see exactly what it is," Olivia said. "I only know that it's there. And it's a threat to not only you but your child."

Alice shouldn't have been surprised that Olivia knew about the baby. She sometimes thought the other woman knew everything there was to know.

Rather like Cheshire, Alice thought wryly, *only considerably less irritating.*

"I will be careful," Alice promised. "More careful than careful can be."

"Don't show them your power," Olivia whispered. "Don't let them see what you are."

"That I'm a Magician?" Alice asked.

"Yes," Olivia said. "I can't read it all clearly, and I can't see from precisely where the threat approaches. I only know that you should be very cautious about using magic in the days ahead."

"That's very annoying. Just when I've learned how to use my magic I'm not to be allowed to use it to keep myself out of trouble."

"Magic doesn't fix everything, Alice. I thought you knew that by now."

"I do," Alice said, chastened. "I do. But it would still be nice to be able to smite one's enemies with a glance."

Olivia laughed. "I think you're still a few steps away from the smiting stage, my dear. Now go, and may all the powers that be protect you and your own."

She kissed Alice's cheek and waved her off, so Alice went.

The morning was fine and fresh, the sort of morning that made one's step lighter simply because the sun shone and the woodpeckers scampered on the tree bark and the squirrels chittered at one another.

Alice felt the shadow somewhere ahead of her, the same shadow that had made Olivia so anxious, but it was too far away to trouble her right now. There wasn't any way to avoid it, that she knew for certain, but that didn't mean she had to worry over it every second.

Besides, Alice thought, *I'm not about to let anyone hurt my baby. Whatever is before me, whatever they want—it doesn't matter. I'll never let them harm my child.*

And Hatcher won't either.

She smiled a little to herself as she thought this, imagining a horde of faceless enemies confronting Hatcher. Whether he was a man or a wolf there could be only one possible end for them—absolute slaughter.

Alice walked on, and by midday she needed to stop—not only to eat, but to rest her feet.

I've gotten soft this winter, she thought ruefully as she took her boots off and dunked her feet into the cool water of a thin, trickling stream.

And she *was* soft, too, soft all over. The hollows in her ribs had filled out and so had her hips. Her cheekbones were not sharp enough to cut any longer. Four months of sleeping in a bed and having regular meals and not spending the entire day walking had taken the raggedy scarecrow look off her.

Though Hatcher will always look raggedy, even if he shaves and cuts his hair and wears clean clothes. No matter what he does he can't shake that air of wildness. It's in his heart and in his eyes.

But four months of walking only about the cottage and occasionally into the woods had meant that Alice was not prepared to march all day. She sat for a while, dangling her ankles in the stream, chewing some of the dried meat that Olivia had packed for her.

After a while her feet felt cold, but she didn't feel any urgency to continue on. The sun was warm so she leaned back and used the pack as a pillow to rest her head.

When she woke Hatcher's mouth was on hers, gentle as the touch of a butterfly. She opened her eyes and found him kneeling beside her, naked and filthy, his face very close to hers.

"You need a bath," she said, leaning on her elbows. She kissed him again to take the sting out of her words. "And a haircut and shave while you're at it. We need to make you look respectable, at least for a while."

"I'll never be respectable," he said, rubbing his beard on her face and making her laugh and push him away.

"There's something coming, or we're coming to it," Alice said. "And I have a feeling that it would be better for us if we looked like a nice pair of innocent travelers, and not a Magician and her wild wolf."

Hatcher frowned. "You want me to stay human for a while, then?"

"If you can," she said. "It would be better."

"Only for you, Alice," he said, and sighed. "Have you any soap?"

She did, some herb-smelling stuff that Olivia had taught her to make, and Hatcher went into the small stream and splashed himself all over until he was soaking and then scrubbed everything with the soap, even his hair.

He rinsed off and climbed out and sat in the sun to dry, completely unselfconscious about his body, and while he did that Alice cut his ragged mane into something resembling respectable. Then he went to the stream again and carefully shaved off his beard.

Once he was as clean as he could be, he dressed in the trousers and shirt that Alice had made for him. He was still a little on the thin side, and his grey eyes seemed more prominent now that the cloud of hair had been removed, but he looked about as respectable as he was going to get.

"Are you hungry?" Alice asked.

Hatcher shook his head. "I ate before I found you."

He picked up the pack and shouldered its weight easily. "You shouldn't be carrying this in your condition."

Alice stared at him. "How did you know already?"

Olivia she could understand, but not Hatcher.

"You smelled different," he said. "Besides, you forget that the Sight runs in my family. I've known that baby was coming for a long time now."

She'd had some idea that she would surprise him with the news. But before she did she'd hoped to have some time alone with her baby, time to accustom herself to the idea of being someone's mother, time to cherish the tiny life inside her.

Alice *had* forgotten about the Sight. It had been some time since she'd heard Hatcher make any kind of prediction. When he fell under the influence of his visions he tended to act more than a little strange and uncontrollable. Alice hoped that he wouldn't have a vision for some time. Olivia had been very sure that it would be a mistake to let anyone know about their magic.

"Are you happy?" Alice asked. She hadn't meant to ask it, but the words were out of her mouth before she knew she'd been thinking them.

"About the baby?"

Alice nodded. Her fists curled up, clenched. She didn't know why but she was worried about his answer.

"Of course," he said. He glanced from her hands to her face and came to her, wrapping his fingers around her upper arms. "There is nothing in this life that makes me happier than you, Alice. And now that happiness will have a name, a little piece of you and of me."

The tension inside her eased but didn't go away entirely.

"What if I'm a bad mother?" she whispered. This was something else she hadn't known she was worried about. "What if he hates me?"

"How could he ever hate you?" Hatcher whispered. "You're going to love him more than any child has ever been loved before."

She would, yes. But she didn't know how to be a mother. The only mother Alice had ever known had given her up the moment she was inconveniently assaulted.

Even before that Alice remembered only moments of affection, moments when her mother or father would kiss or hug or play with her. The rest of the time it was always, "I'm sorry, darling, Mama's very busy at the moment. Go play in the garden."

But I won't be like that. I won't be that sort of mother. I'll be the kind that always says yes when the children ask me to play, because children are only small once, and when they're grown-up they won't ask anymore.

And then she thought, *Children. Don't leap too far ahead of yourself, Alice. You don't even know yet if you can manage one child, never mind more than one.*

Then something Hatcher said finally penetrated, and she said, "Love *him*?"

Hatcher gave her a puzzled look.

"You said, 'You're going to love him more than any child has ever been loved before.' Was that just a word you used, 'him'? Or does it mean that you know that it will be a boy?"

"Do you really want to know the answer?"

"That means it *is* a boy," Alice said, "because you'd never bother being mysterious unless you knew."

"Does it really matter?" Hatcher asked. "Are you happier if it's a boy?"

"Of course not," Alice said. "But it will be a nice thing, a very nice thing, to imagine what the baby might look like and how he might be."

"If he's anything like I was, then he'll be the naughtiest child alive," Hatcher said.

"Were you really so terrible?" Alice asked as they started their walk again.

"Yes," Hatcher said, without a trace of humor. "I was a very terrible child. I never listened, was never grateful for what I had, was always looking for an excuse to run away or steal or fight. I don't wonder that Bess despaired of ever making a proper human out of me."

And Bess never did, quite, make a proper human, Alice thought, but she didn't say it out loud because Hatcher might think she minded and she really didn't. Hatcher was Hatcher, and she wouldn't love him if he weren't exactly that way.

"It might be different for our child, though," Hatcher said. "He won't be abandoned by his parents. He won't grow up in a filthy city with nothing to eat half the time."

It was unusual for Hatcher to be this talkative, and Alice wondered at it.

"Is something troubling you, Hatch?" she asked. "Are you worried about the baby?"

"No," he said.

He didn't say anything for several moments. Alice didn't know whether he was collecting his thoughts or simply had slipped away somewhere else in his mind, the way that he did sometimes. She didn't speak, only went along beside him and waited.

"It's only that I've been thinking lately about when I was young. Some of those thoughts were things I'd forgotten," he said. "I don't know if I'm thinking them because you're going to have a baby, and it's natural to think on one's own past when faced with a new future. Or it might be because my mind is, in some ways, clearer now than it's been in years."

Hatcher saw her expression and laughed.

"I know you don't always think it, Alice. You think I'm still a wolf in man's clothing half the time, that my thoughts are wolf-thoughts because I don't speak them. But it's only that when I'm a wolf for a long while I forget how to talk, and it can take some effort for me to remember."

"I never mind," Alice said, and touched his arm.

"I don't always want to be the mad Hatcher," he said. "I don't want to dream of blood. So when I'm a wolf I run as mad and wild as I want, so that when I return to you I'm a more settled thing, so that I can be a better man."

She stopped him walking then so she could kiss him. There were many things she wished to say but didn't know how to, so she put them all into that kiss.

"I think," Hatcher said into her mouth, "that we ought to stop here for the night."

It was only late afternoon, and a glorious day for walking, but Alice only sighed and said, "Yes."

The next day wasn't quite as gloriously perfect, and while they were still happy in each other's company Alice thought they both felt the shadow ahead, the thing that took the shine off the day. They rarely spoke as their path wove up into the mountains.

Alice knew they must cross these mountains to reach the valley of her dreams. Hatcher seemed to know the best way to go, moving with the same certainty that had guided them through the Old City after the hospital burned down.

"We shouldn't have to cross the peaks," he said. "Though I think there are some tunnels we must use otherwise."

Alice wasn't fond of tunnels. Tunnels sparked a series of vague and unfounded fears—that they might lead nowhere and she and Hatcher would be trapped wandering inside a mountain forever, or that there might be strange monsters inside waiting for foolish travelers. When she mentioned these things to Hatcher he didn't laugh, for which she was grateful.

"If you must worry about something, though, and sometimes I think you like to—"

She hit his shoulder, not hard, and said, "I do not!"

"Then the worst thing you have to worry about with caves, I think, is a cave-in."

"One of those great falls of rock?" Alice said.

Hatcher nodded. "They do happen sometimes. Though you're quite the Magician now, aren't you? I'm sure you could shift a lot of rock with your magic."

"I might," Alice said doubtfully. "But that won't help us if the rock falls directly on our heads."

She imagined it, imagined great slabs of mountain crashing into them, breaking their bodies to pieces. She imagined choking on dust and lightless air.

"Let's avoid caves if we can," she said firmly. "I'd rather climb a little higher if we must."

They soon came upon another of those little villages that seemed to sprout out of the ground here and there, completely unconnected with any other part of civilization. Alice always wondered how these places came to be—how did so many people gather in one isolated spot? Who decided it was a very clever notion to build a village on the path up to a mountain? Why did their descendants decide to stay?

Whatever the reasons, Alice was grateful. She needed an hour or two of rest sitting in a chair instead of the hard ground with nothing except a boulder to prop up against.

The people of the village had a warily friendly look, as if their first inclination was to be kind, but they'd lived long enough to know that not every traveler deserved their kindness. Alice could tell immediately that this place was not the place she dreaded. That dark shadow, whatever it was, still loomed ahead.

"Good morning," Alice said to a woman sitting on the stoop of a cottage. The woman had the slightly faded prettiness that came when beauty met a life of hard work. She was watching two small children, a boy and a girl, run back and forth in the street as they played some game with sticks.

"Morning to you," the woman said, shielding her eyes from

the sun as she stood to get a better look at Alice and Hatcher. "Travelers?"

Alice knew she asked this question not because the woman didn't know the answer, but because she wanted to know where they came from.

"Yes," Alice said. "We've come a very long way, actually. From the City."

The woman gave them a long, keen look. "That is a very long way. And where are you bound?"

It was hard not to feel that these questions were intrusive, and none of the woman's business at all, but Alice knew that information was the currency that would smooth their way in this isolated place.

"We're looking for a quiet place to settle down," Alice said. "Somewhere on the other side of the mountains."

The woman's eyes flashed when Alice said "the other side of the mountains," but all she said in response was, "Hmm."

Hatcher had been watching the children run to and fro while this exchange occurred. He'd dropped the pack at his feet.

"I don't suppose there's a public house or an inn in this town," Alice said. "We'd be very glad to pay for a meal."

The woman snorted. "It's very kind of you to call it a town. More like a bump in the road. But there isn't any inn here. We don't get very many travelers."

The two children had stopped their game, clearly bored. They poked their sticks in the dust, wondering what to do next.

Hatcher quietly walked near the children—not too close, Alice noticed, not close enough to startle—and picked up a stick of his own. He turned the stick in the dust this way and that.

After a few moments the children walked over to him, peering into the dust.

"Wow!" the girl said. She was a little older than the boy. "You're a really good drawer."

"That looks just like a bear that I saw once in the woods," the boy said. "Not from up close, though. From far away."

"Oh, yeah?" Hatcher said. "What was he doing?"

"Trying to get some honey out of a beehive," the boy said. "He didn't seem too happy."

Hatcher didn't say anything, but he kept moving the stick in the dirt, and after another pause the boy said, "Yeah, it was just like that! He had the honeycomb on his hand, but there were bees all over it still and he even *ate* some of them."

"I didn't get to see it," the little girl said sadly. "I was with Mama, collecting herbs, and Calder and Papa were off checking snares."

"What's your favorite animal?" Hatcher asked.

"A wolf!" the little girl said excitedly. "I think they're so pretty."

"Really," Hatcher said, and Alice heard the smile in his voice.

It was sometimes a hard thing to remember that Hatcher had been married a long time ago, and that he'd already had a daughter. That daughter had been taken away from him, and she became a monster, but before that she'd been his most precious child. Hatcher already knew how to be a father, but Alice didn't know a thing about being a mother. What if she was terrible at it? What if all she did was make mistakes and make her child unhappy?

The woman looked from Hatcher to Alice. "You're expecting, aren't you?"

Alice started. "How did you know?"

The woman laughed. "You've got that look, the one that says you're happy and confused at the same time. Come inside and get off your feet awhile. I'm sure I have enough stew left over for you and your man."

"Oh, but . . ." Alice said, worried that if she and Hatcher ate this woman's food that there wouldn't be enough left for her family.

"It's not as hard as it looks here," the woman said, reading Alice's expression correctly. "And besides, your man will pay me back if he can keep those little monsters occupied. It wears me out just to look at them, sometimes."

She said this with the gentle affection of a mother who loved her children but didn't always like them. Alice supposed that was the way of it, really—that you could love your child more than anything in the world and still wish for five minutes of quiet, if you could get it.

The woman, whose name was Thora, settled Alice at the table and spooned out stew from a pot hanging over the fire. She placed a hunk of bread next to the bowl and indicated that Alice should eat.

The bread was a little stale, but the stew was delicious. Alice was already missing Olivia's cooking, even though it had only been a few days.

"You said you and your man were planning to pass through the mountains?" Thora asked.

Alice's mouth was full, so she only nodded. Thora looked troubled.

"There's a place up there," she said. "A very odd sort of place, but I think you should avoid it if you can."

Alice felt the touch of dread slither over the nape of her neck.

"What is this place? Do you know where it is?"

Thora shook her head. "Not precisely, though I know it's even more isolated than our own village. And no one seems to know for sure what goes on there. We have only heard rumours from those who have occasionally passed within reach of that place. There are always storm clouds above the village, and it has a strange name."

"What is it called?" Alice asked.

"The Village of the Pure."

Alice and Hatcher stayed overnight in that village. Thora and her husband very kindly offered Alice and Hatcher the use of their small barn, and Alice found it very pleasant to bed down in the straw and listen to the night murmurings of the donkey and cow and three goats.

She did not, however, find her dreams very pleasant. She dreamt of lightning, and terrible faces, and someone screaming.

When Alice woke her nightmares lingered in a jumble at the back of her mind, disconnected images that wouldn't form a cohesive whole. She'd been warned twice now about peril ahead, and she was certain that the peril came from this Village of the Pure, but knowing that didn't make her feel any easier. She still had no concrete notion of what made the place so terrible, only that it should be avoided.

If they're only interested in purity they certainly won't approve of Hatcher or me. Neither of us is anything like pure.

Alice found she wasn't as troubled by this as perhaps she ought to be. She used to care about being right and proper and good, but whoever that girl was had faded into the far distance.

About midday they were walking on a narrow path that led between two faces of rock. Alice saw that the path widened only a short distance away, and was hurrying to get through this bit, for though the sky was still above her it felt too much like cave walls pressing in on her. Hatcher was being extra careful not to tease her about this, she could tell. The rock walls seemed like they were squeezing inward, like they were trying to squash her between them.

But of course that's ridiculous, Alice thought. *Rocks don't have feelings, or malice.*

She heard a creaking noise above, then a crashing. Alice looked up to see a part of the rock wall had sheared away and was tumbling directly at them.

And it did seem like it was coming *for* them. Alice didn't know why she thought this, only that she felt some rush of magic just ahead of the rock, something enchanted that brushed through her hair.

"Run!" Hatcher shouted, tugging at her arm.

Alice ran, though as she ran she thought that perhaps they wouldn't be able to outrun it at all, that the rock would change direction and chase them no matter where they tried to flee.

This didn't happen, of course, but they did only just manage to clear the area before the rocks smashed into the place where they'd been standing. There wasn't very much of it, certainly not enough to bury them alive, but Alice shuddered. If either of them had been hit they still could have been injured or killed.

"Hatcher," Alice said. "Did it seem to you that those rocks fell just because we were passing beneath them?"

Hatcher gazed upward. "A trap, do you think? A magic one?"

"Yes. That's what it felt like to me."

"I didn't feel it, but that doesn't mean it's not true," Hatcher said. "We should be very careful from now on."

"But who would want to set such a trap? To what purpose?"

It surely can't have anything to do with this Village of the Pure, Alice thought. *Olivia told me that I shouldn't use my magic around them. That doesn't sound like the sort of place that would set a magic trigger on a mountainside.*

Hatcher shrugged, the way he often did when something troubled Alice but didn't bother him in the same way. She could almost read his thoughts—*We didn't get hurt, there's no obvious solution, so why trouble yourself about it?*

But Alice knew it would nag and worry at her, even if she never discovered the answer. It was hard for her to copy Hatcher's equanimity.

They stood for a moment, staring at the pile of rock. Then Hatcher said, "Why don't you try to shift it with your magic?"

Alice gave him a startled look. "I don't think we ought to be standing here playing with the rocks. More of them could fall at any moment."

"I was only thinking that you ought to test what you can do, in the event that we do have to go into a cave."

"But I don't want to go into them," Alice said stubbornly. "So it doesn't really matter, does it?"

"Alice," Hatcher said. "We might have to."

She knew she was being silly and childish about it, and that her fears were very likely unfounded or at least exaggerated, and that Hatcher was quite right that she ought to practice using her magic. But she didn't feel like being sensible at the moment, and the rockfall had given her such a fright that all she wanted was to get away from this narrow space.

"No," she said, and hurried away, knowing that he would follow.

He didn't chide her for her decision, but she felt him staring at the back of her head. Clearly he was more troubled by the fact that she wouldn't go into caves than about the rockfall that had nearly killed them. Alice thought he needed to get his priorities in order.

The path opened up into something less anxiety-inducing and they continued on without discussing the rockfall again. Alice felt some of the tension inside her ease away.

They had to stay that night in the cradle of the mountain. They found a small clearing where they could spread out their blankets and sleep under the wheeling sky.

Alice didn't think she would be able to rest at all, worrying about falling rocks and caved-in tunnels and worst of all—not being strong enough to fix it if such a thing did happen.

She was a better Magician than she had been months before, that was true. But she wasn't, as Olivia had so gently reminded her, at the smiting stage yet. Alice didn't know if she could blast apart a cave-in if they encountered one.

Perhaps the only way to know is to try. If you continue to fear your power you'll never discover the extent of it.

They were sitting quietly by the fire, each of them lost in their own thoughts, when Hatcher suddenly stood. His axe was in his hand, though Alice hadn't seen him grab it. His nostrils flared wide and he stared into the darkness of the path ahead of them.

The path to the Village of the Pure, Alice thought, and she stood too, because she felt it was better to stand up and face whatever might be coming for them.

A man loomed out of the darkness, a man with a bloodless face and rolling eyes, a man who barely seemed aware of their presence at all. He staggered to a halt a few feet from the fire, breathing heavily.

The man's clothes were torn, his face covered in scratches. Alice at first thought the scratches might be from thorns or tree branches, but as she peered more closely it seemed that the marks—long and deep—came from human nails. The tears on his clothes, too, seemed to be the result of grabbing hands— something about the way the cloth had torn.

Perhaps it was just that he had the look of a man being chased by a mob. Or perhaps it was only that Alice's magic was allowing her to see things she wouldn't otherwise see.

Hatcher didn't move toward the man, or threaten him, but Alice sensed Hatcher's tension. If the stranger made any attempt to attack, to hurt them, then Hatcher would dispatch him. Alice didn't think the man was a threat—he appeared terrified—but she knew a terrified person could become dangerous.

"Sir?" she said, taking a step toward him.

"Don't get any closer to him, Alice," Hatcher said in an undertone.

Alice tried again. "Sir? Can we aid you in some way?"

The man's thoughts were someplace far away, someplace that made his eyes dart back and forth, searching the shadows for monsters.

"Nobody would help me," he said, his voice trembling. "Nobody would help me."

"But *we* will help you," Alice said soothingly.

"I thought they were my friends," he said. "I thought I was one of them."

"Would you like to sit down here by the fire?" Alice asked. "We have food and water."

"The lightning," the stranger said, his voice rising. "The lightning. The mercy seat."

Alice and Hatcher exchanged a confused look.

"Sir, I think if you'll sit with us awhile, and be calm, and tell us what happened . . ."

The man suddenly turned on her, seemed to see her clearly for the first time. "The LIGHTNING!" he screamed, spittle flying from his mouth. "The LIGHTNING! I was one of them, but they were going to put me in the mercy seat!"

He took off then as suddenly as he'd arrived, darting around the fire and into the night, back down the path that would take him out of the mountains.

As he ran they heard him calling, his voice a mad and broken thing, "The LIGHTNING! The LIGHTNING!"

It seemed they heard him calling for a long time, his voice echoing back to them long after it should have faded.

That night Alice had another dream, though this one was not as vague as the one she'd had the night before. There was a chair, a strange wooden chair on a dais, and a crowd of chanting people all around. High above there were storm clouds swirling. Alice looked down and saw that she was chained to the chair, and that the chanting people were smiling.

"No!" she called to them. "Help me! My baby! Please don't hurt my baby!"

There was a crack of thunder, and a flash of white, and Alice woke covered in sweat, her hands cradled protectively over her stomach.

"What is it?" Hatcher asked.

"The mercy seat," Alice said.

The next day the path seemed to widen. Strange trees dotted the landscape, trees that clung to the rocky cliffs and set their roots twining into the cracks and crevices. Pretty little wildflowers set white and purple faces toward the sun, and Alice saw several white goats far above them, serenely balancing on rock shelves no larger than their tiny hooves.

They stopped to eat a cold lunch from the provisions Thora had kindly given them. Alice looked at the dried meat and fruit and sighed.

"What is it?" Hatcher asked.

"It's astonishing how quickly one becomes accustomed to hot meals," Alice said. "It's hard to work up an appetite for salted meat and apples."

"I could change," Hatcher said. "I bet I could catch one of those goats, or a rabbit or two. Then we could roast them over a fire."

Alice's mouth watered, and she was about to say it was a wonderful idea when some sharp, sudden instinct warned her against it.

"No," she said. She dropped her voice low and shot a quick glance all around. "I don't think it's a good idea to show your power."

Hatcher's gaze sharpened. He tilted his head to one side, listening to something Alice could not hear.

"You're right," he said. "There's somebody near, watching us."

"I can't see them," Alice said, trying to look about without it seeming like she was looking about. She didn't want to signal to the watchers—for she was certain now there was more than one—that she knew they were there.

"There are at least three," Hatcher said quietly. "By the sound of them they are fairly high above us, scattered over the path."

"There must be a settlement of some kind nearby," Alice said, and thought, *the Village of the Pure*, but she wouldn't say it if Hatcher wouldn't. "Do you think they mean us harm?"

Hatcher shrugged and picked up one of the apples. "We can't tell unless they make some move toward us. Best just to eat our lunch as we planned and act like we don't know about them."

Alice agreed, though it was harder than she imagined it would be to pretend that they weren't being watched. The back of her neck prickled constantly, the sparking feeling that she noticed in the air before a lightning strike.

This is the shadow, she thought. *Or rather, the prologue to it. This is the thing that Olivia saw, the thing that Hatcher and I have dreaded.*

After lunch they packed their things up and continued on the widening path. Alice tried not to look upward if she could avoid it, for she felt that if she saw one of the watchers they might panic and attack. Still, she thought that she caught a flash of fast-moving shadows once or twice, though it might have been her imagination.

"Definitely only three," Hatcher murmured. "One of them has just gone ahead."

"To contact others," Alice said in an undertone. "They must be a part of a larger band."

"Yes, that's what I think, too," Hatcher said. "I don't hear the sounds of a settlement or village yet, though, so I'm not sure how far ahead they're aiming."

"I hope we reach it before nightfall," Alice said. "I don't think I could sleep knowing they were lurking up in the crevices, waiting to kill us in our sleep."

"Nobody is going to kill us in our sleep," Hatcher said. "Have you no confidence in me?"

Alice hastily patted his shoulder. "Of course I do. I know you'd wake up before anything actually happened. But it's not very pleasant to think of someone watching us."

"That's because of the hospital," Hatcher said. "They were always watching us there, you know. Watching through windows and listening at doors. Nothing we ever had was just for ourselves."

Alice had never really considered this but realized then that it was true. There had always been someone watching and waiting, someone writing things down in a notebook or waiting for one of them to step out of line—Hatcher, usually—so they could be punished. She'd been drifting in a fog most of the time then—a consequence of the powders the doctors put in her food.

"Well," she said. "I'm sure you're right and the reason why it especially bothers me is because of the hospital, but I don't think that anyone particularly enjoys being spied upon."

They continued on until the sun disappeared behind the peaks of the mountains. Even though it was spring and the days were getting longer the sunlight didn't last at these higher altitudes.

"Hatch, is there a village close by?" Alice whispered.

He shook his head. "I don't hear or smell one yet. The two above are still lurking, though."

"We're going to have to rest for the night," Alice said. "It will seem suspicious if we don't."

"And you're tired," Hatcher said.

"I didn't say that."

"You don't need to," he said. "It's on your face."

Alice frowned, which made Hatcher laugh.

"It isn't anything to be ashamed of," he said. "You've got a baby inside you and it's using up a lot of your energy. I remember Hattie slept all the time when she was pregnant with . . ."

He trailed off, his face contorting in confusion.

"It's all right to talk about them," Alice said. "I'd never begrudge you the life you had before."

"That wasn't it," he said. "It's just that I can think of them without it hurting. Or rather, the hurt is almost gone, like a bruise that's mostly faded."

"You should remember the good things about them," Alice said. "It shouldn't always be the worst bits."

He nodded, but didn't say anything else, and Alice left him alone. She could always tell when he was in a brooding mood.

They made camp, and Alice was certain that if the watchers hadn't been nearby that Hatcher would have gone off running as a wolf. He stalked around the camp restlessly, unable to settle while Alice drowsed in front of the fire, slowly chewing a piece of bread.

That night Alice dreamed once more, though she thought she would never sleep. She knew the watchers were high above, making her twitch uncomfortably under the knowledge of their gaze. And anyway, she feared what she might see while she slept.

She was right to fear.

There was a wooden chair set on a platform. On the arms of the chair were metal chains that connected to a metal rod. The rod was attached to the back of the chair and ran up high into the air, like it was seeking something. There was no one in the chair, but a large group of people had gathered around the platform. Their faces were avid, expectant, and they filled her with dread.

Inside her dream, Alice thought, *I don't want to see what happens next. I don't want to know.*

Then a scream pierced the air. Alice turned to see who was screaming.

It was a young girl, perhaps twelve or thirteen. Her arms were held by two men at least twice her size. They dragged her across the ground in front of the platform, and the crowd around parted the way so the men could pull the girl up to the wooden chair.

They lashed the girl to the chair with the chains while she shouted and struggled. The men did not acknowledge the girl's pleading in any way.

Once the girl was securely fastened to the strange chair the men left the platform. She continued to scream and plead, her eyes swollen with tears. The girl appeared very tiny in the huge chair. Her slender wrists and ankles looked frail, sticks that could easily be broken. The crowd around her was silent. Every one of them met her eyes, and every one of them offered no sympathy for her plight.

Whatever she's done can't be so terrible that it would justify this. What kind of people would punish a child in this way?

Alice noticed a woman standing alone in the space cleared by the crowd. The woman must have followed the men, but Alice had been so focused on the struggling girl that the woman's presence hadn't registered.

She was a very tall woman, as tall as Alice, but she didn't have Alice's sturdy roundness. The woman's clothes—a plain grey dress and a white apron—hung from her figure in flapping loose waves. Her dark hair was bound tightly to her head, tight enough to see the shape of her skull.

The woman's eyes were an unusual shade—almost purple— and they were lit with a strange fire. She spoke, and all turned to listen except the girl in the chair, who continued to whimper and struggle.

"Jane Blackwood, you are condemned to the mercy seat for the crime of witchcraft. The gods will judge your actions."

"I didn't do it!" the girl screamed. "I didn't do anything wrong!"

"If you are innocent then you shall not be harmed. If you are guilty then you shall die in the way the gods see fit."

At that moment there was a crash of thunder overhead, and Alice looked up to see black clouds circling high above the platform.

"The gods have spoken!" the woman shouted. "Guilty!"

"Guilty! Guilty! Guilty!" the crowd chanted.

Alice wanted to close her eyes, to turn away, to wake up from this terrible dream. But it was like she was bound to that spot, unable to stop watching.

The girl screamed again, and lightning shot from the swirl of clouds above.

It struck the metal rod attached to the chair. Alice saw the lightning course through it and then flow into the chains attached to the girl's wrists.

The girl went rigid, then howled in pain. Alice saw the lightning scorch her skin where the metal chains touched, and there was a terrible smell of burning flesh.

"Guilty!" the woman screamed, and all around the crowd chorused their reply.

"Guilty! Guilty!"

Thunder roiled in the sky, and another flash touched the metal rod. The girl screamed again and again as the lightning struck again and again but nobody could hear her over the sound of the crowd chanting "guilty."

After a very long while, the sky and the girl were silent.

Alice woke in the grey light of dawn and she knew two things.

First, the woman and her mercy seat were the shadow that Alice had been dreading.

Second, the woman might punish witchcraft in her village, but only a Magician could call lightning from the sky.

Hatcher was already awake and warming some bread over a low fire.

"Did you sleep?" Alice asked.

He shook his head. "It didn't feel safe enough to sleep with the watchers above."

Hatcher hadn't modulated his voice at all, and Alice cast a fearful glance around at the cliffs, hoping he hadn't been heard.

"There's nothing to worry over. They're gone now. I heard them go just before dawn."

"I wonder why," Alice said. This news only made her more uneasy, though she should have been delighted that the watchers were gone.

"The one who left earlier returned in the night. After that all three went away in the direction we're heading."

"We must be closer to their village now," Alice said. "They've gone to report to that woman, no doubt."

"What woman?" Hatcher asked.

Alice told him of her dream. "Only I don't think it was a dream," she concluded. "I think that I was seeing something that really happened, or was about to."

Hatcher nodded. "You were sleeping too heavily to hear, but there was thunder in the distance last night, and I saw a flash of lightning."

Alice rubbed her arms, suddenly cold. "That poor girl."

"It seems you were right to stop me from changing," Hatcher

said. "We'd best be very cautious from now on. I don't want to risk you or the baby."

"Why, Hatcher," Alice said. "You're becoming very mature. You used to slash first and ask questions later."

"If I had to do it, and you wanted me to do it, I'm certain I could manage even an entire village of people. But you might be taken by them or hurt in the bargain."

"We both saw the baby," Alice said. "In our dreams, or visions, or what have you. We both saw the baby alive and in our arms in that cottage. So we must be able to get through this, whatever peril is ahead."

"A vision is only a possibility," Hatcher said. "Sometimes they are true—especially if they are close in time, like the one you saw last night as it was happening. But our baby is still only a wisp, a thought, a dream. There are many, many days ahead, and any one of them could change the course of the future. So don't go recklessly throwing your magic about, Alice."

"I never would," she said. "Even with Olivia's help I still don't know how to smite anyone, even if they deserve it."

As they walked, Alice thought of that woman, that Magician with her burning eyes and the power to call lightning from the sky. If anyone deserved to be smote it was her.

But until you learn how to call lightning from the sky, Alice, you won't be doing anything of the sort.

Alice placed a hand over her belly, in the place where she imagined she felt a tiny little flutter, though it was far too soon for such a thing to happen. It was nice to imagine, though—nice to think that her baby could feel her there and waved a friendly little hello.

Hatcher was right. It was one thing to take a risk on themselves, but quite another to risk the life of their child.

I won't let anyone hurt you, she promised. *I can live without my magic long enough to go through this village.*

"I think we should pass through as quickly as possible," Alice said. "Even if it's nightfall when we arrive."

"I don't know," Hatcher said. "That would certainly seem suspicious, and they might come after us."

"Why should they care?" Alice asked.

"Why should they care about travelers approaching at all? Why send the watchers out to follow us? They're obviously afraid of something."

"Not of something—afraid of magic, and anyone who might approach their village bearing it. But if we don't show them any magic then we shouldn't have anything to fear," Alice said. "Anyhow, perhaps we can go around the village. The path is widening. If we're fortunate we won't even need to approach it."

Hatcher shook his head. "I don't think you or I have ever been so fortunate. There won't be a way around, only through."

Alice sighed. "Why can't we have a quiet life? A life like other people, a life without danger and despair?"

"Everyone's life has despair, and even danger. For some it is not as close as ours, that is all."

"I'm not sure I like your very-wise-man act," Alice said. "I rather liked it better when you were a wild wolf."

"Only because you like it better when no one contradicts you."

Alice slugged him in the shoulder.

They continued at a steady pace until about midmorning, when Alice had to stop and have a rest.

Hatcher went a little ahead while Alice sat on a large boulder and wondered if she dared take a short nap. A few moments later Hatcher had returned, however, and his words made Alice feel instantly awake.

"We're very close now," he said. "We should be there by this afternoon. And I hear the watchers returning."

Alice stood. "Let's hurry on, then. If we must stay a night with them then we must, but we can be off at first light."

They walked close together now, so that they could speak in low tones that wouldn't be overheard.

After a little while Hatcher said, "They've returned. Five of them now, all on the cliffs above."

"Should we worry that there are more of them than before?"

"I think we have plenty of worry as it is. Let's not take on any more."

The sun shone and the breeze was very warm. Everywhere Alice looked there were charming little white mountain flowers peeking up out of the grass. But it was hard to take any pleasure in the day or the journey. Alice felt the eyes of those who watched from overhead, felt their menace oppressing her.

Far too soon, it seemed, they crested a little rise and saw the village below. There was a steep downslope from where they stood and then the land leveled out for a bit, allowing just enough flat clearing for the settlement.

Alice expected the village to be a sparse and dismal place populated by folk with hunched shoulders and suspicious glances.

But from above, at least, it appeared to be a typical village. Most of the houses were one-story cottages made of stone with thatched roofs. She saw some farm animals roaming inside pens—chickens, pigs, two cows and a horse. The ringing of a blacksmith's hammer drifted up to them, and Alice smelled wood fires and cooking meat.

Altogether it would have seemed a warm and friendly place were it not for the sight of the strange wooden chair on its platform in the town square.

"They're coming," Hatcher said.

This was the only warning Alice had before five men dropped in front of them, seemingly as if they'd fallen out of the sky.

They were all dressed in homespun wool—grey pants and white shirts, like a uniform. They also wore soft-looking leather boots with thin soles—*The easier to sneak up on strangers in the night*, Alice thought. Every man had a dagger at his waist. They didn't draw them, but their posture indicated that this was a distinct possibility.

The man in the center spoke. There was nothing to distinguish him from the others—in fact, Alice thought all of them rather resembled one another—the same brown hair and eyes, the same shape of the nose and mouth. Perhaps they were brothers, or perhaps the isolation of this village meant that cousins tended to marry cousins.

"State your name and your business."

Alice had been prepared to be cooperative. After the vision of the night before she didn't want to do anything to antagonize these people. But the man's peremptory tone raised her hackles.

"Who are you that I should state my name and purpose? This

is not a very friendly welcome for simple travelers." She felt Hatcher shift next to her, the only indication that he was surprised by her response.

"You may not pass into the village unless you tell us," the man said.

"We don't particularly want to pass into your village. We are bound elsewhere, so if you'll let us by then we will circle around it and continue on," Alice said.

"Where are you bound?" the man asked. His expression hadn't shifted throughout the exchange. He was not angry, or frustrated, or eager. He was implacable as stone.

"I fail to see how that's any of your concern, either," Alice said.

She was half hoping this gambit would work. If she gave enough trouble then maybe this little band of soldiers—for it was clear now they were some kind of organized guard—would simply escort Alice and Hatcher around the periphery of the village and then glare at their backs as they departed.

"If you do not wish to explain your name and purpose then you are free to return the way you came, but you are not permitted to pass through the Village of the Pure."

"Village of the Pure?"

"That is the name of this place. Only the pure of heart, without sin, may live here. And only those who express their purpose may pass through."

Alice noticed the other four men had placed their hands on their daggers, responding to some hidden signal.

Hatcher touched Alice's shoulder, stopping her from replying. She didn't know why she felt the need to suddenly dig in her heels, especially when they'd agreed upon caution. Perhaps it was only that she was tired of being told what she could and could not do, and because the memory of the hospital was fresher than it had been in some time.

"My name is Hatcher. This is my wife, Alice, and she told you true. We are simple travelers passing through the mountains."

Alice knew that Hatcher had only called her "wife" because it was easier than explaining their relationship to this strange folk, but the sound of him saying it made her feel slightly squishy inside. She'd never really thought about marriage, though they lived as a man and wife did.

"And where are you bound?" the lead soldier asked.

Hatcher shrugged. "We left our home in the City and we are seeking a new one."

Alice knew immediately this was the wrong thing for Hatcher to say. The man went rigid.

"The City? You are from the City?"

Hatcher gave Alice a rueful glance. "Yes."

"You will come with us now," he said.

They all drew their daggers and surrounded Alice and Hatcher.

Alice had every confidence that Hatcher could manage these boys and their sharp toys, because that was what Hatcher did. But they would still have to cross through the village, and there would surely be more soldiers, or at the very least angry villagers. So she submitted for the moment, and Hatcher read her face and did the same. The men kept in formation around Alice and Hatcher as they approached the village.

I'm not going to let them throw us on that chair, though. I'll burn down their village before I let that happen.

She was surprised by her ferocity, just as she'd been surprised by the way she spoke to the soldier. Alice had discovered, since she left the hospital, that she was perfectly willing to defend herself, but that didn't mean she had any taste for bloodshed. That was where she and Hatcher differed. But she found that it did not trouble her to accept the death of all the people below if they threatened her or Hatcher.

It's because of the girl, Alice thought. *That small, young girl, screaming in terror as she was tortured to death. And they all watched. They were all complicit.*

As they approached the village Alice saw several of the villagers out and about at their business—feeding chickens, hanging laundry, chopping firewood. When Alice and Hatcher passed by in the custody of the soldiers each person stopped to watch. Alice felt them staring at her.

"Where are you taking us?" Alice asked.

"Be silent," the man beside Alice said, and jabbed in her direction with the dagger.

The blade didn't touch her—it was only a threat—but Alice felt Hatcher tense beside her, coiled to spring.

"I'm not hurt," Alice murmured, and he subsided, though she felt his tension. If these men threatened her again then there would be no mercy.

The soldiers marched Alice and Hatcher up to a cottage in the center of town, just across the square from the platform that held the terrible chair.

The mercy seat, that's what the woman in my dream called it. That's what the screaming stranger at our fire called it. Though I don't know what kind of mercy that was supposed to be.

The soldier knocked on the door of the cottage. The woman from Alice's dream answered.

She was even more skeletal up close, the skin pulled tight over her bones. Alice had the strong impression that the woman was being consumed from within by some fever.

"Yes, Matthew?" the woman said, addressing the lead soldier. She gave Alice and Hatcher a cool, disinterested look.

"They're from the City, ma'am," Matthew said.

The woman's gaze sharpened. "I wish to speak to them alone. Stand guard outside the door."

The men in front of Alice and Hatcher parted. There was only one place for them to go—into the cottage. Alice dearly wished to dart away, to surprise them into chasing her, to surprise herself by escaping. But then she remembered her baby, and the agreement that she and Hatcher had made to not take any unnecessary risks. Besides, there was little chance that they would be able to escape—at least for the moment.

The interior of the cottage was cool and dark, but there was an underlying odor that made Alice gag. It was something both sweet and rotten at the same time, like fruit that had been too long in the sun.

The woman lit a candle, which cast strange and flickering shadows all around the cottage. Alice wondered why she didn't open the shutters and let in the sunshine. She gave Alice and Hatcher a long look, but before she could speak Alice did.

"Who are you, and why are we being treated in this unacceptable manner?"

The woman was clearly surprised. Alice had used her mother's voice—the one that said she was rich and powerful and accustomed to being obeyed. She hadn't realized that her mother's voice was still inside her, or that it would come so easily to her tongue.

"Well?" Alice demanded.

The woman visibly gathered her dignity and her authority around her. "My name is Wilhelmina Ray, and I am the mistress of the Village of the Pure."

"And what is that to us?" Alice asked, her tone dripping with contempt. "We had no intention of stopping in your village, but those men threatened us and claimed we could not pass through without revealing our names and business."

"No one may sully the Village of the Pure, even a traveler," Wilhelmina Ray said. "Any who may be impure must be brought before me so that I may determine their worthiness."

"And what is it that made us impure, precisely?" Alice asked.

Wilhelmina Ray raised her eyebrows. "Why, you are from the City, of course. And there is no greater source of wickedness in all the world."

Alice remembered all the terrible things that happened to her in the City. But she also remembered all the terrible things that had happened outside of the City, and thought that wickedness was wherever people were, not the sole property of one geographic location.

"We escaped the City because it was wicked," Alice said.

"We are seeking a home where we can settle. We mean you and your people no harm."

"That is a very admirable thing," Wilhelmina Ray said. "To escape the net of sin. Yes, a very admirable thing. But you'll forgive me if I say that I will be the judge of your intent."

"No," Alice said.

"No what?"

"No, I will not forgive you. Your behavior has been abominable and so has your people's. Even the meanest peasant shows more generosity to travelers."

Alice didn't know what had taken hold of her again. She only knew that she did not wish to submit to Wilhelmina Ray's will. She thought, too, that she could smell the lingering stench of burned flesh in the air. Everything about Wilhelmina Ray revolted Alice.

"You have quite a sharp tongue for a woman who is at my mercy," Wilhelmina Ray said. "I notice your husband has not spoken in all this while. Perhaps he has more sense than you."

There it was again—a word that implied marriage. Alice wondered what Hatcher thought of it.

Don't allow yourself to be distracted like a lovestruck girl. What would Cheshire say if he saw you?

(He'd tell you to use your magic.)

Alice didn't want to reveal her power unless she must. And Olivia had warned against it. Perhaps Alice could still get them out with her bravado, though a part of her longed to use magic, to show this terrible woman what magic could do.

Hatcher gave Wilhelmina Ray a bland stare. "My wife and I are partners in all things. I assure you, the only reason I don't speak is because it isn't necessary."

"You, too, believe our behavior unjust?"

Hatcher shrugged. "Whether it is just or not is not for me to decide. But it certainly is rude."

Alice rather thought that Hatcher could have passed as a New City toff at that moment, no matter how ragged his clothing. It made her realize how adept he could be at pretending, if he chose to do it.

But then she looked closer, and saw the very faint lines of strain around his eyes. He was holding himself back at the highest cost, his feral nature hanging by the thinnest thread.

He's wanted blood ever since those watchers started following us, Alice thought. She was half inclined to let him have his head, but there was still a chance that they would be able to escape without bloodshed.

Though that chance is dwindling by the second. Wilhelmina Ray doesn't realize how close she is to dying at this very moment.

"Whatever you think of my hospitality the fact remains that we won't have impure souls in our village. Now, you will submit to me while I determine the quality of your soul."

She grasped Alice's chin before Alice realized her intent. Wilhelmina Ray's fingers were sharp and hard, talons digging into Alice's flesh. She forced Alice to stare into her strange purple eyes.

The air crackled. Electricity arced between them. Alice thought, *Let go of me NOW.*

Wilhelmina Ray cried out and released Alice's chin. She backed away, staring at her fingers. They were scorched and smoking where she had touched Alice.

"You're a witch," Wilhelmina Ray spat.

"And so are you," Alice said. "What will your villagers think if I tell them that it's you who calls the lightning down on them?"

Wilhelmina Ray shook her head. "That is not me. That is the judgment of the gods."

Then she paused, staring at Alice.

"How did you know about the lightning?"

Alice laughed, a long reckless thing. "You said it yourself. I'm a witch. And as I said before—so are you."

Though I'm not really a witch, I'm a Magician, but I suppose it all comes to the same thing in the end.

"I'm no witch," Wilhelmina Ray said. "I am only an instrument. I do the gods' will. I use my ability only to keep the village safe, never for selfish purposes."

"Is that what you called it when you burned that little girl? Keeping the village safe?"

Yes, Alice realized. *It's because of the girl.*

This strange recklessness, this uncharacteristic lack of caution—it was all because of the girl. It was because Alice felt the girl's anguish burning in her own belly. It was because Alice knew that she could have been that girl, that in some ways she was that girl—a girl punished simply for being herself.

"Little girl? Do you mean Jane Blackwood?"

"I don't know what her name was but she was just a little thing. She couldn't have been more than thirteen and you all watched while she screamed."

"That 'little thing,' as you call her, was no innocent. Her own mother caught her using spells to complete her chores. And what was the girl doing while the broom swept on without her? Lying about daydreaming, no doubt thinking of her master, the devil. We don't need that kind of child in this village."

"Her mother told you?" Alice said. "Knowing that would happen?"

Just like me. My mother gave me to that hospital because I didn't suit her anymore, because I'd become nothing but a problem. She knew what might happen to me there and she left me there anyway.

My mother left me. I wasn't important enough not to give up.

Then she thought, *I'll never let you go, my child. I'll never do that to you.*

"Of course her mother told me," Wilhelmina Ray said. "She knows her duty to this village."

"I think you are a wicked person," Alice said. "And I think the gods will judge you, and find you wanting. Let's go, Hatcher."

Alice turned toward the door. She felt Hatcher's presence behind her, could sense the heavy straining of his will, the effort it took for him to remain human in the face of such provocation.

Wilhelmina Ray grabbed Alice's arm, hard, and Alice cried out.

That was when Hatcher broke.

Alice saw him out of the corner of her eye. He was a man and then he was a wolf, all in an instant, and he growled at Wilhelmina Ray, ready to strike.

"Witch!" Wilhelmina Ray cried. "WITCH! WITCH! A witch and her familiar!"

She pushed past Alice and threw open the front door, running out into the crowd of soldiers that stood guard. Several more men had arrived while Alice and Hatcher were inside her house. Wilhelmina Ray dashed into the middle of the group and then pointed an accusing finger at her own house.

"Another witch for the mercy seat! Take her! Take her!"

"Now we've done it," Alice said to Hatcher, but he was already gone.

Hatcher leapt into the crowd of soldiers, biting, clawing, rending. Blood sprayed and men cried out, swinging wildly with their daggers to try to stop Hatcher. One man aimed for Hatcher, throwing his blade, but Hatcher was too quick and the dagger was buried in the neck of his fellow soldier.

"Witch! Witch! Seize her! Seize her! Bring her to the mercy seat!"

Two of the men separated themselves from the melee and ran toward Alice.

Alice calmly stepped out of the cottage doorway and stared at the men who reached for her. They both paused, their hands hovering inches away.

"Don't touch me," she said. "If you do, you'll burn."

The air all around Alice felt scorched, the shimmering heat over a fire. She knew in that moment that she could do anything.

This power is a dangerous thing. I could kill them all the way I killed that boy in the house of horrors. I could crack open the ground and make their village fall into it. I could set every man ablaze from the inside and make them burn, make them burn the way that beautiful little child burned in the mercy seat last night.

More people were coming now, running at the sound of the screaming and shouting, and more men tried to catch Hatcher, to stop him, but he was an instrument of death now, his mind nothing but tooth and claw and warm, wet blood. Anyone who approached him paid for it.

The men who had come for Alice fell away from her, their eyes filled with terror. She hadn't done anything in particular except tell them not to touch her. She hadn't done anything overtly magical. But the magic was there nonetheless, like an aura all around her, and only a fool would have tried for her then.

"Witch! Witch!" Wilhelmina Ray shouted.

She sounded like a crow, cawing and cawing the same tune over again.

Most of the villagers had gathered in a frightened half circle around Hatcher and the soldiers. Several women were weeping, clinging to each other.

For a moment Alice thought, *What have we done?* And then she remembered that these weeping women had stood around Jane Blackwood last night and cried out their pleasure while the girl burned. One of those women might even be Jane's mother, the mother who'd betrayed her, the mother who'd given her daughter to the mistress of the village without a qualm.

They all deserve what they get. All of them.

Hatcher stood alone now, his muzzle drenched in blood, and all around him were broken men who'd tried to stop him.

He growled low in his throat, his teeth bared, at Wilhelmina Ray.

Wilhelmina Ray stood alone too, and the villagers watched her with frightened eyes. It seemed that none of them dared approach the mistress of the village. Wilhelmina Ray's accusing finger pointed at Alice, but she'd stopped screaming. Her strange purple eyes were lit with the same fire that Alice felt all around her.

Above the square, dark clouds circled. There was a rumble of thunder. Alice realized that Wilhelmina Ray was going to call the lightning down, strike at Alice and Hatcher and prove to the village that they were impure souls.

"We won't be having any of that," Alice said.

She swept her hand out, almost carelessly, and Wilhelmina Ray flew into the mercy seat. The chains wrapped around her arms.

"No!" Wilhelmina Ray shouted. "I am pure! I am the instrument of the gods!"

A tremendous crack of thunder shook the mountain. Alice heard rocks sliding from the cliffs above.

"I think it's about time you had a taste of your own mercy," Alice said.

Lightning sizzled out of the sky and struck the mercy seat. Wilhelmina Ray screamed.

The villagers all gathered around the platform as if they'd been called there. After a moment Alice heard their voices rise in chorus.

"Guilty, guilty, guilty."

"I am not guilty!" Wilhelmina Ray screamed. "I cannot be guilty!"

"Guilty, guilty, guilty," the villagers repeated.

There was another bolt of lightning, and another scream.

Hatcher came to stand beside Alice. None of the villagers took any notice of them now.

"I think you should change back into your clothes," Alice said. "And you dropped the pack in there, as well."

He nuzzled her leg before trotting back inside the cottage.

Two more bolts of lightning struck the platform. Alice wondered why Wilhelmina Ray would not save herself. She didn't have to feel the lightning.

She must know, deep down, that what she's done is wrong, Alice thought. *She must believe that she should be punished.*

Alice found she couldn't feel very sorry for Wilhelmina Ray.

Hatcher touched her shoulder. "We should go, while they are distracted."

"They won't try to harm us now," Alice said. "They're afraid of us."

"This is an unhappy place," Hatcher said. "I don't think we should stay any longer than we have to."

"You're right," Alice said.

They turned and left the village, though they could hear the crack of thunder and see the flash of lightning for a long time after.

Alice and Hatcher did not speak of that village for many days.

One day, almost three weeks later, Alice said, "What kind of mother would give up her child like that?"

They were walking downhill for a change, and Alice found she preferred it to the constant climb of the mountain paths. Even though her belly wasn't any larger she found herself more tired every day, and most days they had to stop in the midmorning so she could nap. Hatcher didn't seem to mind it, though. She often woke to find he'd gone off and caught a rabbit or two for their lunch.

"Do you mean Jane Blackwood's mother, or your mother?"

Hatcher asked, in that way he had of knowing what she meant without her saying it.

"Both, I suppose. It doesn't seem a very motherly thing to do," Alice said.

"What are mothers supposed to do?" Hatcher said.

"Well, they're supposed to love their children, and care for them, and play with them. They're supposed to listen and understand. They're supposed to make sure they are never harmed. That's what my mother used to be like, before I went to the Old City and came back broken."

"You weren't broken, Alice," Hatcher said. "You were only cast in a new mold, and she didn't like the shape of it."

Alice tried not to feel the hurt of this, the fact that her mother could do without her so easily.

"I never had a mother at all," Hatcher said.

"You didn't sprout from beneath a mushroom," Alice said.

Hatcher shrugged. "I know I had one, in the sense that someone gave birth to me, but she left me with Bess and she disappeared. And most mothers in the Old City are tired and cross, for they have to work all the time, and as soon as their children are old enough the children have to work, too. I didn't see many happy families.

"I think that kind of mother you're talking about doesn't exist, not really. She's only the idea of a mother, a perfect person who can't be true. It's sort of the same way your mother thought you were the perfect daughter, and when you weren't she couldn't reconcile it with the real you."

Alice considered this. Perhaps she was being unfair to her

mother, as unfair as her mother had been to Alice. She knew that they had loved each other once.

It wasn't so easy to be a mother. Alice hadn't even given birth yet and she already knew that. It had to be hard to know just what the right thing to do was, especially when it came to your children. It had to be hard to know you were responsible for someone else's life, someone else's happiness.

Maybe she ought to remember what she loved about her mother. Maybe she ought to forgive her.

As she thought this, something inside her unknotted, some hurt she'd been holding on to for too long.

The path they were on leveled out, and Alice and Hatcher rounded a high cliff wall.

Below them was a clear silver lake stretching across a wide valley. Wildflowers sprouted all around in a riot of color. Above the valley the high peaks of blue mountains watched.

This was the place she had dreamed of for so long. This was the place where they would raise their child, and perhaps more than one. Alice felt something catch in her throat, for she could almost see them, their children, running and playing in that field of wildflowers, their high sweet cries echoing all around the valley.

This was the place where they could be quiet, and content, and leave their terrors behind.

Alice could finally see the exact spot where they would build their cottage, and their life.

"Hatcher," she said. "We're home."

Christina Henry is the author of *The Girl in Red*, a postapocalyptic version of the classic "Little Red Riding Hood" tale. She is also the author of the Chronicles of Alice trilogy—*Alice, Red Queen* and *Looking Glass*—a dark and twisted take on *Alice's Adventures in Wonderland*, as well as *The Mermaid*, a historical fairy tale based on the P. T. Barnum Fiji Mermaid hoax, and *Lost Boy: The True Story of Captain Hook*, an origin story of Captain Hook from *Peter Pan*.

She has also written the national bestselling Black Wings series (*Black Wings, Black Night, Black Howl, Black Lament, Black City, Black Heart* and *Black Spring*), featuring Agent of Death Madeline Black and her popcorn-loving gargoyle, Beezle.

Christina enjoys running long distances, reading anything she can get her hands on and watching movies with samurai, zombies and/or subtitles in her spare time. She lives in Chicago with her husband and son.

CONNECT ONLINE

ChristinaHenry.net
 AuthorChristinaHenry
 C_Henry_Author
goodreads.com/CHenryAuthor

Ready to find
your next great read?

Let us help.

Visit prh.com/nextread

Penguin
Random
House